I0819542

THESE FAMILIAR WALLS

ALSO BY C. J. DOTSON

The Cut

THESE FAMILIAR WALLS

C. J. DOTSON

ST. MARTIN'S PRESS
NEW YORK

This is a work of fiction. All of the names, characters, organizations, places, and events portrayed in this work are either products of the author's imagination or used fictitiously.

First published in the United States by St. Martin's Press, an imprint of St. Martin's Publishing Group

EU Representative: Macmillan Publishers Ireland Ltd, 1st Floor, The Liffey Trust Centre, 117–126 Sheriff Street Upper, Dublin 1, D01 YC43

For information, address St. Martin's Publishing Group, 120 Broadway, New York, NY 10271.

www.stmartins.com

The Library of Congress Cataloging-in-Publication Data is available upon request.

ISBN 978-1-250-33658-3 (hardcover)
ISBN 978-1-250-33659-0 (ebook)

First Edition: 2026

10 9 8 7 6 5 4 3 2 1

For my mom. I've been sitting here staring at this page for ten full minutes trying to find the words, but nothing I can think of feels like enough, so we'll have to settle for this: Thank you, all the time, for everything. My family is so lucky to have you in our lives. I love you.

PROLOGUE

TOO DIM TO SEE

JANUARY 2020

Snow obscured the neat lawns and sloped roofs, weighed down needled pine boughs, and shrouded the skeletal branches of bare trees. Fuzzy yellow streetlights softened the darkness, and here and there the multicolored glow of holdover holiday lights broke the cold night's monotony.

A sharp crack and soft, tinkling scatter interrupted the snow-softened silence. A door creaked once as it swung open and again as it eased closed.

Quiet resumed.

Minutes passed in the slow way of deep, unobserved night.

The violence that followed stayed within one house, did not spill out to disturb the sleeping suburb.

Inside, a man in his pajamas crawled from the master bedroom into the second-floor hallway. His steel-gray hair stuck out at messy angles. As he crawled, he favored one arm. His mouth gaped but he drew no air. Pain filled his eyes, tears shone on his cheeks. He scrambled down the carpeted floor.

Footsteps sounded behind him, uneven but picking up speed.

A man in all black, wearing a ski mask and clutching a baseball bat in both hands, stumbled out of the bedroom in pursuit.

The crawling man came to the edge of the stairs. Through a bared-teeth grimace, he sucked in a breath at last.

"Theresa! *Theresa!*"

The baseball bat struck him between the shoulder blades. His hands slipped out from beneath him, and he tumbled end over end down the steps. The fourth stair up creaked as he thumped it. He sprawled at the bottom, in the entryway hall.

"Dave!"

His wife's voice pierced the ringing in the man's—Dave's—skull. He picked up his head, slow and unsteady.

Two figures stood before him. His wife Theresa, nightgown askew and eyes wide with panic, hands raised in pleading self-defense. A second masked intruder blocked the front door.

A knife gleamed dull and silvery in the intruder's gloved hand.

"Please!" Theresa cried. "Don't!"

Shaking, limbs loose, Dave lurched to his feet. Hot, breathless pain lanced through his leg and he wheezed, shuffling sideways to get his weight off it. Broken for sure. No time for that.

The knife flashed.

His wife screamed.

One of the stairs creaked. Despite the pain in his leg Dave shouted and lunged for Theresa.

The baseball bat clattered to the floor behind him.

Something passed before his face. A rope flung over his head and around his neck from behind.

The slack went out.

Dave's attacker pulled him back against his chest. The rope tightened. Dave gagged. The man behind him grunted and pulled harder, and Dave couldn't even choke. His mouth hung open, his lungs burned. The rope dug into his skin, but that was nothing compared to the pain building in his chest.

Desperate to make slack, he shoved his body against his attacker. He threw his head back, hoping to feel his skull break the stranger's nose. Instead they wound up almost cheek to cheek. Dave reached up, groped for some purchase, and yanked the man's mask off.

The face he glimpsed in profile, pressed against his own from over his shoulder, struck Dave with unexpected familiarity. Did he know this man?

Nearly forgotten images bubbled to the surface of Dave's frantic mind. A troubled neighborhood kid, an angry confrontation, a fire. What had the boy's name been?

Nathan.

Across the entryway the knife caught Dave's whirling, panicked attention as it flashed again. A sick sound, slick and meaty. Theresa's scream climbed abruptly—then cut off.

She collapsed.

Shuddering on the floor, she made a wet wheeze but didn't cry out anymore.

The figure with the knife knelt before Dave's wife.

The knife rose, paused, then fell. Theresa's bubbling gasps stopped. Her quivering ceased.

Dave thrashed, nearly broke free, and managed to draw in a single rasping breath. The rope tightened with cruel fury. Tears turned the front hall into an unrecognizable wavering nothing. He grabbed for the rope, his fingernails tearing helplessly at his own skin.

Nathan grunted, breath hot on the back of Dave's neck. "Get over here and finish this fucker, will you?"

The blurred figure before him stood and moved closer, leaning a little to the left. The knife flashed again. The blade ripped into Dave's stomach. It stuck for a second, but with a vicious jerk was yanked back out. The pain made him want to scream. All he managed through the strangling hold was a high keening. Warmth oozed down his belly, seeped into the waist of his pajama pants.

Dave tried to grab the second attacker's hand as the knife came back in. His fingers clumsy, he took a slice on the palm instead. Such a small cut, but his terrified mind brought up the phrase *defensive wounds.* A tremor shook him as the knife sank into his intestines. When it pulled free he swooned, the sick, hot pain more total than anything he had ever experienced.

The rope around his neck loosened. Nathan shoved Dave forward. He dropped to his knees next to Theresa, pressed his palms against the ragged tears in his guts. The flow of his blood pushed against him, seeping between his fingers. He fell belly down, arms trapped beneath him, face twisted to one side.

Dave watched his life seep away—the wet, red current traveled first through the cracks between the floorboards. Beyond that stared the glassy, terrified eyes of his wife and oh, no. No, please, Theresa's agonized, motionless face couldn't be the last thing he ever saw.

He turned his focus on the attackers standing over them, blurred by distance and the darkness crawling in his peripheral vision. His mind slowed, drifted, but he wouldn't let his gaze wander.

One intruder still wore a mask, and that one had dropped the knife. Nathan grinned, his expression disconcertingly exultant, almost lustful, despite the blood splattering him.

Dave's lips tried to form the word *why*, but he didn't have a voice or the breath to ask the question. He hadn't seen Nathan in more than two decades, hadn't thought about the boy he'd been in years. How could a long-forgotten neighborhood troublemaker be standing over him and Theresa now, as Dave bled out on the floor of their home?

"Let's get outta here," Nathan said to his accomplice, fishing a key ring out of his pocket.

The other figure reached down as well. It took Dave a sluggish moment to comprehend what the gun rising between the two murderers meant.

Nathan's expression crumbled, first into betrayal, then rage. "Wait, hey, wait!"

Dave's eyes blearily tracked the motion as Nathan took a step toward his partner but slipped on the gore-slickened floor.

The muzzle of the gun followed Nathan as he stumbled to his knees between Dave's legs and Theresa's. Bearing witness to this moment brought Dave no satisfaction. The nauseating, burning pain in his belly and the growing horrified confusion left no room for anything else.

Still, he watched.

"You'll be fucking sorry if you do this," Nathan growled.

The gun went off with a flat crack. Dave barely heard it.

Gray emptiness crept over his sight. Every sound came to him as if from a greater and greater distance. He only knew Nathan fell because the body landed with heavy finality across his legs. Dave no longer perceived anything farther than the motionless form of his wife, whose eyes he still avoided.

She, too, grew too dim to see.

From impossibly far away came the sound of a smartphone beep and a hoarse whisper. Light gleamed on the red saturating the floorboards of the foyer as the lone intruder opened the front door and left.

The door closed again. The pale illumination faded.

The darkness deepened.

Dave died.

PART ONE

CHAPTER 1

THE ONLY ONE LEFT

MAY 2020

Amber Hughes pushed open the front door and forgot herself, standing framed in the threshold, staring into the house in which she'd grown up. The POLICE LINE tape she'd seen strung around in the crime scene photos was gone, as was the stain on the hardwood floor. At half past eight in the morning, the sun already warmed the back of her neck. Across the street insects buzzed in the undergrowth lining the little creek she'd explored as a girl, somewhere in the distance a child gave a happy shout, and the wind whispered through the branches of the tree she had climbed to the top of in her teens. That breeze pushed past her, bringing the powerful scent of the hyacinths growing along the front of the house and freshly mowed grass from a nearby yard, and that was the smell of her childhood.

Inside, yellow squares of sunlight fell on the floor beneath the east-facing windows. The carpeting was new and the wallpaper in the kitchen had been replaced by a cheerful, pale yellow coat of paint, but the neighborhood glimpsed through the windows looked exactly as it always had. The house might have had some touching up, but its bones were the same; at any second she might hear her sister calling from the backyard or her parents puttering around together.

Instead, a strained voice behind her said, "Ma'am? Where d'you want this couch?"

She snapped back to the present. Amber would never again hear her sister's footsteps or her parents chatting in the kitchen. She was the only one left. The realization didn't bring the rush of emotions she expected, only a weary numbness that she didn't have time to try to understand right now. She shoved it to the back of her mind, stooped to pick up the boxes she'd set down on the front porch, and stepped through into the house.

"Sorry," she said, scooting aside to let two movers follow her in with a huge sofa. She gave the first a warm smile but didn't offer any explanation for her absentmindedness. These strangers didn't need to know her business. Or any more of her business than they might have read in the paper a few months ago. Amber kept her expression pleasant and added, "That can go right over here. Thanks, guys." She pointed them to the living room, trying to ignore its emptiness.

The house stood as bare as if it were brand-new; the notion of going through her parents' belongings after the murders had given her sleepless nights, so she'd had everything put into storage. She just couldn't imagine *living* with all of it, every framed photo and throw pillow another silent reminder of a family from whom she had been distant even before they were gone forever.

By the end of today, the house would be full of her and Ben's furniture and the kids' toys, their photographs and prints ready to hang. Until then these familiar walls belonged to bygone times, not to Amber.

A car door slammed and the high, excited voices of Xander and Marigold broke the morning stillness. Their shouts threatened to pierce Amber's already fragile composure; she'd wanted to have kids since even before she met her husband, and she'd honestly, maybe naively, thought she'd anticipated the challenges and difficulties in parenthood . . . but slogging through the mud of one day to the next through the pandemic, especially with Xander out of kindergarten since the schools shut down back in March, left her worn out even before the move. And until today, his first of four in a row off, Ben had been at the firehouse more than he'd been home all week, so every last-minute preparation had fallen to Amber.

When was the last time she'd had a moment alone? Or any real downtime?

Marigold shrieked at the exact frequency that made the skin on the back of Amber's neck crawl. She closed her eyes for two heartbeats, and when she opened them she saw the front hall again as it had been in the crime scene pictures, the bloodstain spreading across the floor. She blinked hard and flinched. The image dissipated, and with a grimace Amber straightened her spine and took a firm hand on her emotions, trying to ignore the stinging of her eyes and the trembling of her knees. Still, she skirted the spot on the floor where that bloodstain had been.

If she'd checked where she was going first, she and Xander wouldn't have collided. The six-year-old's wiry body crashed into her legs. He rebounded and caught himself on the nearest wall, and pushed his dark blond hair away from his face to throw her an apologetic grimace. Meanwhile, Amber shuffled in a clumsy sidestep, then fell on her tailbone. Her stack of boxes, small but full of precious things, toppled.

One cardboard corner split in a wide tear. An antique wrought iron jewelry box tumbled out and popped open, revealing black silk lining, and for just one moment the sunshine seemed to dim in a way that made the back of Amber's neck prickle. The moment passed and Amber sighed as new bracelets and old date-night earrings, a class ring from 2005, a necklace that had been her mother's, and a handful of glittering rings slid and rolled and tumbled in every direction. Something glinted near one of the air vents in the floor, followed by a prolonged clatter that grew increasingly faint. The fading of the sound gave Amber a shivery little pause, but this was not the moment to pick apart the strange unease.

Instead, she scrambled around on the floor, trying not to think about anything worse than the dropped jewelry and the human traffic jam at the doorway. And Xander, who should've known better than to run in front of people.

"Honestly, Xander!" she scolded, her voice closer to a shout than she meant—especially in front of these strangers—as she scooped up necklaces and earrings. She made herself stop narrowing her eyes, relaxing her face into a calmer expression as she went on with a tone of gentle correction, "We need you to be more careful, buddy."

Amber fumbled the jewelry back into the silk-lined box, trying to will the heat of an embarrassed blush out of her cheeks, when the realization that she was crawling around in the exact place where her mother and father had been murdered not six months before struck her like a blow. A shiver crawled up her spine, and she snatched the last bracelet with a flutter in her chest and a quick, shaky breath.

She made way for the steady stream of boxes and furniture again, meeting the eyes of the movers. They all wore matching white shirts with N.E. OHIO PRO MOVING CO. emblazoned on the chest, they all had masks, and all but one of them wore the masks incorrectly, pulled down under their noses.

Xander was watching her, his eyes wary, almost untrusting. A dull, resentful ache bloomed behind her rib cage—it wasn't fair that he'd turn that expression on her, especially now; this whole painful, stressful move would make everything better for him and Mari.

But Amber knew how to handle difficult situations: take control of them, starting with herself. No more counterproductive yelling at the kids, especially in front of strangers. She forced herself to smile instead and landed on the perfect distraction—the kids hadn't visited her parents' home in long enough that they certainly wouldn't remember the yard, and it hadn't been a good idea to go to public play areas for a few months now.

"Hey, bud," she said, "why don't you take your sister out back and play? There's a swing set out there that my sister and I played on when we were little."

Hannah and her husband Greg had died in a house fire when Xander and Marigold were too young to remember them, and Xander knew the family history well enough to be more intrigued by a swing set than by the passing mention of Amber's sister. His eyes lit up.

"Mari!" he shouted, running out of the house, this time avoiding any wipeouts. "Mari! Mari*gold*! Guess what! There's *swings*!"

Marigold's answer was loud, high-pitched, and largely unintelligible from inside the house, but Amber heard the joy in it. Moments later both children came racing back through, dodging obstacles, and disappeared through the doorway into the kitchen, where the sliding glass door let out on a half acre of fenced-in yard in which they could play without Amber having to check on them every ten seconds.

Ben entered the house and a little of the tension in Amber's shoulders and jaw eased. Her husband was square-shouldered and solidly built, with hair so dark a brown it was nearly black, streaked now with the first touches of gray. His job required him to stay pretty fit, but there was a growing softness to him that Amber found, to her surprise, endearing. He stood a couple inches shorter than his wife, with smile lines drawing themselves a little more deeply across his face every day. The kids took after her side of the family: a bit clumsy, tall but ungainly thin, all knees and elbows, with tousled dark blond hair and brown eyes. Xander was the spitting image of Dave, Amber's father, and the older Marigold got the more Amber saw her mother in the little girl's curls and her delicate features. Both kids emulated Ben more in their mannerisms, and when her husband brushed his hair out of his eyes the same way Xander had a moment before, a pang of guilt stung Amber for how sharp she'd been with the boy.

Amber set her boxes on one of the steps, crossed the front hallway, and leaned into her husband. He regarded the house with bright eyes and a small smile, showing none of her growing misgiving. Well, he didn't have a lifetime of strained memories waiting around every corner and hiding in every shadow.

"I should have claimed the property and then sold it," Amber murmured. "We could have bought a whole new house if we sold this one *and* our old condo."

Not that handling her parents' estate really could have been *that* straightforward with all the legal nonsense tying things up. She didn't want to think about that unpleasantness now, though, not when she didn't have time to do any proper research into the problems, and especially not on top of the hassle of the rest of this long day. And at least they *had* been able to move in, after all.

"Come on, babe, you know it wouldn't have been that simple. Plus, the house is great, and we really needed the space. You made the right moves," Ben said, his words smooth and reassuring and the hug he wrapped her in more comforting still. "You'll feel better once we're settled in."

Amber rested her head on his shoulder and nodded. "Sure."

She allowed herself a few more moments in his embrace before she broke away, slapping her palms together and rubbing them briskly. They had a lot to do. She picked her boxes up once more. On the first step upstairs she paused and said, "Oh, hey, I sent the kids out to play in the back. Could you check on them, make sure the swing set isn't going to come down on top of them? Maybe look for a spot to put in a bonfire pit."

She didn't wait for his answer. The bright sunlight filling the foyer faded the higher she climbed, dulling the gleam of the wrought iron jewelry box, and she failed to suppress another shiver.

Maybe this had all been a mistake.

CHAPTER 2

A SHADOW SHIFTING

MAY 2020

Amber squeezed between the headboard and a stack of cardboard boxes, sliding through until she reached the bedroom wall with the biggest window. She crossed her arms on the windowsill and rested her forehead against the glass, trying to will herself not to need a break yet.

"Screw it," she muttered to no one, then turned and sank to the floor.

They'd been going for hours, and Amber had already been up and down the stairs more times than she cared to count. The desire to get this over with was so powerful that she wanted to cry, but the need to get off her feet for a minute or two was just as strong. Her back ached, her bad knee throbbed, and her arms hurt down to the tips of her fingers. To give herself an excuse to rest, she pulled her phone and charger out of her pocket to plug in, checked her notifications more out of habit than the thought that anyone might be trying to reach her, and set it down next to her.

The whole time she and Ben had been planning this move,

Amber had known they would have the largest bedroom and en suite bathroom, and the kids would have the two smaller rooms. But some deeper part of her, some part not engaged in the present and in active thought, was still surprised that she was setting up to live in her parents' bedroom and not her own. Surprised, and uneasy.

They had died in the middle of the night. This room was the last place in their lives where they had felt safe. What had her mother been dreaming about before the night had turned bloody? Amber found herself mulling that over often in the months since the triple murder.

Police had identified the killer-turned-victim as Nathan Teldegardo, a man who had lived in this neighborhood when they were both kids. Amber tried hard not to think about the cops still working to identify the second killer, tried not to worry over whether they'd made any progress or if they knew anything they hadn't shared with her, or the million other things to fret about. To distract herself, she gave in to a morbid thought—one that made her breath catch and her eyes squeeze shut, but didn't fill her with the kind of paranoia that would have her checking over her shoulder for the rest of her life: Had her parents recognized Nathan that night? Had knowing one of their murderers given them some context, or had it made their final moments worse?

With a grunt, Amber forced herself to stop poring over these thoughts. It wouldn't help. She and her parents hadn't even been close, and in the four years since Hannah's death the distance between them had only grown wider, more strained.

Soft rattling brought her back to the present moment. The sliding door to her parents' walk-in closet—*her* walk-in closet now, no longer off-limits, she reminded herself firmly—had shifted slightly on its track. The skin on the back of Amber's neck tightened, but she snorted at herself and shook her head. There were men coming in and out of the house, shutting doors, setting down heavy objects, going up and down the stairs. In fact, the fourth step up creaked loudly at that moment, same as it had done when she was a kid if she forgot to skip that one while sneaking downstairs after bedtime.

She was about to stand up when the closet door rattled again. It slid an inch farther open. Amber's body reacted before her mind did, her mouth drying and heart rate quickening. A sluggish moment later the conscious thought—*is someone in there?*—caught up with her central nervous system. As soon as the thought occurred, it took root. In that moment she was sure she could see a shadow shifting, sliding, into the deeper darkness at the back of the closet. Was that a gleam? Like eyes glittering in the shadows?

The sounds of the world outside the bedroom faded into the background, thumps and bangs and voices growing muted, distant. The sunlight pouring down on her from the window above lost its summertime cheer. All the warmth bled out of Amber. She sat in cold illumination, brilliantly spotlit. At the same time the flat light dazzled her, blinded her to what might wait in the darkness.

Muffled grayness settled heavily upon her, isolation wrapping her up totally, as if more than mere drywall separated her from the houseful of people.

The closet door shifted again.

Amber's heart lurched, sped up. She sucked in a breath that caught in her throat.

A soft, barely audible voice made her jerk back against the wall.

Her spine crawled, and her scalp tingled. How long had that voice been whispering without her noticing? The hairs on the back of her neck stood up. Had it been going the whole time? Another shiver prickled over her skin, starting at the base of her spine and spreading. She couldn't discern the soft words, but she felt their hateful bitterness down to her bones.

The closet door. The voice hissed and hissed from the shadows behind that door, of course it did, the room held no other hiding places. Someone was in there. The certainty sat like a stone in her chest, filling up the space where her lungs should go, making the next breath a struggle.

Amber tried to call for Ben, or for one of the men effortlessly hauling furniture into the house. Anyone. But her voice faltered; she managed only a dry, high-pitched wheeze.

Fight and flight both failed her; fear pinned her in place. No. *No.* Amber refused to allow that. Though her heart raced, she braced her damp palms on the wall behind her and forced herself to her feet.

The whispering intensified as she stood. But the moment she was up off the floor, some of the shuddering fear subsided, edged out by a hot rush of anger.

Someone was trying to frighten her, trying to make her feel small and helpless. She clenched her jaw, her hands curled into fists, and she leaned into the outrage. She let it build, hot and steady, to push her momentary weakness away. Whoever was in that closet, they were going to be sorry for it.

She wanted to storm across the room; instead she had to pick her way around the disassembled bed frame and detour past a pile of bags full of clothing. By the time she reached the closet door some of that rush of fire had cooled. The whispers intensified. Amber steeled herself, gritted her teeth, and slid the closet door all the way open.

Light poured in to illuminate a bare space, no one crouching in the corner or whispering venom into the air. Fear collapsed on itself, crumbling to ash and leaving her hollow and buzzing with only the anger.

The light of the day grew warm again with the suddenness of a wave crashing on a beach, and the sounds that had become dim and distant came roaring back. Amber leaned against the closet doorframe and took a long breath, trying to slow her heartbeat. Nothing there. *Of course* there was nothing there. Everything was fine.

Her next breath was calm. She eyed the emptiness, remembering when this closet belonged to her parents. Its vacancy was somehow unnerving, and Amber told herself that the first things she'd unpack in this room would be for that closet.

From below pounded the rapid thumping of the children running back and forth in the front hall, the solid wood floor making each hard footfall reverberate through the house. Marigold shouted something that Amber couldn't make out, her voice wild with laughter, and Xander called his sister's name over and over. This move would be good for them, at least. The isolation of this year had been hard on them; this was probably more adventure than they could remember having. The new house, the new yard, the swing set, it was all going to help Xander and Marigold, maybe more than Amber could guess. Which she hoped would help her, too—handling them lately felt like more than she had bargained for.

Stress. That's what it was. The year had been stressful. It was no wonder that now, on a day that would have been difficult even under good circumstances, she was getting the creeps. Imagining things.

Amber ran a hand over her hair, making sure it remained smoothly gathered into the ponytail. She schooled her face into pleasant normalcy, took care to breathe steadily.

She probably wasn't even imagining things. That sounded so dramatic. Like she was hallucinating. Amber shook her head. No, it was nothing that serious. The door had rattled on its runner because of the kids racing around downstairs and the movers dropping furniture less carefully than they should. She hadn't dreamed up a disembodied voice. This house was just older than the condo had been, the AC made noises she wasn't used to anymore, and the vents certainly carried echoes strangely through the rooms.

From beyond the bedroom came the sound of a door being opened too hard, swinging wide to bounce off the wall behind it. Amber nodded. No creepy-crawlies, no hallucinations. Just strain and noises she wasn't used to.

Another childish cry echoed up from downstairs. From the upstairs hallway, one of the movers muttered to another, "Those fucking kids need to shut their mouths."

They didn't know she was upstairs, didn't know she was standing right there and could hear them. She gathered herself to march out into the hallway, to say something sharp, remind them that the kids were four and six, had been stuck in a two-bedroom condo with a tiny balcony and no yard since the shutdowns started, and their energy was normal—and didn't reflect badly on her and Ben as parents. She suffered an unexpected wave of exhaustion instead. It left her feeling limp. If she tried to confront them, she wouldn't find the right words. She'd sound like a bitchy-customer person, not like a reasonable-parent person. Maybe they'd find an excuse to drop a box of plates if she pissed them off too much. It wasn't worth it.

Rather than step authoritatively into the hallway, she moved quietly to the door, leaving the closet wide open behind her, and peered through the crack. The hall was empty, the movers busy in what was going to be Mari's room. Amber crept silently out and made her way down the stairs, skipping the fourth step although the maneuver made her bad knee twinge. She ignored the sinking in her belly, the way her shoulders wanted to hunch forward a bit. She couldn't tell which shame stung worse—that she had so little control over the children that people would comment on it in her own home, or that she hadn't said something to defend them.

When she stepped down into the foyer, she saw the sliding door standing wide open, an invitation to flies or wasps. Xander and Marigold's voices chattered from the living room. They'd been careening inside and out, not staying outside like she'd asked. Anger flashed through her, as bright and hot as a lightning bolt, and as brief. In its wake was the certainty that if the kids had been playing in the yard like she'd told them to, they wouldn't have embarrassed her.

Why did their behavior always fall to Amber? Where was Ben? Her jaw tightened. Then she forced herself to stop gritting her teeth and loosened her hands, shaking her fingers out. She needed to master her irritation before she rounded the corner to find the kids. They didn't need her snapping at them, and it wouldn't help the situation.

She neared the family room, and from out of sight she heard Marigold asking her brother, "Who lives in this house?"

Amber paused. She and Ben had tried to prepare the kids for the move, and this was a good chance to see how Xander was handling things.

"*We* do," he said, and Amber smiled. Xander elaborated, "We live here now."

"No, I don't mean *us*," Marigold answered, her voice casual. "Someone else lives here, too." Cold oozed through Amber. The little girl added, perfectly matter of fact, "Hiding."

Did the whispers from upstairs sound in the air around her again, distorted and unintelligible, a noise more felt on the skin than heard in the ears?

A heartbeat later it was gone, if it had been there at all. Amber's pulse fluttered. She swallowed hard, breathed deeply, and settled herself. Being back here played with her imagination, brought back childish thought patterns, nothing more.

Anger forgotten, Amber stepped around the corner with her arms crossed over her chest. Xander and Marigold looked up from where they sat cross-legged on the floor in front of the fireplace. Marigold gave her a bright, sweet smile, but Xander's still held a touch of reservation.

She forced a grin and said, "Hey, you punks. I thought I told you to go play outside. The movers are going to be bringing more stuff in here soon."

Xander jumped to his feet and hauled Marigold up after him.

She giggled and went limp, making herself harder to pick up. Marigold could very well get up on her own, but Xander had been trying to do everything for her since before she could crawl, and he wasn't letting her perfect ability to take care of herself stop him.

"Go on, get outta here," Amber said, shooing them. "I'll make lunch." The pots and pans and baking sheets were all packed away, but she'd asked Ben to pick up bread, peanut butter, jelly, and disposable tableware. "Peanut butter and jelly sound good?"

"*Only* jelly," Marigold declared, and before Amber could answer that an only-jelly sandwich wasn't a great choice, the little girl bolted. Xander let out a laugh and gave chase, leaving the door open behind him as they ran out into the yard.

As soon as they were gone the oppressive sensation that had been following her closed in again, but she shoved the feeling down and went into the kitchen. Briefly she debated offering the movers some sandwiches, then snorted at herself and shook her head. Maybe she hadn't had the energy to confront them when they'd been rude, but that didn't mean she had to feed them.

CHAPTER 3

SECRET PLACE

MAY 2020

After a poor night's sleep in what she still thought of as her parents' room, Amber spent the next morning trying to get *anything* done despite the children's exuberance and interruptions. Weariness slumped her shoulders before lunchtime, and as she slapped together a couple more peanut butter and jelly sandwiches, a prickly irritation—unearned and aimless—smoldered to life in her chest.

"Hey, seen my box cutter?" Ben asked, appearing in the kitchen doorway.

"Not now, Ben," she said, curt and a little sharp.

His eyebrows rose. Amber caught the look, surprised and just a touch defensive, and before he could respond she sighed and pinched the bridge of her nose, saying, "Shit. Sorry. You caught me at a bad moment." She'd have to be better at dousing her temper while they handled the irritating process of unpacking and getting settled. Pushing the sandwiches away, she stepped back. "I think I need a break. Can you take care of lunch? Please?"

Ben hesitated, then nodded. "Yeah, I can do lunch duty. You okay?"

She ran a hand over her hair, smoothing her ponytail, and shrugged. "It's all just . . . a lot. I need a few minutes."

Ben stepped closer, reaching out. She tucked herself into his embrace, but there was too much to do to linger in his warm hug. She drew away and slipped past him, out of the kitchen.

"Thanks. The kids are outside. Love you."

Amber made her way to the room off the hall to the garage, formerly her and Hannah's playroom, where she'd had the movers leave her home office supplies. As Ben called the kids to lunch, Amber shut and locked the door. She turned, letting her gaze wander. If she set her desk in the corner under the window, filing cabinet and printer in arm's reach, the room would still be half empty. Maybe she could get a small sofa, and the built-in shelves were perfect for jigsaw puzzles and books.

Tightly wound muscles in her back loosened, and Amber savored a bubble of growing pleasure in her chest; her office, a space for no one else, and the quiet to work in it, all alone.

The movers had left the furniture along the wall farthest from the window, and boxes filled the middle of the room. Amber shifted the cardboard stacks out of the way. When she lifted the last box, the contents within slid with a series of soft *clack-clacks*. Opening that one first, she found a surprising number of candles, a handful of trinkets, a little green lighter, and a small decorative mirror with an oversized, ornate frame.

Amber had no plan for these things, but it might be nice to arrange them on the built-in shelves, at least until she had a better idea. She started with a candle, a vanilla-scented pillar of creamy off-white. She set it on the shelf, scooped the lighter out of the box, and lit the wick. The soothing glow heightened the relaxation of this much-needed alone time. Amber let her gaze linger for a moment on the small flame.

Next, she pulled the little mirror from the box. As she

turned, an impression of motion in her peripheral vision made her pause. She glanced back down at the glass, and when she blinked—was her reflection slower to open its eyes than she'd been? The impression left as fast as it had come, and she saw nothing more than her face, tired and small in the overwrought frame.

Come to think of it, Amber didn't actually like that mirror much. Rather than prop it up next to the candle, she set it to one side, face down.

The next candle came in a glass jar, dark green, with three wicks. She set it next to the first, began to turn away, then paused and picked up the lighter. Eyeing her desk, considering whether she could lift it or if she'd have to drag it across the carpet, Amber touched the flame to each wick. Artificial pine scent mingled with the vanilla.

Lifting the desk proved possible, if strenuous. Amber walked it halfway across the small space before she set it down, leaned over, and pulled another candle from the box. This one was pink, in a holder with beads on it, and she lit it as well and set it with the others before she finished moving her desk. Everything would be right where she wanted it. When had she last felt this content? On her way back across the room, she stopped to fish out another candle, bright red and never burned. She lit it and set it down. A handful of tealights followed. Her wheeled office chair rolled easily to the desk. She put a sculpted-wax sea turtle candle on the shelf, one she'd had for so long she didn't remember getting it, and lit the wick. Like the desk, the filing cabinet was too heavy to move in one go. That was okay, Amber didn't have to rush. While she paused, she lit two more candles. A smooth, shiny wax sphere in swirling, glittering shades of brown came next, but the shelf was too full. That candle went onto the next one up. She set another simple pillar next to it and lit them both. Three more tealights fit in one hand, easy to set out in a little cluster. Two thin candles in old fashioned holders went one on each end.

Time to start unpacking the office supplies. First, Amber reached into the box of decorations again. She felt around, paused, and glanced in at a clutter of odds and ends. She pushed aside a framed photo of her wedding day and moved a clumsy, handmade mug from Xander. No more candles.

Irritation marred Amber's relaxation. She wanted to light another candle. The annoyance gave way to perplexity. Wasn't it strange that she'd run out? Hadn't she just been surprised by the number of candles in this box?

Amber turned to the shelves and her last scrap of soothing calm melted away.

Nearly twenty candles flickered there, the flames small but numerous enough that the room had grown warm. The tall ones singed blackening spots onto the bottom of the shelf above them. Grimacing, Amber leaned forward and blew them all out. Ribbons of smoke drifted up from the wicks and Amber stared, her mind moving slowly.

Why had she lit that many candles?

She retraced her actions and shook her head. The furniture was arranged how she wanted it, she'd been working until the moment before, but the details were fuzzy. Strange.

"I'm tired," she told herself, surprised by the rasp in her voice. "It's been a long couple days and I just had a . . . a weird blank moment."

The wicks left the room vaguely smoky, a scent that brought Nathan Teldegardo to mind, as he'd been the summer they'd met. A smell of smoke had always hung around him, sometimes faint but never missing.

All the tension she'd banished while setting up her office crawled back up her spine, across her shoulders. Her one relaxing moment, spoiled. She wasn't ready to go out again and put all the priority back on her role of parent and wife, but it was either that or keep working in the too-hot room, trying to ignore her unease and the hint of smoke.

Rubbing her temples, Amber went out to face the rest of the day with a hesitant stride.

When the kids' bedtime finally arrived, eight long hours later, it came as an unmitigated relief. With fraying patience, Amber helped them through their nighttime routines, then crossed the hall to the room she'd always felt like an intruder in.

Ben sprawled across his side of their bed, reading a paperback. Trying not to disturb him, Amber kept her silence as she shed the jean shorts and tank top she'd been wearing all day, sighed with relief as she unhooked her bra and dropped it into the hamper, and pulled a nightshirt on before sliding into bed next to her husband.

"Good night," she said, and rolled over to face away from his lamp.

"I love you, Amber."

"Love you, too."

Sleep came on fast, but it didn't prove very restful. In deep stillness, Amber woke all at once. Her heart raced and her mouth tasted dry and sour. Sweat dampened her pillow and the sheets tangled around her legs. A nightmare, but she remembered nothing, only a sinking in her belly and a whisper in the back of her mind that said *coming back here was a mistake.*

She glanced at the clock. Just past six in the morning. Might as well just get up—she could make coffee and unpack in the kitchen before the kids needed breakfast. With luck she'd be able to actually cook today.

By eight, when the kids came downstairs, she served them pancakes on real plates instead of dry cereal in paper bowls. When Ben appeared a little later, his gaze fell on the kids, and he did a brief double take.

"Amber, who're these children?" he asked, committing a little too much to the bit; the confusion in his voice was convincing enough that Mari frowned up at him.

"C'mon," Xander said, his smile hesitant. "It's *us.*"

"Us?" Ben repeated, face blank. Then he blinked, his expression cleared, and he grinned. "Us who?"

"*Us* us!" Mari giggled, frown vanishing. "Marigold and Xander!"

"Never heard of 'em," Ben said, ruffling Xander's hair as he sat.

Ben always ate fast, so he cleaned his plate first and then hung their small fire extinguisher before pecking Amber's cheek and heading toward the garage once more. When the kids finally finished, too, Amber sent them outside to play again. Quiet filled the house, and though she'd been awake for hours, the day still stretched ahead of her. It'd go more easily if she took care of herself a bit. Time for a quick shower.

She went upstairs to grab fresh clothes. Instead, she found herself in her childhood bedroom. After she'd moved out at eighteen, her visits here had been infrequent and brief, and she'd rarely gone into her old bedroom again. The last sixteen years took on an almost physical weight, but in that same moment Amber hardly believed that her childhood had fallen so far behind. Time seemed flimsy, fake. Closing her eyes, Amber imagined that when she looked again Xander's bed and boxes of toys and clothing would be gone. It'd be her own childhood bed, her bookshelf full of adventure stories and teddy bears, and her desk.

Of course, it didn't work.

Amber crossed the room and peered out the window at the sun-filled lawn. Her dad's old shed, still mismatched after painting over smoke damage decades ago, took up the far corner near the swing set. The trees were bigger than Amber remembered, the flower beds unchanged, and the concrete patio showed weather stains and cracks. At least her parents had replaced the fences. Before, they'd been four-foot pickets with a wooden gate in the center of the back fence. Now they stood a foot taller, built solid for privacy. Much nicer.

She turned her gaze out into the neighborhood. The home directly behind hers used to belong to the Nowaks. Immediately to the right, the next house drew her attention. A few families had lived there over the years, but only once had she known the inhabitants well enough to have visited.

The Teldegardo house.

Thinking of Nathan again made Amber's skin prickle. He'd been in the crime scene photos, dead on the floor. His accomplice—his betrayer—had never been caught. In quiet moments Amber worried over whether the police would ever catch the second intruder, but she tried not to dwell on it. The real threat had been Nathan, she was certain of that. And, to put it crudely, he was taken care of. Besides, between the pandemic and the move, she could hardly muster much more fretting.

Shifting movement pulled her focus to the corner of her yard nearest the old Teldegardo house. Long after those troublesome neighbors had moved away, Hannah had planted a pine sapling in that corner for a high school project. Now a healthy tree, its lower branches dipped close to the ground, creating a concealed place beneath it.

Xander and Marigold sat in the cool shadows there, and with a smile Amber realized they'd found a little hiding place. Something half seen, mostly obscured by the trunk of the tree and the needle-covered branches, caught Amber's eye. Something that moved. Her smile froze. Barely discernible, a figure hid on the other side of the trunk. It leaned forward, as if softly speaking to the children.

Amber sucked in a gasp, tried to exhale, but her breath caught. Fear sank into the pit of her stomach.

Hot on its heels came a rush of rage. This was *her* house now, just like that was *her* yard and those were *her* kids. No one had a right to try to—to try to—to what? Amber didn't know, her mind raced too fast, almost buzzing. There was something wrong, fundamentally wrong, down to the core of the world, with the thing beneath that tree, and Amber couldn't think.

Well, if she couldn't think, she'd act.

Rushing through the house called up visceral recollections—playing tag, being sent outside, fighting with her sister, a hundred childhood excitements and crises. Body memories so real that for a moment Amber was fifteen, or twelve, or eight again.

They passed when she darted around Ben in the foyer, through the kitchen, to throw the back door open. From here the dark leaves of a pair of Japanese maple trees obscured the view of that pine.

On the threshold, Amber stopped, sudden dread filling her. She did not want to go check under that tree. Whatever hid beneath it—*whoever*, she tried to correct herself—Amber couldn't force herself to lay eyes on it.

She stood, one hand on the sliding glass door and one on the frame, and called, "Kids?"

No answer. It was all wrong; they knew Amber hated being ignored.

"Answer me *right now.*"

"Amber? What's wrong?" Ben asked at her shoulder. Amber jumped, her foot hit the runner at the bottom of the sliding door, and she stumbled. To catch herself she took a step forward, outside. She opened her mouth to tell him about the figure she'd seen in the yard, but the words stuck like glue on her tongue.

"I can't see the kids," she said instead, then raised her voice again. "I said *answer* me!"

A car door slammed nearby, a bird let out a harsh call, and the yard remained silent.

The breeze trailing across her skin brought goosebumps despite the day's warmth. Which was ridiculous, wasn't it? She had to get this fanciful nonsense under control. But first the kids needed to obey her, so she could show herself that they were fine.

"Xander, Marigold, get your butts over here or you'll spend your first week at the new house grounded!"

"Amber, let's not make a scene." Ben's voice was soft, tinged with a reproach that stung all the more because she deserved it.

With a rustle of branches, Xander and Marigold finally emerged around the trees.

"Mom?" Xander asked, eyes distant and voice full of confusion. His uncertainty doused Amber's anger as abruptly as if she'd been plunged into cool water.

"Xander, buddy, are you all right?" Ben said. Xander's head snapped toward Ben as if he hadn't noticed him. Amber saw no recognition in the boy's gaze.

Without warning, Marigold burst into tears. Xander put a protective arm around her shoulders.

Any neighbor looking out a window might see the new family's kids having a tantrum. They'd be assessing Amber and Ben, and this could be their first impression. Amber shook herself, then hurried to the children. They needed to stop fussing. Amber needed to get the situation under control. Sternness wouldn't work just now. Amber made herself soft instead.

Sinking to her knees, she gently pulled both children to her. Xander tensed, leaning back, his body stiff in her arms. His fingers tightened on his sister's shoulders, pulling her back as well. The resistance lasted for the space of a few rapid heartbeats, before he softened all at once. The confusion left his eyes and he took a shaky breath. Marigold's wailing gave way to sniffling. Xander frowned.

"I'm sorry," he said, and his tone—apologetic without quite understanding why he should be—sounded more mature than Amber had ever heard it.

A confused swell of emotions swamped her; her eyes prickled, her palms itched to clench into fists, her gut tightened, and her shoulders sagged. When the rush receded it left a strange ache in her chest.

"I got confused," Xander continued. "I dunno . . ." He rubbed the back of his neck. "I thought you . . . Never mind . . ."

He trailed away, and Amber didn't press him. She didn't want to know what he'd thought.

"Hey," she said, keeping her voice soft and soothing, "people get confused sometimes. You're okay." They were okay. *She* was okay. Being back here simply called the overactive imagination of childhood to the front of her mind. As the children calmed, so did she. Until she added, "Everything is all right."

Her heart skipped a beat. The words felt like a lie.

PART TWO

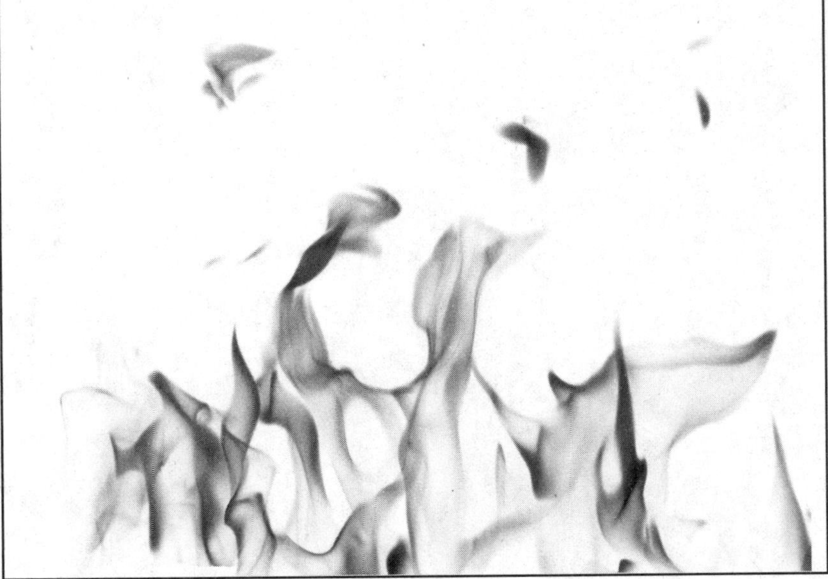

CHAPTER 4

GET IN GOOD

JUNE 1998

The swing's chains squeaked faster. Amber breathed hard, her chest fluttering. She grinned as she hit the right speed and height to create an instant of slack in the chains, a single moment of free-falling. On the downswing her momentum caught up to the slack with a jerk that drew a breathless laugh from her. She'd need to slow down a little to jump off safely, but not too much or she'd lose the game.

Hannah stood by the edge of the swing set, the fingertips of one hand on the bar, straining as far forward as she could without losing contact with the wood. When Amber jumped, her nine-year-old sister (*almost ten*, Hannah had started insisting over the last week) would be allowed to let go, and the chase to the picnic table at the other end of the yard would begin. If Amber got there first, she'd get to start on the swing next turn. If Hannah tagged her first, they'd have to switch. Hannah had started on the swing four times in a row before this turn, but now Amber had the advantage.

At the next sweep forward she jumped off, sacrificing a little distance to time her leap for a solid landing, keeping her feet from simply going out from under her on impact. She hit the ground running, her sister's footsteps thumping in the grass close behind her. Amber let out a laughing shout, putting on an extra burst of speed, but the exultation of the jump and the run didn't last.

Hannah was catching up. Amber wasn't going to win.

So, she took a dive.

Years of losing at tag during recess had led Amber to perfect the art of a realistic trip and fall, allowing her to call a time-out rather than be caught. The trick had worked the day before, in fact, during her final elementary school Field Day. Amber wouldn't miss Field Day, the big event the PTA put on after the last *real* day of school every year, now that she was going into sixth grade. It was basically an all-day gym class disguised as a party, and her fake tumble had gotten her out of the whole end of it.

She'd never told anyone, not even her sister, that she took falls on purpose.

Which meant the tactic worked as well now as it did on the playgrounds and soccer fields.

She faked a stumble and went down.

"Ow!" She took a hissing breath in between her teeth. Sliding a little with the landing put some convincing grass stains and a dirt smudge on the skin of her left knee, even though the fall hadn't been hard enough to bruise. Hannah skidded to a stop next to Amber as she rolled over. She grabbed her knee, gritted her teeth, and repeated, "Ow, ow, owww."

"Are you okay?" Hannah asked.

Amber wanted to grin at the success of her ruse, but instead she made a show of checking her leg and sniffling. She nodded slowly, hiding her satisfaction behind a display of reluctance. Hannah reached down and Amber allowed herself to be pulled to her feet. She pretended to wince, took a fake shaky breath, and gave her sister a thumbs-up.

"I think I'm okay, yeah," she said, and allowed her voice to quaver a tiny bit as she added, "but can we start over?"

"Yeah," Hannah answered. "And maybe—"

"That was some wipeout," a strange voice interrupted.

Hannah's eyes flicked over Amber's shoulder, and Amber turned. A kid stood in one of the neighboring yards, next door to the Nowaks' house, his arms on the fences where the corners of their backyards touched. The Nowaks' bullmastiff, Lacey, sniffed around the bottom of the fence near the boy, tail wagging.

Every other kid in the neighborhood was either Hannah's age or younger, like Hannah's on-again, off-again best friend Steph Nowak and her baby brother, or was old enough to have babysat Amber and her sister when they were little. But this kid looked about twelve, same as Amber. He was pretty much the same height as her, not as awkwardly, gangly skinny but still almost slender, with tanned skin. He ran his fingers through his brown hair and regarded the sisters with a kind of stuck grin, somewhere between fake and friendly.

The rush of excitement that coursed through Amber was the same as she'd had back in the middle of fifth grade, when there had been a new girl in the school she'd been going to since kindergarten. Back then, Amber had tried honesty, admitting as part of her introduction that she was an unpopular kid, to give the new girl a chance to choose whether befriending her was a risk she wanted to take. It hadn't worked out.

Well, she wouldn't be trying that again, and—better, best—it was summer break. Sixth grade didn't start for almost three whole months. She'd have plenty of time to make friends with the new kid, to get in good before he could discover exactly how bad that would be for his own reputation.

"Who're you?" she asked.

The boy put his hands on top of the chain-link fence that separated his yard from the Nowaks', palms between the metal points, and heaved himself up, his lower body pressed against the links and his upper body leaning over a bit, feet dangling above the grass.

"I'm Nathan," he said. "I just moved in." He jerked his head behind him. Past the backyards all facing one another, at an angle between Nathan's new house and the one directly behind Amber's home, she glimpsed the cul-de-sac and a big moving van parked there. Now that she was listening for it, the occasional unfamiliar shouts of the movers rang out.

"I'm Amber," she said. "This is my sister, Hannah."

"Nathan!" a man's voice shouted, and though Amber's attention was on the way the new kid's eyes darkened at the sound, she didn't miss how Hannah flinched at the harsh tone. A man about her father's age, with a less impressive mustache and darker hair, came around the far side of the house. His face was red and drawn in a frown, and he carried a plastic clubhouse, sized for younger kids but designed like a castle—which, in Amber's opinion, nearly made up for the fact that it was basically a baby toy.

"I'm gonna go inside," Hannah murmured, shifting her weight uneasily. She gave a halfhearted wave to the kid before she turned to run back across the lawn. After a few steps she paused and added over her shoulder, "C'mon, Mom's gonna have lunch ready soon anyway."

At that moment the man dropped the castle playhouse and straightened, scowling as he glanced at his son until his gaze took in the two girls. Hannah gave another awkward wave and ran inside. Amber let her unfocused eyes drift to a spot over the top of the adult's head as she prepared herself for the inevitable barrage of boring conversation. He'd ask her what her name is, introduce himself as Mr. Whatever, ask her what grade she's in, what she likes to do. He'd probably put a hand on Nathan's shoulder and say something embarrassing, and Nathan would either roll his eyes or find a way to blame the embarrassment on *her*, and if that happened, she wouldn't get to make a friend.

"Nathan," the man said, and the boy dropped back to the ground and turned. "Go see if you can get lunch over there." He jerked a thumb toward Amber's house before turning to go back to the front of his own. Without looking back, he added, "Don't get in any trouble."

"Okay, Dad," Nathan answered, and before Amber worked out whether or not she should remind them that he hadn't been *invited* for lunch, he was climbing over the fence into the next yard, then hoisting himself over the next fence into hers.

"What's for lunch?" he asked.

The boy pulled his shoulders back and puffed out his chest, head high, jutting his jaw forward a little. On an adult the pose would be aggressive, but coming from another kid Amber recognized it as posturing. Daring her to tell him to go back to his own yard now that he was already in hers. She probably should. His dad hadn't even said hello to her, which wasn't polite, and Nathan simply coming into her yard and expecting to be fed without anyone telling him it was okay was even less polite. But the thought of telling him off—maybe getting sneered at, maybe getting yelled at—made her stomach tighten a little. Worse, though, she was certain if she made him go away now it'd ruin this unexpected chance at starting middle school with a friend.

Instead, she smiled at him.

His pose relaxed, and by the contrast Amber realized part of his tension had been fear. No one had ever been afraid of *her*, so Amber's eyes flicked in the direction Nathan's dad had gone. The new kid was walking across the grass now, though, toward the back door of her house, and she had to hustle to get there ahead of him. If he barged into her home the way he'd barged into her yard, her sister and parents could still scold him. Which might ruin everything.

"Mom!" she called through the screen door before she got to the patio. "Can the new kid come for lunch?" She heard Hannah's voice start to murmur something from within, and she cut her sister off, improvising, "His dad said they haven't unpacked enough to make anything to eat yet."

The hesitation before her mother answered was slight, probably Nathan didn't notice it, but Amber knew what it meant. She was going to get a talking-to later about putting Mom on the spot, forcing her to either send a kid away with the kid right in front of her, or give in whether she wanted to or not. Amber would deal with the scolding when it came, but for now Mom answered, "Sure thing, honey."

"Come on in," Amber said, taking a step toward the house.

Before she could take a second, Nathan grabbed her upper arm. The skin on his palm was warm, and from this close he smelled like smoke, almost unpleasant.

"My dad didn't say that," he said in a low voice, his brows drawn and his eyes flat. "My family has *plenty* of food."

"I didn't say you don't have food," Amber whispered back, giving her arm a shake. She frowned when he didn't let go, but at the same time her cheeks warmed, and she hoped the boy wouldn't notice. Rather than wasting time trying to understand those mismatched feelings, Amber leaned closer to him and said, "I only said your food isn't *unpacked* yet. So my mom wouldn't get mad I invited a friend over without asking her first."

Nathan let go as quickly as he'd grabbed her, the thundercloud frown blowing away as if it had never been there. Puzzlement replaced it. "Your *mom* gets mad about stuff like that?"

She shrugged, trying not to rub her arm and also trying not to grin too broadly when he didn't correct her after she'd called him a friend. Mom's voice drifted out from the kitchen, something about macaroni and cheese, and Amber stilled for a moment to listen for any hint of irritation in her tone. When she realized Mom was only rebuffing Hannah's nearly weekly plea for a jelly-only sandwich for lunch, Amber tuned them out and turned her attention back to Nathan.

"Doesn't everybody's mom?" she asked.

"Nah." He shook his head and moved toward the door again. She expected him to keep his voice down, because she knew if Mom heard the end of this conversation, she'd figure out that they'd been whispering about her. But he spoke at a normal volume. "My dad gets pissed all the time"—Amber winced at the cuss, hoping her mother wouldn't embarrass her by reprimanding him—"but my mom doesn't get mad at me for anything."

Nathan opened the screen door and stepped into her home without waiting for Amber to go first or introduce him.

CHAPTER 5

NOT FAIR

JULY 1998

"Gotta get the right angle," Nathan muttered. He held a magnifying glass, aiming a beam of sunlight at a pile of twigs in his yard. With a tilt of the glass, the light narrowed to a point and Nathan made a victorious noise, but no trails of smoke or licks of flame appeared. Hannah let out a quiet breath, her expression one of guarded relief.

For her part, Amber did a better job of hiding her boredom than Hannah handled her nerves. Dad told her once that the best way to make someone think you were interesting was to let them do the talking. Though Mom had been quick to say he'd been joking, Amber took the advice to heart anyway. So, she hoped she looked interested, and she didn't ask—

"Is anything gonna *happen*?" Hannah said.

Nathan glanced up at her, his eyes flashing and lips pressing together. The anger disappeared so fast Amber thought she might have imagined it. His eyes stayed flat, but he gave an easy grin and pulled a little square of thin cardboard out of his pocket.

"Yeah, something's gonna happen," he said, and flipped the

cardboard open. A matchbook. The back of Amber's neck prickled, but she didn't check the nearby windows. Nothing caught a grown-up's attention faster than acting like she didn't want to be noticed.

"My dad left these out after Fourth of July, been saving 'em for a couple weeks. The magnifying glass trick *usually* works, but I could just use these."

He struck a match with a practiced ease that Amber envied. It hissed as it flared, and Nathan let it burn down, eyes on Amber and Hannah, smiling a little as the flame crept closer to his fingers. At the last moment he tossed it onto the twigs. In stark contrast to the pitiful attempt with the magnifying glass, the kindling caught in a rush. The sun-dry grass turned brown, crisped. The fire spread.

Amber and Hannah scrambled to their feet. Amber's mind filled with an image of the whole yard awash in fire, and her parents' faces if they burned somebody's house down.

Nathan stood, too, but calmly and with that same small smile, his eyes fixed on the flames as they expanded.

"Nathan—" Amber began.

"Yeah," he interrupted in a soft voice, then licked his lips and repeated in a normal tone, "Yeah. We gotta stomp this out."

"No *way*," Hannah exclaimed. "I'm not getting my shoes melted."

"Don't be dumb," Nathan said, rolling his eyes. He put the fire out himself, and his shoes weren't scorched at all. Then he turned and added, "What'sa matter with you, Hannie?"

"Don't call me Hannie."

"You scared of a little fire?" he taunted.

"*No.* I'm just careful."

"Now," Nathan flipped the matchbook open and lit another match, his grin widening, "are you scared?" He watched Hannah, lips set in a wooden smile, eyes flat.

"I don't think—" Amber began.

Hannah must not have seen the warning in Nathan's expression, because she spoke at the same moment, "I'm still not scared of fire, and I'm not scared of you."

"Okay, then," Nathan said. The next moment slowed way down. Like a distant spectator, Amber watched Nathan dart his hand toward her little sister.

Then the stretched-out instant passed and Amber yelped, "Hannah, move!" She grabbed her sister's tank top and yanked her backward an instant too late.

"My hair!" Hannah shrieked, a small flame licking up one of her braids. Amber leaned in fast and blew hard, then licked her fingers and frantically pinched the last smoldering spark out.

In the second of shocked silence that followed, the stink of burned hair in the air, Amber turned her gaze on Nathan. He wiped the grin off his face, replaced by wide-eyed horror.

"I'm sorry!" he gasped, dropping the matches as if it were he who had been burned.

But when his eyes met Amber's, she thought she saw contempt beneath the contrition.

"You did that on purpose," she yelled, pushing Hannah back, stepping between them.

"No, I didn't, I swear," he said, holding up his hands.

"Yes, you did! Yes, you did, you liar!" Hannah shouted.

"No!" Nathan protested, his eyes still on Amber. She scowled at him, but unaccountably found herself struggling not to let the corners of her mouth tug upward—the hot anger that he might've hurt her sister shouldn't have been so easily cooled by the way he made his half apologies to her rather than Hannah. She couldn't help but feel a little bubble of pleasure, though, as he insisted, "I was just trying to scare her!"

"I don't know . . ." Amber said. He deserved to sweat it a moment longer.

"Wouldn't be a *huge* shame if I burned half your hair off, though," Nathan said with an abrupt shift in focus to Hannah, his tone becoming conspiratorial and amused. "You'd still be pretty, and it might even up the score a little between you and Amber, huh?"

The comment hit Amber in the chest, squeezing her breath out. She'd only known this boy a short while; his opinions shouldn't hurt. And so what if Hannah—who took after Mom with her graceful features—*was* prettier, anyway? It's not like Amber even cared about stupid stuff like that. Still, she was mortified to feel her eyes sting. A hot blush rushed up her neck and cheeks. When Hannah let out a weak chuckle the laughter cut, a sharp betrayal.

Nathan's gaze shifted to Amber and he playfully mock-punched her shoulder. "Aw, c'mon, I was just joking," he said. When she didn't answer, he grimaced. "Man, I'm sorry, girls. Hey, lemme make it up to you?"

"How?" Hannah asked. Amber stayed quiet; she didn't trust herself to say anything yet.

"One of the reasons Mom and Dad wanted this house was 'cause it's got a *bar*," Nathan said, his tone rich with hushed importance. "I'll show you, but you gotta be quiet. Mom's asleep."

The novelty of being inside a neighborhood house she'd never visited before slowly replaced Amber's hurt as he led her and Hannah in, through a dimly lit kitchen, into the living room, and across to the shadows behind a counter separating a small space on the far side of the room, where they settled down on the tile floor. Despite the lingering sting of the insult, Amber allowed her gaze to wander. She didn't know anything about bars outside of TV shows and movies, and Nathan had been acting like the bar would be impressive, but Amber gave it a brief inspection and found it lacking—a counter with stools on one side and cabinets on the other, some shelves across from the counter, and barely bigger than a bathroom.

Nathan opened a cupboard and, reaching inside, asked, "Wanna try some wine?"

The bottle he removed seemed big and unwieldy in his hands,

one of which wrapped around the graceful taper in a clumsy contrast that made Amber think less of cool teens partying in a movie and more of herself and Hannah dressing up in Mom's clothes when they were little. Dark glass glinted with a muted gleam in the low light, the liquid inside darker yet. Nathan set it down on the floor in the ring made by three pairs of crossed legs, then leaned back into the cupboard and pulled out three plastic cups. With effort, he uncorked the wine and began pouring.

"I don't want any," Hannah said before Nathan could fill the third cup.

He paused, the bottle poised over the cup, and anger swept his face for half a second before he glanced at Hannah, then Amber, and wiped the expression away. He shrugged.

"Fine, if you wanna be like that," he said, jamming the cork back into the bottle before putting the wine away. After closing the cupboard, he eyed Amber's untouched cup. He raised his eyebrows at her, challenging, and she hoped her reluctance didn't show as she picked it up.

"This is a bad idea," Hannah murmured, not looking at their neighbor.

Amber frowned. Hannah always did stuff like this, telling her what to do, acting like she knew better, acting like *she* was the big sister.

"It's fine. Back off," Amber muttered. She raised the cup to her lips. It smelled sour. Nathan smirked and drank. Amber took a smaller, slower sip, then kept the cup in front of her face a moment, hiding her expression. Terrible, with an aftertaste that reminded her of vomit. Maybe she'd get used to it? Nathan seemed to like it—he'd nearly emptied his cup.

Hannah leaned in close, one hand held up to mask her mouth, her body pressing against Amber's right arm and shoulder as she whispered, "I want to go home."

Amber shrugged her off and didn't whisper at all when she answered, "Then go home."

"*Amber,*" Hannah hissed, blushing and turning her face away from Nathan, but she didn't get up and leave.

Amber shrugged again and took another tiny sip, suppressing her grimace. Nathan had already finished his wine, faint purple coloring his lips, and Amber licked hers self-consciously. Nathan saw and grinned, raising his eyebrows in a way she didn't entirely understand.

Awkward silence fell. Hannah sat with her arms crossed, her body angled away from the others. Nathan picked at a scuff on the cabinet, scratching away at it a little at a time. Amber took another, longer sip of her wine and tried to think of something cool or funny to say.

Instead, she asked, "Is it always so dark in your house?"

In her own home, Mom would have all the curtains pulled aside to let in the light. Here the shades had been drawn over every window, and had been that way anytime Amber had glanced at the house since Nathan's family moved in.

Nathan shrugged. "Mom doesn't like people looking in our house."

"No one cares about looking in your house," Hannah muttered without turning back to the others. Amber ignored her, but Nathan gave her a hard look.

A moment later he was on his feet, holding his hand down to help Amber stand. She let him pull her up, angling her cup to keep him from noticing how little she'd drunk yet. Nathan offered his hand to Hannah as well, but she pushed herself upright without accepting his help.

"Good thing no one's looking, then," he said. "I got something to show you. Come on."

Amber felt a little strange, her head sort of floaty and her limbs sort of loose, as she kept sipping while she followed Nathan, Hannah trailing farther back. Through the kitchen a door opened to the basement stairs. Amber glimpsed an unfinished room, all concrete floor and cinder block walls, piled up with unopened cardboard boxes. There must have been small windows out of sight, because dim light cast the room in blues and grays and deep shadows.

"Come on," Nathan repeated, starting down the steps without turning on any lights first.

Amber lifted her cup to take another sip of her wine. It was empty. She felt unsteady, and thought the uneven stairs might be hard to navigate.

So, when Hannah crossed her arms and said, "There is *no* way I'm going down there," a secret rush of relief coursed through Amber. "I'm going home," her sister added. This time she didn't whisper and didn't wait for Amber to join her. She turned the corner out of sight and a moment later the sliding back door closed a little harder than necessary, almost a slam.

A creak from upstairs followed the sound, and Nathan grimaced. "She woke up my mom," he said in a furious whisper. He ran back up the steps, snatched the cup from Amber's hand, and sprinted back to the bar and his own discarded cup. When he returned he opened the kitchen trash and pushed aside the top layer of garbage, shoving the cups in and down, then covered them over.

"I better go," Amber said, not wanting to be present for whatever fallout would occur if Nathan's mom wasn't fooled. "I gotta make sure she's okay."

"Yeah," Nathan said, and he pointed at the door. He didn't walk her out; instead, he hurried into the living room and threw himself onto the couch, snatching up the remote control and turning the television on. Amber let herself out as quietly as possible.

Still a little disconcerted, Amber fumbled through the gate to cut through the Nowaks' yard and almost forgot to close it behind her so they wouldn't lose their bullmastiff, Lacey, next time they let her out. She turned back and pushed it shut, then set off toward her own yard. Perhaps drawn by Hannah's arrival home alone, Mom stood at the back door, waiting for Amber with a concerned frown. The nearer Amber drew, the more the concern melted away, replaced by growing anger.

"What's on your mouth?" her mother asked, suspicion sharpening her voice.

A thin haze drifted between Amber and the shaky nerves Mom's tone inspired. She wiped her lips with the back of one hand and answered, "Nothing."

When she spoke, Mom leaned down and sniffed, then straightened with a scowl.

"You reek of wine."

She yanked Amber inside. Hannah lurked just beyond the kitchen door, her arms crossed. The haze that separated Amber from her nerves did no such thing for the wave of fury.

"You *told*," she hissed, pulling her arm out of her mother's grasp.

"Did not," Hannah whispered.

Their mom cut off the argument before it could begin by slamming the sliding glass door shut and drawing the curtains. "Go to your room," she said, pointing at Amber. Ignoring Hannah, Mom brushed past to get her address book. "I'm going to have a talk with that boy's mother before I talk to you, so you sit on your bed and think about what you've done."

Holding the railings with both hands, Amber stomped up the stairs and slammed her door once she got to her room. All alone, she burst into furious tears. On the phone in the kitchen downstairs Mom was practically yelling at Nathan's mom. Amber's anger withered away into mortification. Nathan definitely wouldn't stay her friend after this, and it was all Hannah's fault.

Moments after the angry call ended, Mom barged into Amber's room. Amber wiped her nose and blinked hard in an effort to look as if she hadn't been crying.

"*What* were you *thinking*?" Mom asked, arms folded. "Wait until Dad hears about this!"

"About what?" Amber failed to keep belligerence out of her

tone, and almost without noticing it she narrowed her eyes and jutted out her jaw.

"Drinking! Getting drunk!"

"You *never* said I couldn't try wine."

"I assumed you knew better." Mom's voice was cold. "That's not a mistake I'll make again. You're grounded."

Amber's stomach clenched with the injustice—punished for a rule Mom *admitted* had never actually been given to her. Tears stung her eyes again, but this time Amber didn't try to hide them. This time she used them like a weapon, letting her lip quiver and her face crumble.

She sniffed, then wailed, "It's—not—*fair*!"

Mom didn't even answer, just left the room, the disappointment in her eyes so intense that Amber thought it bordered on disgust.

Only a moment later the door opened again with a slow creak, and Amber ground her teeth to keep in a furious shout when Hannah tried to peek in.

"Amber, I tried to tell you—"

"Get out!" Amber snapped.

"I didn't tell on you!"

With a feeling like something was digging out of her chest, Amber's temper broke through any semblance of control and she shouted, "Liar! Liar! I said get out of my room!"

When Hannah still hesitated in the doorway Amber trembled with a barely restrained urge to cross the room and slap her sister. She snatched up her pillow and threw it at Hannah, followed immediately by a teddy bear.

The projectiles had no impact other than prompting Hannah to repeat, "I didn't tell!" Then she held up her singed braid and added, "Not even about this."

"Out!" Amber reached for one of her hardcover books and chucked that at Hannah's head.

Her sister barely dodged in time, then stared from the book

to Amber. Her eyes glittered, but her voice held more scorn than tears as she declared, "You're crazy."

"I'm not crazy, you just won't listen! *Get out of my room!*" This time she screamed, rasping and raw. Hannah finally retreated, giving her one last wide-eyed stare before shutting the door.

Amber stormed over to jab the lock on the doorknob. Sliding down to sit on the floor and lean on the wall, she gave in to a bitter, tearful tantrum.

For about an hour after that, nothing happened. The tears dried and the fury drained. She felt sick to her stomach and thick in her head, and sleepier than a good hard cry normally made her. It wasn't bedtime, but she dragged herself up to lie atop her covers. She fumed and seethed, staring at the ceiling until her eyelids grew heavy and she sank into sleep as if into dark water.

Darkness shrouded her room when a sharp sound pulled her into a bleary wakefulness.

She sat up. From downstairs drifted the murmuring voices of her parents and the canned laughter of a sitcom. The out of place noise had been nearer than that. It came again, to her right. Next time it happened she was ready, and saw a small shape clatter against her window. Someone was throwing rocks at her room.

Nathan stood in one of Mom's flower beds out of sight of the family room window, which cast a yellow square of light onto the ground not far from where his sneakers crushed a patch of heat-withered daylilies. In one hand he held a handful of pebbles, the other drawing back for another toss. His face was blank, almost robotic, until he met her gaze through the glass. A scowl spread across his features.

Amber slid the window open and leaned her forehead against the screen.

"If my mom sees you out there, we're both gonna get it."

"I *already* got it. When my dad got home from work my mom told him I was trying to get the neighborhood girls drunk and . . ." He trailed away, his scowl deepening.

“It’s not *fair*,” Amber whispered. “It’s all Hannah’s fault. She told on us!”

Nathan’s shoulders stiffened, and his expression turned into a thoughtful, cold anger Amber had never seen before. It made her uneasy.

In a calmer voice than anything she would’ve expected, Nathan said, “What a bitch. Maybe she’s cuter, but you’re *way* cooler. She really screwed us over.”

The sting of this second dig at her appearance vanished almost as quickly as it came, erased by his solidarity. Though the combination of lingering wooziness and anger fed a growing headache, Amber smiled with relief. Whatever risk the growing friendship had been at a moment before was gone, their alliance solidified against a common tattletale.

CHAPTER 6

THE INTENSITY UNDIMINISHED

AUGUST 1998

The first week of her grounding, Amber followed the rules. She spent seven sullen days in her bedroom, emerging only for the restroom or to silently join increasingly strained family meals. Rereading her books quickly lost its appeal, and after the first few vitriolic pages she had nothing new to write in her diary. Through her window she heard the sounds of summer break in full swing, but she had nothing but boredom.

Within that boredom, defiance simmered. Her parents had already grounded her for the whole summer, hadn't they? What more could they do to her if she simply . . . kept breaking rules? So when Monday of the second week came, Amber listened at her door as Mom and Dad got ready for work, itching to do *something* other than rot in her room all summer.

"Amber! Breakfast!" Mom called, and Amber decided to dawdle. She immediately shut herself in the bathroom, glancing once at the mirror before dropping her gaze; she hadn't really liked seeing herself ever since Nathan's dig about how much prettier Hannah was. She turned the faucet on and leaned over the counter, watching the water run. The longer she loitered, the less time she'd have to spend at the table with her family, but eventually the smell of bacon enticed her down.

Amber walked downstairs to the sound of Hannah mumbling around a mouthful of food and getting scolded for it. A pause followed, and Amber stepped into the kitchen while her sister gulped a glass of milk before starting over.

"There's an *Angry Beavers* marathon today," Hannah said. "Steph's dad is gonna let us watch it on his big TV, and he said I can have lunch there. Can I stay at the Nowaks' for the day? Please?" Hannah and Steph must have been in an on-again phase of their on-again, off-again best-friendship.

"I don't see why not," Mom said, glancing at Dad with a shrug, which he returned.

"Thanks! It starts at nine, I gotta get ready!" Hannah exclaimed, and stuffed the rest of her breakfast into her mouth with reckless speed.

Half an hour later her parents were out the door and Amber sat on the floor beside her bedroom door, ear pressed to the wood, waiting for Hannah to leave. An unexpected knock startled her, and she scrambled a little away, not wanting Hannah to know she'd been listening, before answering.

"What?" she grunted, the first she'd spoken to her sister all week.

"You used all the toothpaste," Hannah said. "I had to squeeze the last tiny bit out."

"So?"

"Mom left the new toothpaste on the top shelf of their medicine cabinet. I can't reach. You need to get more and put it in our bathroom."

"Fine," Amber said, willing her sister to be done fussing at her and *leave*.

But Hannah lingered. "Amber," she said, voice hesitant now, "I really *didn't* tell on—"

"Whatever," Amber interrupted, impatient with the lie. "Leave me alone."

Hannah let out a frustrated grumble, then—finally—her footsteps thumped down the stairs. The squeaky step creaked. A moment later the back door slid open and shut.

Peeking out her window, Amber watched her sister run across the backyard, through the gate, and vanish into Steph Nowak's house.

Amber let herself out of her room at last.

Now what? A snack wasn't tempting. The only games on the family computer were *Solitaire*, *Math Blaster*, and *Write, Camera, Action!*, and after two years with only those to play, they bored her. She wasn't in the mood for cartoons or channel surfing.

Well, while she figured it out, she could at least grab the toothpaste, give Hannah one less thing to get her in trouble for later. She crossed the hall and pushed open her parents' door, stepping into their bedroom.

There were windows on two walls, one facing the next-door neighbor's house and the other facing the street, and with Mom's thin curtains pushed to the sides the room was brilliantly lit. It was tidy and smelled like them, a comfortable scent even when she'd been angry with them for a solid week.

Amber slipped into their master bathroom and slid open the side of their mirror that concealed the medicine cabinet. She had to stand on tiptoe to reach the toothpaste, and as she pulled the new tube out it tapped a little orange bottle and sent it tumbling down to rattle into the sink.

This wasn't some over-the-counter painkiller; this was a prescription with her mother's name on it. But Mom hadn't been sick, not a sneeze or a sniffle. Amber picked the bottle up and read, "Prozac. Take one tablet once per day by mouth."

Amber had seen commercials for this medication. So, Mom had depression. Amber's notion of what that meant, mostly based off those same commercials, was fuzzy and extremely general—Mom must be sad a lot. It took a moment to muster some sympathy for that as she replaced the bottle and closed the medicine cabinet.

Toothpaste in hand, Amber stepped back into her parents' room.

She paused.

What else might they be hiding?

Maybe she should do a bit of snooping, see what she could find out on purpose instead of accidentally. She stuffed the unopened tube of toothpaste into her pajama pocket, then put her hands on her hips, studying her parents' space.

Nothing interesting jumped out at her.

Amber pressed her lips together. Where would *she* hide something?

With her own diary's hiding place in mind, she made her way to their walk-in closet, a narrow but deep and ill-lit space. She stepped in and a little to her right, letting more sunlight stream in past her and giving her an angle that let her see onto the shelf above the hangers.

It held mostly off-season clothing and a small plastic tub labeled HATS/SCARVES/GLOVES in Dad's blocky printing. At the end nearest the door sat a small cedar box where Mom kept weird stuff like her and Hannah's lost baby teeth and scraps from their first haircuts. At the end farthest from the door towered a stack of old shoeboxes nobody ever threw away.

Amber huffed. She should've known she wouldn't find anything good in here; Mom and Dad were boring.

Something about the stack of shoeboxes caught her eye again, though, as she turned to leave. The one at the bottom was different, its colors more faded, the design old-fashioned, its corners and edges worn.

"Now what's this?" Amber whispered. It wouldn't be anything good, that was sure. Worth a little peek, nothing more, simply to stop herself from wondering about it later.

With care, she slid the whole stack off the shelf. Once in her hands, the slightly shifting weight made it clear that this bottom box was not empty like the rest. Amber sat cross-legged on the floor at the back of the closet, then set the extras to one side, still stacked so she could return everything to its place in the correct order. She lifted the lid on the last shoebox.

Papers filled it.

Amber picked up the first neat bundle, tied with ribbon. Rather than untie it and risk being unable to exactly replace everything, she slipped the whole bundle out of the loop of ribbon and unfolded the first page to find a letter in Mom's handwriting, dated January 3, 1982, before Mom and Dad got married.

A love letter.

"Oh, *god*," Amber muttered. Her *mother*, the woman who lived in a constant state of frazzled distraction, wrote all *this* frilly sweetness? Amber folded the first letter and picked up the next. She read the first few lines, then skimmed. It was mostly the same, letter after letter. Mom obviously loved Dad a lot, but without much imagination.

After that, she set anything that looked like a love letter to one side, unexamined. At the bottom of the shoebox lay a scatter of loose papers. Letters in Dad's handwriting, and the salutation on the first caught her eye: "Dear Mom."

Amber hardly remembered her paternal grandparents. She had a distant understanding that they'd had Dad late in life, and they'd already been really old when she was born. She sorted the loose letters by the dates in the upper corner, from September of 1974 through August of 1975. Dad would've been eighteen or nineteen.

"Dear Mom," the earliest read, in an untidy teenager's version of Dad's writing. "I don't know what to say. I know I been gone a while. Mostly everything's okay. But I thought you should know I got arrested."

Amber gasped out loud, startled herself, and nearly dropped the paper.

"I'm in Montcalm County Jail in Michigan. I don't want you and dad to worry forever I didn't even mean to be gone this long I just needed to cool down and now I'm going to be stuck here for a whole entire year. I'm real sorry I ran off. Could you send me some stuff? Maybe some magazines or some better food than they got in the cafeteria?

"Tell dad how sorry I am. I'm real REAL sorry. I miss you both."

Amber read the letter three times before she set it aside and picked up the first one that was addressed to Dad from her grandmother. It was much longer than the letter he'd sent to her, and the tone jumped around: anger, weepy recrimination, guilt, comfort. Mostly she had questions. "Why did you run away?" "What have you been doing the last five months?" "How have you been keeping yourself?" And most importantly, "Why are you in jail?"

Amber all but snatched up the next letter, as eager to know the answer to that question now as her grandmother had been more than twenty years earlier. Dad's reply was shorter, terse—glancing at later letters, Amber saw the same in every response.

He'd been caught shoplifting beer from a gas station and had punched the middle-aged passerby who'd tried to stop him. He gave little in the way of detail, and though Amber read every last letter in that stack, she didn't learn anything new.

No matter. What she'd discovered was worth the violation of her parents' privacy.

She hurried back to her room, fetched her diary from her own closet, snatched a pen off her homework desk, then darted back to her parents' room. She scribbled down the name and address of the jail where her father had been kept for the better part of a year, then carefully replaced every letter in the box and returned everything exactly how she'd found it.

Diary and pen in hand and toothpaste still in her pocket, Amber went back to her room to check the time. Nearly noon.

Hannah could be home any minute. Which meant getting on the family computer in the corner of the living room and using Ask Jeeves to find out more about the county jail would have to wait until the next time her parents and Hannah were all out of the house at the same time.

Hiding her diary, Amber tried to shove away her teeth-grinding frustration. She forced herself to relax her jaw. The opportunity *would* present itself sometime. When it did, she'd just have to figure out a way to use what she'd learned. Amber was certain she could.

Unfortunately, a series of summer thunderstorms rolled in, so Hannah stayed home every day that week. The sun returned with the weekend—Saturday the fifteenth dawned hot and bright, but Amber's mood remained cloudy. It was Hannah's tenth birthday, the party had been planned for weeks, and although Amber refused her parents' invitation to be un-grounded for that one event, she found no safe time to snoop any further that day, either.

After the last of the screaming kids had gone home—more than ever showed up for Amber's February birthday parties—Amber picked at her dinner of leftover pizza and sheet cake and tried to tell herself that next week would be better.

"Did you have fun at your party?" Dad asked Hannah, settling himself into his seat.

"Yeah," Hannah replied, but she flicked a shadowed gaze at Amber. Neither of them had missed the other's birthday before. "Do you wanna play a board game after dinner?" Hannah asked her, the bright false cheer in her voice belied by the hesitation on her face.

"Sounds like fun," Dad said, his voice too hearty, trying to prompt her to answer.

Amber didn't oblige. Hannah didn't deserve forgiveness just because it was her birthday. Two weeks of Amber's summer had already been wasted, and she had another week of it ahead of her.

After dinner she went back to her room, skipping the board game and keeping to herself until bedtime. Most nights Amber stayed awake after lights out, staring up at the dark. Nathan didn't always come and throw rocks at her window, but he did often. In the dark, the hours crawled by. Flat on her back in bed, Amber's eyelids sagged. She blinked hard, pulling them open again with difficulty. Widening her eyes as far as she could, she willed them not to close again, but her arms and legs felt heavy, her body soft and warm. Amber's breathing slowed. She didn't want to fall asleep, told herself she wouldn't, then did.

Tap.

The small, sharp sound jolted her awake. Her bedside clock told her it was nearly two in the morning.

"About time," Nathan said when she opened the window, his voice soft.

She grinned down at him. These moonlit conversations were the most she'd talked to anybody since getting grounded. Her tummy fluttered every time with the thrill of having a secret, of the secret being a boy calling up to her bedroom window at night. Imagining her parents catching her leaning on her windowsill talking to the neighbor kid while he stood in the dark flower beds gave the feathery excitement a buzzing edge.

"About time yourself," she answered. "It's two in the morning."

"Yeah, something at work pissed my dad off," Nathan answered with no hint of apology. "He stayed up ranting about it forever." He was always complaining about his parents; annoyed when he mentioned his mom, shoulders hunching anytime he said something bad about his dad. "Whatever. When are you gonna hang out again?"

"When I'm not grounded anymore."

Nathan snorted. "It was just *wine*. My dad says your parents must be real stuck up, making a big deal outta *nothing*. Just 'cause of Hannah."

He launched into a complaint about stuck-ups and tattletales, and Amber folded her arms on the windowsill and let him talk. By the end of these conversations, no matter how calm he'd seemed at first, the anger would turn Nathan's voice flat and hard and sharp. His eyes would go cold and distant, his brow furrowed, lips thin and hands in fists. Amber had never met anyone so open about being angry all the time, his intensity undiminished after weeks had passed.

"It's not fair." This line always closed out his tirades. Nathan had rigid ideas about fairness. "You've been in trouble *forever.*"

"I know," she whispered. "I can't do anything about it."

"Well . . ." Nathan rubbed the back of his neck, then grunted. "Huh. Yeah. We'll see."

"What?"

"Don't sweat it. Hey, I gotta go." Without any further goodbyes he turned and crept back through the yards.

For three nights after that, Nathan was a total no-show, and waiting up for him—just in case—wore Amber down. After the third night she picked at her breakfast with disinterest, and between the muzzy-headed sleepiness and her sulking, Amber almost didn't catch it when her sister's mood shifted.

"Mom, outside," Hannah whispered, her voice tense, staring out the screen door.

Amber followed her sister's gaze and her heartbeat sped up. There was Nathan, stepping out from behind one of the Japanese maple trees. He had his hands in his pockets, shoulders hunched a little and head ducked, a sheepish grin plastered across his face. He didn't look at Amber, but instead at her parents, each in turn.

"He was watching us eat," Hannah muttered.

"Don't be ridiculous," Amber countered. So, the daylilies by the back door were crushed again. That didn't prove he'd been standing out of sight, watching them have breakfast.

"He's not—"

"Um, hi," Nathan said through the screen, his hands still in his pockets and the hesitant smile still on his face. He spoke to their parents, his entire demeanor radiating apologetic embarrassment. "I came over to say sorry," he said, a hint of a regretful grimace pulling his smile to one side. "I thought it wouldn't be bad to try a little bit of my mom's wine, except I guess we tried too much."

"That's beside the point, Nathan," Dad admonished.

"I know. I'm sorry. I shouldn't have." Nathan hung his head, the sheepish smile melting into remorse.

Amber marveled. If they hadn't had all those midnight talks, she'd have been totally fooled. A trick like this could come in handy; maybe she'd get him to teach her how to pull it off.

He went on, "I shouldn't have asked the girls to try it. I feel awful for scaring Hannah—"

"I wasn't *scared*," she whispered.

"—and getting Amber in trouble. So, I came over to say I'm really sorry, and if you ever let the girls come play again, I promise, no more alcohol. Not ever."

An uncomfortable pause followed. Amber wanted to chime in, to ask if it was okay now, but Nathan didn't pose the question himself and she was pretty sure he knew what he was doing.

In fact, before her parents could respond, he added, "I'll just be going home now. Bye." He turned and left, his departure abrupt. Was that awkwardness deliberate, too?

Mom and Dad exchanged a measured glance. Amber watched in amazement as Dad's face softened and he quirked his eyebrows questioningly, and Mom sighed and shrugged. Nathan had pulled it off.

Amber wasn't sure she could be as convincing as Nathan, but maybe after two weeks of silence they'd be happy if she simply talked to them again. Eyes on her plate, she said, "I didn't know I was doing something so bad, but I'm sorry, too."

"We can talk about it again another time," Dad said.

The conversation around the table lightened, and Amber

made an effort to answer questions asked of her, in full sentences even.

Once breakfast was done and the kitchen was tidy, she steeled herself for disappointment and asked, "Mom? Can I be done being grounded now? *Pleeease?*"

"Well . . ."

"I wanna go to Nathan's house," she said, then added a small lie. "I wanna apologize to his parents, too."

"What do you think, Dave?" Mom asked.

Dad took off his baseball cap and scratched the back of his head.

"I don't think a kid's whole summer should be ruined over their first big mistake. But"—he held up a hand—"if there's a second big mistake I'll take that all back. Got me?"

"Gotcha," Amber said with a grin. "Thanks!"

"Be home by lunch," Mom said.

Amber glanced at the clock. Nearly three hours. She nodded, grabbed her shoes from the front hall, and let herself out the back door.

Before she'd finished tying the laces, sitting in the middle of the patio, the screen door slid open and closed behind her. She glanced over her shoulder at Hannah, who was pulling her long, curly hair into a ponytail as she paused behind Amber.

"What're you doing?" Amber asked.

"I'm coming, too," Hannah said. "I wanna hang out."

"I don't need my kid sister keeping an eye on me," Amber said, struggling to keep her voice neutral. "If you don't like Nathan, you don't have to come." She finished tying her shoes.

Hannah shrugged, helping Amber to her feet and answering, "Yeah, well. There's nothing else to do. Pete and his friends are too little and Steph's not talking to me right now." Hannah paused, but Amber didn't ask what she and Steph were fighting over this time. After an awkward moment Hannah added, "I'm bored."

"Whatever," Amber said, heading toward Nathan's house. She

didn't try to examine her feelings, a blend of amicable comfort in her sister's presence and niggling hostility at the intrusion. They weren't at odds within her; the emotions mingled seamlessly into a frustrated love.

"You're not really gonna apologize to Nathan's mom and dad, are you?" Hannah asked in a soft voice as they crossed into Nathan's yard.

"Probably not, unless you tell on me if I don't."

"Good." Hannah's voice was relieved. "That woulda been *so* embarrassing."

Amber grinned as she knocked on the door. When Nathan answered he gave Hannah a long, blank stare.

"Hannah's gonna be cool," Amber said at last.

"Sure," Nathan said, his tone skeptical, but he stepped aside to let them in, adding, "Dad's not awake yet, so we gotta be real quiet, okay?"

The girls nodded and followed Nathan to the living room, where he turned on the television and hooked up his game console. Amber could never remember what button to push or when, and by the end of an hour when she'd crashed her frog's jet again, she sat back to watch Nathan and Hannah take on the final boss. In the end they won, and when the scores were displayed Hannah had done the best.

"I'm bored with this," Nathan said with a dark look at the game's results. "Wanna see something really cool instead?"

"Sure," Amber answered. Hannah nodded with an obvious reluctance that made Amber embarrassed to have let her come along.

"C'mon," Nathan said, and as he had on the day of the wine, he led the girls to the basement steps.

"I'm still not going down there," Hannah muttered. "It's creepy, and it's even *darker* today."

"My mom just put some curtains up. But if you're going to be a baby . . ." Nathan gave a disappointed sigh. "You might as well just go home."

Amber snorted and Hannah turned surprised, hurt eyes on her. Chagrin tugged at Amber for a moment—she hadn't meant to hurt her sister's feelings, the sound had just come out. Before she could backtrack, she heard again the little laugh Hannah had given when Nathan said Amber wasn't as cute as her, and so instead of apologizing, Amber turned the snort into a full-on laugh, chuckling the words "Such a baby" as she let the forced mirth trail away.

"*I'm* a baby?" Hannah repeated. "You're the one who can't even sleep at night if your closet door is open."

Amber's cheeks heated and she half turned, angling herself so that if Nathan was smirking at her, she wouldn't have to see it. "You *should* just leave if this is how you want to act," she told Hannah, going for lofty and mature but sounding sullen instead, even to herself. "But we're not doing anything wrong, so when you do go home there's nothing to tell. *Right?*"

"It's not like that," Hannah hissed, but Amber only shrugged. After another moment of watching Amber, clearly hoping for a response or—Amber ignored a small, guilty pang—some sisterly reassurance, she huffed and left.

"Well?" Nathan said, standing at the open door to the basement steps with his arm out to usher Amber down before him.

"Will you turn a light on?" she asked.

"It's got a pull cord, can't turn it on from up here."

She hesitated for one second. Weeks ago, when afternoon light seeped in through high windows, the basement had been ghostly blue and gray. Now shadows had taken over. The stacked boxes took on an ominous quality, and she had the sudden and impossible idea she might get lost among them and never find her way back up.

Stupid. She pushed the thought away and preceded Nathan

down the steps, nearly stumbling when he closed the door behind himself and cast them into deeper darkness.

Nathan must have heard her falter, because his voice muttered, “Careful,” and his hand settled on her shoulder. She’d never been so alone with a boy in her whole life, and it finally occurred to her to wonder what he wanted to show her.

At the bottom of the steps he slid past her, his chest brushing her back. A moment later came the rasp of a pull chain. She stood blinking in the harsh light of a bare bulb in the center of the basement’s ceiling.

“Over here,” Nathan said, and she trailed behind him as he wove between cardboard box skyscrapers.

In the back corner sat a small, boxy shape. Nathan waved her over, and she came closer. The dim shape turned out to be a wire trap with a mouse inside, circling the cage. On the floor lay a pair of leather work gloves. Nathan pulled them on; they were clearly his father’s, much too big for his hands. He picked up the trap and fumbled with the latch, the oversized gloves making him clumsy.

“Ever heard how *loud* one of these can get?” he asked over his shoulder.

Amber frowned, puzzled. The door to the trap sprang open with a rattle and Nathan jammed his hand inside quick as a snake. He grabbed the mouse and pulled it out, and now Amber saw why he needed the gloves. The little animal squeaked and squirmed, biting the leather.

“Listen,” Nathan said.

He squeezed the mouse. The noise it let out was louder than anything she thought could have come from something so small. His grip relaxed and the mouse fell to scratching and biting again, frenzied now. He tightened his fist once more, and it made the same piercing, sickening squeal.

Amber’s teeth ached in sympathy. Nathan squeezed the mouse again and the pressure built around Amber’s lungs, too. Her mouth was dry. Nathan didn't let up. Amber couldn't blink, couldn't look away from the black little eyes. She tried to draw a breath, failed, couldn't fight past the pressure to expand her lungs. From the corner of her eye she saw Nathan, watching her the way she watched the rodent in his fist. Her belly twisted into a hard knot.

If she told him to stop, would he? She doubted it, and under that doubt tugged a thread of fear.

Without a word, he stopped and put the mouse back in the cage. He set the trap and the gloves back where he'd found them. Amber couldn't make herself check to see if the mouse was still running around. Good thing Hannah had left early after all.

And on the subject of leaving, Amber thought of the breathless stillness that had caught her up, and lunchtime or not, she needed to go and be alone for a little while.

"Mom said I couldn't stay too long," she lied. "I better head home."

Nathan walked her to the door, following close behind her. The skin on the back of her neck prickled. The dim kitchen seemed bright after the basement, making everything that had just happened feel like a nightmare—unreal and strange, but dismissible. Nathan opened the back door for her, and she didn't flinch from the nearness of him as she slipped out into the hot summer sun.

"You'll come back tomorrow," Nathan said, and was he asking her if she would or telling her to?

A ghost of that breathless pressure made her lungs catch. After all that, did she still want to?

"Yes."

PART THREE

CHAPTER 7

KEEP AN EYE ON IT

JUNE 2020

"Take those back inside," Amber called to Xander, catching him as he stepped out with a stack of paper plates in his hands.

"I'm *helping*," he protested.

Amber breathed deeply, slowly. A handful of the neighbors were out in their own yards enjoying the mild mid-June evening, having Father's Day cookouts. Even busybody old Mrs. Jones next door, the one person still living on this block who had been here back when Amber was a kid, puttered around her garden. Amber didn't need to turn her head; from the corner of her eye she glimpsed Mrs. Jones near the privacy fence, where the sound of shears clipping had stopped and the top of her head appeared to peer over at Xander after his indignant exclamation.

Amber used to find Mrs. Jones intimidating—always acting superior to everyone else all through Amber's childhood, always giving local kids the stink eye or a shrill scold. Adulthood had shown Amber the truth, though: Everyone pretended to be more respectable in public than they actually were. Mrs. Jones, no matter what she might tell herself about the rest of them, wouldn't be any different or better than anyone else.

Still, spending time outside like this when everyone else was, too, strained Amber's nerves. Her family might as well have been on display, and she and Ben didn't subscribe to these fake holidays. But they were new in the neighborhood, and there was value in showing people what they wanted to see, at least at first. Which meant grilling—and no displays of temper even if they were warranted.

Taking care to keep any sharpness out of her voice, Amber pushed herself to be patient instead as she said, "I've already told you three times, Xander. *Three.* We can't bring the plates out until the food's all ready, or the wind will blow them away. Take them back in, and go watch a show with your sister until we're done grilling, okay?" She paused, and when Xander didn't answer right away she repeated herself with a little more force, "*Okay?*"

"Okay, okay," Xander huffed.

He went back into the house, and Amber's irritation diminished. The lingering summer evening settled down over the neighborhood and the sky shone bright without any unpleasant glare. A warm breeze fluttered the pristine tablecloth pinned to the picnic table, set exactly how Amber wanted it. Ben had mowed the grass earlier. Anyone peering into the yard wouldn't find any detail amiss, and the privacy fences did keep them from being *too* exposed. On top of that, the smell of the burgers promised a meal that would taste as good as Amber had made sure the picture-perfect family dinner on the patio was going to look.

"Kid's getting an attitude," Amber remarked, moving up behind Ben, standing by the grill, monitoring the burgers. He maneuvered carefully to stir the coals, and flames licked higher. She leaned her cheek on his shoulder, and with his free hand he reached back to give her arm a pat. Breathing in the smell of him, Amber smiled.

Ben picked up the white, red-topped bottle of lighter fluid and carefully squeezed some onto the coals. Light and heat flared up.

Ben sounded more indulgent than frustrated when he agreed, "Yeah, he's at the age when it kind of starts."

It was on the tip of Amber's tongue to make a joke—if she'd known they'd be so difficult, she might not have wanted to be the first one in the family to have kids—but it was, perhaps, a little too harsh. Xander's behavior had been leaning toward defiance lately, but that wasn't really out of the ordinary for a six-year-old. They weren't angels, children.

So instead Amber said, "Yeah. Kids stop being sweet and start being just . . . adults, but smaller, way sooner than people realize, I guess."

Ben shrugged but gave an agreeable hum and they lapsed into a comfortable silence. Xander had left the door to the house open—flies would get in, but the worry slipped away from Amber—and the over-the-top *boings* and *bonks* of cartoon sound effects drifted out, followed by a peal of laughter. Too much screen time was supposed to be bad for kids, but they were being good and clearly enjoying themselves, and giving her and Ben a moment to just be together.

A lawnmower buzzed in one of the yards down the street, someone splashed in a pool nearby, and Amber closed her eyes, relaxing into the easy quiet between herself and her husband. He stirred the coals again. Had he always used the long-handled metal spatula for that? Wasn't that for flipping the burgers? She didn't remember him actually flipping the burgers in a while, though.

On the ground near the grill sat a second bag of charcoal, and Amber stopped leaning on Ben when he reached down to rip open the top. He hefted it over the grill, held the bag carefully, and poured slowly, letting the little black chunks clatter down into the fire. The heat rose, washing pleasantly over Amber, then the breeze shifted, blowing the smoke into their faces. Amber's eyes watered as Ben reached for the lighter fluid again, squeezing a stream onto the new coals. The fire expanded with an audible *whoosh*, and the skin on her face tightened a little in response to the heat. Ben stopped squeezing the white bottle, cutting off the flow of accelerant, in time to stop the flames leaping up the stream.

He stepped back, and Amber leaned on him again, wrapping both of her arms around one of his. When he turned his hand so his palm touched her thigh, she tightened her fingers over the subtle shifting of the muscles in his arm. She coughed, the smoke blowing over them rasping in her throat. Ben glanced at her, the contentment on his face marred by mild concern. Amber gave him a small smile and the hint of worry eased out of his red, watering eyes.

Amber's eyes stung and dripped, too. Pressing her face against his arm, she wiped them on his sleeve.

"Hey," he protested, laughing. He pretended to try to pull his arm away from her. Amber chuckled and tightened her grip. This time when he squeezed the lighter fluid, he aimed the arc of it directly onto the burgers. Orange light flared and the flames reached higher. Amber's lungs burned and her skin prickled. The smoke took on a scent of burned meat. Amber let go of Ben's arm as he reached for the long-handled spatula again. She hooked her thumbs into the pockets of her shorts, still smiling as she watched the way Ben moved. The fire in the grill roared and Amber reached for Ben's hand even though he was still holding the lighter fluid. Her fingers trailed over his.

"What are you doing?" a voice called from nearby.

Amber glanced up.

"What?" Ben said.

"I said, *what* are you *doing*?" Mrs. Jones repeated, standing on the other side of the fence between their yards, her hands curled around the wood at the top. The older woman must have been on tiptoe in order to shout at them. Her frown hovered somewhere between puzzled and angry. "I never saw anything so foolish in my life!"

Amber followed her gaze back to the grill.

The quiet peace of the moment with Ben shattered.

Alarm spiked through her, sharp and electric. With a cry she jumped back—away from the raging fire, out of the reeking smoke.

Her eyes burned. A cough wracked her and wouldn't clear. Heat *poured* off the grill. Amber's face stung, her skin hot and tight. Like a sunburn. All down the front of her neck and her arms, too. That warmth didn't penetrate deeper than her skin. The pleasant glow in her chest collapsed to nothing. It left in its place a crumbling cold.

"Ben," she coughed, covering her mouth and nose with one hand and swiping at her eyes with the other. "What the fuck?"

"Oh, *shit*," he exclaimed.

Snatching an oven mitt off its hook, Ben shut the lid on the grill. He turned the vents at the top to close them. Inside the fire crackled, but without fresh air it would soon sputter and die.

"The whole neighborhood stinks! What were you thinking?" Mrs. Jones said with a shake of her head. Without waiting for an answer, the older woman snorted and turned to storm away from the fence. She hadn't really been asking them, she'd been using the question as a way to scold a pair of adults she barely knew. Sick, ashamed anger coursed through Amber, but she couldn't very well go shouting at a little old lady.

Instead, she rounded on Ben. "What was that, Benjamin?" she asked, keeping her voice low, refusing to allow herself to be overheard in any other yards, but trembling with embarrassed fury.

"What? What was that, yourself? You just watched me do that!"

Amber's eyes widened and her lips thinned. Heart hammering, her thoughts moved as if through a fog. What had happened? Why had they stood there, doing that? Unease was a cool twist in her belly, thick and heavy. Amber summoned another tide of fury to overwhelm the fear and push it away.

"I'm not your mother, Ben. It's not my job to hold your hand and tell you how to cook dinner. You're a fucking firefighter—I shouldn't have to remind you not to play around with fire."

She whirled and stormed back into the house. When her mind tried to drift back to the hazy way she had stood there, blissfully watching her husband build up the fire and scorch the food without a second thought, she reined herself in. *She* wasn't responsible for Ben's actions. *He* was the one who'd done all that. Damned stupid. And on top of the ruined dinner and the uncomfortable scene in front of the neighbors, she had to figure out what to cook before the kids started acting up, too. Ramen noodles, she guessed, and grunted at the thought of eating that garbage instead of a good, juicy burger.

When Ben followed her inside her spine stiffened and her shoulders tensed. If he got defensive, she'd let him eat whatever was left of his burgers for dinner before she'd make anything for him.

He came up behind her and put his hands on her shoulders, squeezing tentatively. "I'm sorry," he said, and Amber let out a long, slow breath. "Dunno what came over me, but you're right. I shouldn't have blamed you for not stopping me."

"Thanks."

"That was really weird."

Amber hesitated. "We're just . . . tired. It's been a weird summer," she said, turning. "Ramen for dinner, I guess?"

He made a face. "I still have beef, I'll pan fry some new burgers and we'll salvage the night."

Amber forced a smile. The smell of the scorched meat lingered in her nose. But the kids would be happier if they still had their hamburger-picnic-table dinner, and letting the neighbors see them all fine and acting normal might help erase whatever strangeness they'd just done.

So she nodded and helped him get the last of dinner ready. They ate outside, and if a lingering unease tightened her chest and darkened Ben's eyes when either of them glanced at the grill, it was easy to ignore. The kids behaved well, and one of the neighbors—not Mrs. Jones—walked closer to their yard to call out a friendly introduction.

By the time the day was over everything returned to normal, and Amber put the grill and the burned meat out of her mind. She got the kids to bed, then took a shower, leaving the ventilation fan off to allow the steam to fog up the bathroom mirror too much to see her reflection clearly. When she emerged, a towel wrapped around her hair and her pajamas clinging a little where her back had still been damp when she got dressed, Ben glanced at her from the bed where he waited with the television remote in hand.

"One sec," she told him. "I'm starving again, I'm gonna go get a snack." She crossed to the bedroom door.

Marigold lay face down on the floor outside the door.

For a moment the small form was too still, too lifeless. Amber winced, sucking in a breath, the images she'd seen in the crime scene photos flashing before her eyes. Her stomach clenched, and in spite of the humidity rolling out of the bathroom, a chill shivered through her.

Then she shook her head and Marigold murmured in her sleep and stirred a little, rolling her head to one side and putting her thumb in her mouth.

"What's up?" Ben asked from behind her, and Amber moved to one side, letting him see past her to the sleeping child. He sighed. "Last night I found her in a linen closet," he said, shaking his head. "Just about scared the shit outta me."

Amber bent, scooped Marigold up, and carried her back to her own bed. She tucked the little girl back in and slipped out without waking her. Taking care to skip the creaky step on her way down, Amber fetched a bowl of white cheddar popcorn from the kitchen and returned up the stairs as silently as she'd gone down. When Marigold finally settled she always slept like a stone, but Xander was a light sleeper, and Amber didn't feel like having to waste her evening soothing him if he woke up.

After she'd shut her bedroom door behind her, she said, "I wouldn't care where she sleeps, honestly, as long as she does sleep. And as long as she's not getting freaky with it."

"Getting freaky?" Ben repeated, laughing.

"Dangerous, I mean," Amber groped for an example and settled on a couple of extremes, as much to make her point as to forestall any more teasing from Ben. "She's not trying to climb into the oven or shut herself in the refrigerator, y'know? No, for real though, she can sleep on the floor every night, I don't care. It's when she creeps around all night that it makes me crazy."

"What d'you mean?" Ben asked.

"You always sleep through it," Amber said, rolling her eyes with an indulgent kind of envy. "A bomb could go off on the bed and you'd never know it."

Ben laughed but didn't deny it. "So, what? She sneaks around at night?"

"You saw that movie about Manson? The scene when his cult guys snuck into houses and rearranged everything at night?"

"Nope."

"Huh. Well, they did that. Anyway, sometimes Mari goes around at night and moves shit. Sometimes she makes a *huge* racket. No clue how Xander sleeps through it," Amber snorted. "But he's always in bed. And the damnedest thing is the kid's getting sneaky. I can't even catch her. I just follow the sounds of her thumping around from room to room until she stops. Whenever I talk to her about it the next day, she says she doesn't remember." Amber paused, considering, then added with a hint of uncertainty, "I think I believe her. Unless she's getting better at lying."

"Sounds annoying," Ben said.

"It is. And . . ." Amber trailed off for a moment, took a breath, and reminded herself that this was *Ben* she was talking to, the one person she didn't always have to be rock solid in front of. Sighing, she finished, "It's getting to me, Ben. I sleep badly enough lately as it is. I'm going to have to think of some way to get her to stop."

"Come here," he said, holding his arms open to her, and since his tone was commiserating, not condescending or dismissive, she smiled and settled down next to him, offering him some of the popcorn. They watched a couple episodes of a comedy show, then Ben got up to use the bathroom while Amber went to each window in turn, twitching the curtains to be sure they were drawn all the way closed against the night.

Checking the curtains before bed had become a nightly ritual for Amber in recent weeks. Amber's old bedroom—now Xander's bedroom—faced the yard, and it was still that view a deep part of Amber's mind expected to see when she glanced out of the master bedroom windows. Instead she found herself gazing out through the branches of a tree growing too near the house—and beyond them, the street—on one side, and on the other she peered across the narrow divide at the side of nosy old Mrs. Jones's house. It was jarring every time. The blackout curtains she and Ben had hung helped, but not much.

Most evenings, Amber could even convince herself that this was the only reason for the curtains. Most evenings she could force herself not to accidentally glance at the night-dark window reflecting the room behind her and her own face. But sometimes she glanced, sometimes she couldn't help herself. Her reflection never glanced back, window-Amber's eyes remaining downcast. If she stared long enough, would it look up at last? If she got Ben, would he see it, too, or would he think she was losing her grip?

She should get her phone. She should film her reflection and see if the camera picked up what she saw. But at that moment the toilet flushed in the en suite bathroom, and the last thing she needed was to worry Ben before she could figure out what was going on. With another quick twitch of the curtains, Amber cut off any chance of an accidental peek, whether at the jarring view or at her own face.

They had kept their old bed—her parents' king-sized mattress and frame sat in storage with everything else, gathering dust while Amber figured out what she wanted to do with it all—and on nights that Ben was home he slept still as a statue, and the white noise machine was as soothing as ever, and the curtains were tightly drawn, and still she tossed and turned through most of every night.

Amber managed to get an hour, maybe a little more, of fitful sleep before a nightmare jarred her into full wakefulness.

Lying flat on her back in the bed, she stared at the ceiling, trying to remember what the dream had been. She could recall almost nothing; a memory more in her body than her mind of heavy suffocation and a piercing, sickening noise, a faint taste of copper and the pricking on the back of her neck and heat in her cheeks of being watched, judged.

It took a long time to banish the shallowness of her breath and the trembling of her hands. She had barely begun to sink back into sleep when the bedroom door rattled in its frame. A small, hesitant sound, it nevertheless woke Amber up as fully as if someone had shaken her.

Her eyes snapped open, fixing briefly on the clock. 2:02 in the morning.

She rolled over slowly, careful not to shift the mattress too much with her movement, and peeked past Ben's solid, sleeping form toward the door. She couldn't sleep at night unless it was locked, and the kids knew that. One of them needed her for something—Marigold had wet the bed *again*, or she was engaging in her new strange habit of sneaking around at night, or Xander woke up from a nightmare of his own.

Amber didn't jump out of bed right away, though. Sometimes if she pretended not to hear them lingering out there, they'd go back to sleep on their own. In the interest of encouraging self-reliance (and getting back to sleep sooner, herself) Amber stayed quiet and waited for whichever one of them it was to either go back to bed or knock.

What followed instead was a dry scraping sound.

The dim glow of her alarm clock provided scant illumination for the room; even so, Amber was certain the doorknob moved. The house had the kind of doors that were locked by pushing a round little button into the doorknob, which Xander had discovered to his great satisfaction were terribly easy to pick.

The doorknob moved again, and Amber knew he was out there, bending over the lock with a toothpick or some other slender poking thing he shouldn't have, trying to break into her room in the middle of the night by the dim glow of the hallway nightlight. She shouldn't let this behavior go, but the idea of being able to just go back to sleep proved a stronger temptation. So, as long as he didn't succeed in picking the lock, Amber decided to stay silent and hope he'd get bored and go back to bed on his own. At least he was being quiet about it. She sighed and closed her eyes, forcing herself to keep still in the bed though her legs wanted to move now that she'd been woken up.

The first lassitude seeped into her limbs, the first soft touch of sleep, and at that moment the expected knock sounded at the door.

Amber sat straight up in bed, heedless of whether the abrupt movement would jostle Ben out of his own sleep. He mumbled and turned his head away.

The knock had been . . . wrong.

There was no other word for it. Amber knew the way the kids knocked. That one single, dull thump had been more like something falling against the door. Too dull, too low. A soft sound, almost furtive. Stealthy.

Amber reached out to shake Ben awake but paused just before her fingertips brushed his shoulder.

What was she thinking? How could a knock be wrong? It had

startled her just as she was falling asleep, that's all. Whichever kid was out there had bad timing, nothing more sinister than that. She drew her hand away without touching her husband.

It came again.

A muffled thud, too low to the ground. Right by the floor. Was it Marigold? Lying with her face against the carpet outside, trying to peer under the crack in the door? Somehow the simple image—innocent, almost cartoonish—squeezed the breath out of Amber. Cold oozed through her.

The next knock struck high on the door, way up at the top. Amber sucked in a thin gasp, throat tight, then couldn't exhale until the knock repeated, still impossibly high. The air blew out of her, shaky and rushed. She pushed the covers off in a slow fumble.

From the hallway, soft and sibilant, whispered a voice, the words lost under the white noise machine and the muffling of the door. It could have been either child. It could have been neither. Amber's mouth dried and her eyes stung. The whispering went on and on. Her stomach tightened.

Whoever stood out there muttering softly in the night never took a second to draw breath.

The tingling on the back of her neck and her palms became painful, prickling. Cold needles crawled over her skin.

Waking Ben didn't cross her mind a second time.

She pushed herself out of bed. On legs made of wood she went to the door. The moment her fingers brushed the doorknob it rattled again. Another knock sounded—she imagined a body falling against the door, heavy but muffled and lacking intent—from too high up. Amber slapped her hands over her mouth to keep in the scream pressing into her throat from somewhere within her chest.

Dredging up what strength she could against the spine-deep dread, Amber reached for the one thing she knew could buoy her above any other feeling. Anger.

The kids were on the other side of that door trying to frighten her, trying to play a prank, thinking they were fucking funny scaring her in the middle of the night like this. Probably hitting the top of the door with a broom, taking turns whispering so it would sound like one never-breathing mutter, covering their own mouths to muffle not screams but laughter.

The anger flared high and bright. Amber seized it, leaned into it. It drove the cold away, pushed the weakness back. Waking her up in the night? Ruining her sleep for some bullshit prank? Trying—yes, only *trying*—to scare her? Her blood ran hot. This was out of line, the kids had gotten out of hand, and, oh, Amber was going to put them back in their place. Twisting the knob and throwing open the door, Amber put on her most wrathful face. The one that promised not merely consequences but *punishment*.

After the pitch dark of the bedroom, the ghostly blue glow of the night-light illuminated the hallway perfectly.

It was empty.

A terrible weight settled in Amber's chest, smothering the fire of her anger, leaving her cold and breathless. Where were the children?

The hallway bathroom door stood ajar, a second night-light glowing peacefully within, showing the toilet and the sink and no hiding shadows. Xander's door was closed, Marigold's cracked open a little bit. A decorative table stood to her right, too small to hide under or behind. The top steps of the staircase at the end of the hall harbored no giggling or cringing fugitive children.

The emptiness made her skin crawl.

No way, there was *no way* she had imagined the voice and the knocking. Her breath came faster. The comfortable haven of the bedroom behind her lost its familiarity, became the only looming pool of unlit blackness on the second floor. She stood in the doorway, on the border between the hallway—empty as a fake smile—and the shadows gathered at her back.

The skin up her spine and atop her scalp tightened.

Dread settled in her belly, a certainty that if she turned to look, her room would be gone. There would be nothing but a gaping impenetrable void. She *had* to turn, had to show herself that the darkness was only darkness. She had to, or feeling that nothingness behind her would make her scream. But Amber went cold at the thought of what she would not see in the hallway if she didn't keep an eye on it—what would move through it or exist in it the moment she turned her back.

Indecision turned to paralysis. This went beyond not wanting to turn. Amber couldn't move. Her feet stuck to the floor. Her muscles coiled with tight tension that had no release, that locked her in place. Amber's breath came faster and faster, more and more shallow—

The sharp crack of a door closing echoed up the steps.

Marigold.

The fear broke like a dam, a wave of relief washing through Amber so strong her knees went rubbery and she braced herself on the doorframe. Why should the relief be this powerful? It was silly. No, it was *ridiculous*, a testament to how badly the little girl's antics had frightened Amber. She straightened her spine and scowled.

Marigold's odd little post-move rebellion, sneaking out of bed in the night when she'd never done anything like that in the old condo, had gone on long enough. Amber was done with it. Several times since the move, she'd come out of her room in the morning to find Marigold asleep on the floor outside her bedroom door, stretched face down on the carpet. Once she'd found Mari curled up on the bath mat, and twice when Amber went downstairs in the morning Marigold was snoring on the couch.

Talking calmly about the behavior during the days after clearly hadn't worked. As if Amber had room for only one emotion, anger pushed the fear down and back once more. Before she knew what she wanted to do, she was halfway down the stairs. The time had come to put a stop to this. Marigold needed to understand who was in charge in this house, and it was not a four-year-old girl.

"Marigold," Amber hissed through gritted teeth. "Where are you hiding? Come out right now or you're going to have a *big* time-out before you even go back to bed."

Silence in the foyer. Moonlight filtered through the window in the front door, falling on the floor, and images from the crime scene photos swam before her eyes again. She could almost see . . .

No.

No.

A soft voice called, impossible to understand. Sour bile rose in the back of Amber's throat. She strained to hear the unintelligible words, but a ringing built in her ears. The whisper ebbed and flowed, never clear but always sharp and hateful, always from the same direction.

The kitchen.

Amber turned that way, ignoring the cold creeping up from the base of her spine as she put the entryway behind her.

In the kitchen she considered fumbling for the light switch but thought better of it. What would it feel like if she reached for the switch and something grabbed her instead? The true fear, not of the dark but of what lurked in the dark. But that was ridiculous. No. That wasn't the reason she kept her hands clutched close to her chest. If she turned the light on and let her eyes adjust to the brightness, she'd have a harder time getting to sleep again once Marigold was caught and settled, that was all. Nothing to do with the things in the dark that she didn't want to see.

What things?

The question came to her sharp and sudden.

What things in the dark that she didn't want to see?

Light footsteps thumped through the living room. With an uneasy blend of relief (at the thought of resolving this midnight escapade and returning to bed, *only* at the thought of bed, *nothing* to do with leaving the kitchen and its thick blackness) and buzzing nerves, Amber hurried to follow the sound.

"Marigold?" she called and cringed at the sound of her own voice. She sounded like a child herself, crying out in the night. Amber cleared her throat and tried again, "Marigold."

She meant to say it sharply, but it came out meek.

The back hall that ran from the living room to the door into the garage was a shadowed pit. Amber's eyes watered, her chest constricted, as she stared down into it. When she'd been about five, she'd developed a terror of this hallway, had nightmares about it for a year, then abruptly forgot her fear. Until this moment.

At the far end, in the deep darkness, a scrape came low and soft. Fingernails scratching down the walls? It grew louder.

No. Closer.

With a strangled squeak, Amber finally flicked a light switch, turning on the hall light.

A shadow lingered at the end.

Amber blinked her stinging eyes, and the shape was gone. Nothing more waited there than the far door seen through the blur of frightened, unshed tears.

The tiled hallway stood empty.

Amber's watering eyes made her nose run. When she sniffed, the sound of her own inhalation made her jump. Where was Marigold—what had made that scraping noise?

The hall offered no hiding places; her office stayed locked and the open laundry room door displayed a clearly empty space. Nothing could've been there.

She must have imagined the sound, the shape. Had to have. No other explanation . . . unless the child had gone through the door into the garage.

Amber's mouth went dry. She forced herself down that hallway, picturing the scene: coming to the halfway mark, out of reach of the light switches at either end of the hall, and plunging into sudden darkness. Her next breath rattled in her throat. Her gaze fixed on the deadbolt on the garage door.

It was locked. Marigold absolutely could not be in the garage, she couldn't have locked that deadbolt behind her. Amber's relief nearly knocked her off her feet; she leaned against the wall and slid down, sinking lower and lower until she sat on the floor in the narrow rectangle cast by the hallway light into the living room.

From the shadows beyond that illumination, a glitter reflected on a pair of eyes.

"Marigold!" Amber gasped, shooting back to her feet. She stumbled, threw a hand out for balance, and struck the light switch.

Darkness engulfed her.

Amber blinked. She'd grown accustomed to the light and now could see nothing. She squeezed her eyes shut and said, "Marigold, this is not funny, you stop this right now."

A cool exhalation breathed across her cheek. Amber's eyes snapped open and her hands flew up and closed on nothing.

No one was there.

A gaping pit, icy black and sharp, opened up in her chest. It squeezed the breath out of her. Her heart stuttered, lurched, and kicked into a painful hammering. A faint taste of copper rose from the back of her throat. Where the breath had brushed her cheek, the skin tingled. The chill of it crept through her, struck down to her bones, and a violent shiver wracked her.

Amber fought to suck in a loud, shuddering breath. The house settled into a deep, still silence in which nothing moved or spoke. The wind in the trees outside died away. In a world of mute, motionless darkness, Amber trembled. The back of her neck prickled, sharp with the sensation of being watched. Her thoughts ran in circles, a whirl of barely coherent terror that abruptly slammed up against one stone-solid certainty looming out of the swirling fog of her mind.

Marigold was not out of bed. Marigold had not been out of bed all night.

A soft whine escaped her, and Amber clapped her hands over her mouth. If she cried out now, she wouldn't be able to stop. She'd scream and scream.

She'd lose her control.

Bed. She had to get back to bed. Get back to Ben. Make this all not be happening anymore. Her stomach flipped and her feet were lead, weighed down to the floor. The first step was a wrench, took all of her will. Her fingers pressed into her cheeks where she still covered her mouth as the very act of turning for the exit from the living room made the urge to scream surge higher, a physical force pushing up her throat.

With that first step the paralysis broke. She didn't run—wanted to so badly her legs trembled, but walked stiff-legged and shaky instead. If she ran back up the stairs instead of walking, whatever was happening would start again and worse. Much worse. The knowledge dropped into her mind wholly formed and unquestionable. To run would be to bring it all down on herself.

Her spine tingled and her scalp crawled. Amber's breath whistled in and out of her nose, mouth still covered. The back of her neck itched but the last thing in the world she wanted to do was look behind her. By the time she reached the upstairs hall her pajama shirt clung to her, damp under her arms and breasts and down her back. Her breath hissed, fast and strained.

The hallway at the top of the stairs waited, unchanged in the cool, dim night-light's glow. Amber paused and shook herself, dropped her hands from her face. The thunderous pace of her heartbeat began to slow, her breathing grew less ragged. Before her, the door to her own bedroom still stood open, revealing not the terrible void of her fears but the safe haven of her covers and her husband.

One thing had to be done before she could retreat to that comfort, that normalcy. She had to check the kids' rooms. Had to be sure, would never be able to settle or go to sleep again if she didn't.

Xander was easy. She pressed her ear to his door and listened to his buzzing snores for a moment. She'd never known a kid could snore so loudly.

Marigold, though, slept silently. Amber had to ease her door open and creep in.

She expected the malicious shifting of the shadows and hissing whispers to lie in wait for her here, but the moment Amber stepped into the room the fear dropped away. In its place a gut punch of guilt nearly doubled her over.

Where had that *come* from?

She'd never done wrong by Marigold, by either child, so why suddenly did the thought of checking on Mari in her sleep—as she had a hundred, hundred times—make Amber want to wail? She wiped her eyes, fighting to keep her feet under the overpowering burden bowing down her shoulders and pressing on her spine.

The small shape under Marigold's cover rose and fell in the deep rhythm of a sleeping child's breath.

That was more than enough. Amber stumbled as stealthily as possible from the room, easing the door shut behind her.

Back in her own bed, she lay on her back and stared at the ceiling. What time was it? How much more rest could she get before she had to wake up and lock herself in her home office for the day? Wearily, she turned to the clock.

It was 2:34 in the morning.

Plenty of time to try to calm herself. She didn't think she would sleep, but as the night drifted on her breathing slowed, her body grew heavy, and at last Amber slid back into unquiet dreams.

Morning came groggy and gray, and Amber would have slept through her alarm if Ben hadn't shaken her shoulder after it failed to rouse her.

"Another bad night?" he asked, the sympathy on his face and in his voice underscored by a sense of routine. All of Amber's nights were bad nights, after all.

It was a short step from routine to boredom, though, and from boredom to dissatisfaction. And from there, who knows? No. Amber couldn't risk pushing him away.

Even if a little voice inside whispered that just feeling less alone might help. . . .

Amber shut that thought down. She couldn't risk it. What would she do? Tell Ben the truth? He'd think she was nuts. He'd stop trusting her. Or, maybe worse, he'd think she was lying to him. She needed Ben with her, on her side. She needed Ben to trust her, to believe her.

So, she made herself meet his gaze and said, "Just drowsy this morning, that's all."

Still, when Amber gave Ben her most natural, most normal smile, she couldn't help the touch of disappointment when he bought it, returning her smile without guile before going on with his morning.

CHAPTER 8

AS FAR BEYOND RECONCILIATION

JULY 2020

"You've been on my ass about these mirrors for two months, Amber," Ben huffed, running his hands through his hair, then cupping the back of his neck and tilting his head back toward the ceiling. In a tightly controlled voice he went on, "Now you're telling me you don't like them."

Amber stood at an angle, not facing the mirror directly, but not letting it loom behind her, either. She shrugged, her arms crossed, shoulders hunched.

"They're just wrong," she said. She couldn't tell him that it wasn't only the ones he'd switched in the bathrooms. The mirror built into the top of their dresser, same as they'd always had, gave her chills now, too.

And if she couldn't bring herself to tell Ben that it wasn't the *new* mirrors but *all* of them, she certainly couldn't tell him why. She needed to be calm, after all, she needed to be in control, and there was nothing calm or controlled about the prospect of telling her husband that every time she looked in a mirror, her reflection stood there with its eyes firmly shut. Her mouth went dry just thinking about it, and maybe she should tell Ben, maybe she could show him. If it was real, of course. If it was real, and he could see it, then she wouldn't be alone with this strangeness anymore. The problem would be if he didn't see it. Amber didn't think she could stand it if he didn't see it, too. That would mean admitting weakness, it would mean Ben questioning her decisions and her plans and her very state of mind.

Even with that in mind, part of Amber wished she'd told him the truth about her experience that night last month. The longer she insisted she was fine, the harder it became to tell Ben how deeply she was struggling in this house. And she could insist whatever she wanted, but the truth was that Amber was not fine and hadn't been for a long time. Maybe it was time to—

"I finally did what you wanted, and after the *shitty* weekend I had," Ben began, snapping Amber out of her thoughts.

"Whoa, no, I didn't ask you to hang the new mirrors *today*, you decided to," Amber protested, but under the defensiveness was a thread of relief; his poor attitude answered her question for her. This was not the right time—if there would be a right time—to try to show him what she was seeing . . . or thought she was seeing.

"Whatever. I don't know what was wrong with the mirror your folks had in here, anyway," Ben added. As soon as the words were out of his mouth, he winced.

They hadn't talked about Amber's parents since the murders, just like they hadn't talked about Hannah since the fire. After Hannah's death Ben had tried to get Amber to talk through it, to process all her conflicting emotions by explaining them fully to the one person who understood how things had been between Amber and her family, and who wouldn't judge her for anything that had happened or anything Amber might feel because of it.

He probably had meant well, but he'd pushed her too hard and they'd had the worst argument of their marriage over it. Realization had struck Amber that night—one time, powerful when it came, deeply buried and mulishly ignored ever since—that the sole reason she hadn't left him after that argument was because she was afraid. Before Ben she'd been so alone, the idea of being that lonely ever again made her chest tight. And she couldn't stand the thought of him out there, if she left him, talking to people about her behind her back, telling people the things only he was supposed to know.

The fear came almost entirely from the part of her stuck in her own unhappy past, the part of her that still sat alone in the school cafeteria every single day and still moved through the halls with head ducked to avoid catching unkind attention. Amber hated the memory version of herself as much as she'd ever hated her family; the girl she'd been was as far beyond reconciliation as they were now.

"You *had* to bring them up, didn't you," Amber said into the cold silence that followed Ben's words, her voice sharp and brittle, like broken glass.

"I'm sorry," he said, too fast. "I'm just . . . it's been a hard week. It's only my second day off. It was *just* Fourth of July, and thanks to the shutdowns a million more idiots were trying to set off their own fireworks this year than any other year. I get home and the yard's full of used up sparklers and smoke bomb trash, and you've been all over the place lately. I'm feeling stressed, is all."

"All over the place?" Amber repeated, heat blooming in her chest. He was always like this after he'd been out of the house too many days in a row, boorish and combative with her. This was nothing new. Why did it hurt her feelings this time?

"I didn't mean it like that." Ben turned his gaze away from her and sighed. "I'm trying to apologize."

"Not doing a great job," she muttered, covering the sting of his words with a scowl, but her arms tightened across her chest. She drew in a breath to say more when the alarm on her phone beeped. She blew the breath out and shook her head. "Break's over," she said, squeezing past Ben and out of the master bathroom. She didn't go out of her way to jostle him as she passed, but neither did she take care to move gently by him. Without turning back, she added in an emotionless monotone, "I have a whole list of potential customers to call back today, so keep the kids outside."

It was a long, bad day in the home office. Selling homeowner's insurance did not make for a fulfilling job at the best of times, and now with the world falling apart the stress wound her up more than ever. All morning, Amber had taken calls from people who didn't have insurance and either just figured out they needed it or were being forced by their landlords to get it for liability reasons. Half her callers lived in wildfire states, which meant Amber had to deny them getting so much as a quote in the first place. The vitriol they heaped on her, as if she had the power to change these decisions, gave her a stomachache. She'd reserved the afternoon for calling back people who had gotten quotes from her but hadn't bought—wheedling, making herself subservient, trying to get them to come back and buy a policy after all. Debasing herself.

At the end of her workday she hung up her headset, turned off her computer, slid her work notes into the bottom of her filing cabinet and made sure both the business and personal documents drawers were locked, and told herself again that maybe it was time to throw in the towel on a sales job and go back to retail. Except that wasn't the easily available option it had been before this year. What would Ben's coworkers think if she quit her job without lining up a new one and he let it slip? That she was lazy? Comfortable living off his salary? She sneered at the thought.

No, Amber was stuck in this job until something better presented itself. Trapped. An old memory—a dim room and a mouse in a cage, an aching sympathy with the desire to bite and scratch and fight back—hung ghostly before her eyes, and for an instant Amber felt the pressure close in on her, taking her breath away.

"Grow up," she hissed to herself, and banished the memory.

She pushed herself out of her chair and stood, glaring at her office. The computer and the modem sent by the company, the cheap desk and swivel chair she'd provided for herself, it was loathsome. Here she was, stuck in a job she hated, knowing she'd have more wiggle room to find a new job if her parents hadn't arranged their affairs in a way that made everything harder for her. Amber took a harsh breath and blew it out forcefully. Her careful research into how to navigate the labyrinthine tangle of issues caused by probate laws was moving forward, at least. She might be able to get out from under all this bullshit yet, maybe in as short a time as a couple more weeks if she was clever. For now, time to put this room behind her for the day.

In the back hallway she paused, raising a hand to her cheek unconsciously. Her fingers were cold. *Like the breath that night—* she cut the thought off, scowling. There had been no breath that night. There had been nothing at all. She would not think of it.

A clatter of pots and pans rose from the kitchen as Ben made dinner; she caught the scent of something briny. Amber smiled. Seafood wasn't his go-to and the kids could take it or leave it, which meant he was trying to make her night better. The effort alone went a long way toward soothing her feelings.

And the sly, arched eyebrow and exaggerated wink he gave her after dinner, when the kids weren't paying attention, helped, too. It was transparent, an obvious attempt to get back into her good graces without having to apologize, but what the hell.

"Kids, go watch TV," she said, pulling her eyes away from her husband but unable to banish her small smirk. "I'll get you some ice cream, you can eat on the floor in the living room if you don't make a mess. We have to have a grown-up talk, so you guys gotta stay down here, all right?"

The promise of unsupervised time with ice cream and the television was sufficient to forestall the natural inclination of all small children to never allow a pair of adults a moment alone.

With a cheer Xander ran out of the kitchen. Marigold copied his jubilant cry, and within moments both of them were screaming gleefully from the living room.

As Amber scooped a much more modest amount of ice cream than the kids would have preferred into two small plastic dishes, she grinned and asked, "Do you think I overdid it?"

"Nope," Ben said, making a show of leering at her. She laughed and flapped a hand at him. He added, "Hurry up, though."

Amber deposited the ice creams in front of the children with a reminder to be good, paused in the kitchen doorway to give Ben a smile, then ran up the stairs ahead of him. She wanted to slip into the bathroom before they started—seafood dinner made brushing her teeth imperative before any intimacy might go down, no matter that they'd been married for six years.

Amber dropped her gaze the moment the light came on in the bathroom, unwilling to glance at her reflection. Even so, the thought of it there, unavoidable, right in front of her, inches away while she brushed her teeth, made a shiver crawl up her spine. She turned quickly and snatched a towel off the bar next to the shower and shook it open. Lifting it before her, blocking her view, she stepped right up to lean against the counter to tuck the top edge of the towel behind the mirror.

"What are you doing?" Ben's voice behind her made Amber jump, the towel slipping from her fingers. She spun fast, as much to face her husband as to avoid the risk of looking at herself in the glass.

"What?" she asked.

"I said, what are you doing?" Ben frowned, and it troubled Amber that she couldn't tell if the frown was of confusion, or concern, or displeasure.

She didn't want to ruin the moment, didn't want to spoil their planned time together by making him worry about her, and so rather than tell him the truth, Amber shrugged and said the first thing that came to mind. "Nothing. I don't like these mirrors, that's all."

Ben gave her a flat look. "Don't be a child, Amber."

Amber leaned back, eyebrows raising. "Excuse me?"

"I mean, give me a break. I've already told you I'll replace them when I can. I don't need this passive-aggressive stuff."

Again with the way he acted after shifts at the firehouse—quicker to blame her, quicker to judge her. She hated it. The anticipatory warmth that had been building in her dissolved, and Amber straightened, putting her hands on her hips.

It was so stupid, him being mad at her for this. The whole reason she'd made an excuse about the towel on the mirror was to avoid ruining the moment and then he had to go and do it anyway. Now, of course, she couldn't admit that there'd been a different reason. He wouldn't believe her, he'd think she was backtracking, and that would be too much like letting him get away with talking to her like that.

So instead, Amber sighed. "Fine." She turned back toward their bedroom. "I'll go get the kids' baths ready," she added as she headed for the bedroom door Ben had only a moment ago locked behind himself for privacy.

"Wait, wait, wait, Amber, no," Ben said, following after her and catching her hand in his. Amber could have pulled away from his gentle grip if she wanted to, but the soft conciliation in his voice made her pause. He rubbed his thumb over the back of her hand. "Come on, look."

She turned, and Ben pointed to the dresser and the bedside tables. He'd placed candles around the room, and Amber smiled in spite of herself. A hazy recollection of too many small candle flames tried to surface, and Amber pushed it back down without letting it come into focus. She loved the ambience of candlelight for sex, but Ben always said he'd seen too often the results of people not paying attention around them.

"It won't make you too nervous?" she teased.

Ben shrugged, but grinned and said, "Nah, not every once in a while. Besides, I shut the windows so the curtains can't blow around, and none of the candles are close enough to bump, so . . ." he trailed off, raising his eyebrows.

Amber glanced one last time toward the bedroom door. He followed her glance and squeezed her hand once.

"I shouldn't have called you passive-aggressive," he said, and while that wasn't really an apology, it was good enough for now.

"Well, what're you waiting for? Light the candles for me," Amber said. She waited until his back was turned and he was busy with the matches, then undressed in a hurry and settled herself onto the bed. She smiled as she watched him move around the room, increasing the warm glow every time he paused to light another candle. Amber loved to watch him move, especially when he didn't know she was watching.

When he turned back to her, she was ready in the center of the mattress, trying hard not to appear posed. The way his eyes turned hungry as he took her in made her smile. Her body wasn't as firm as it used to be—tonight she'd carefully positioned one hand over her stomach, and lately she regarded herself with growing discomfort—but when Ben looked at her like that it eased those worries.

At a little shy of seven in the evening darkness hadn't fallen outside yet, but the blackout curtains dimmed the room enough for the candlelight's warm illumination and flickering shadows to set the mood. Ben moved over her and Amber smiled as she traced her fingertips up his sides, reveling in the warmth of him. When he leaned down, she lifted her face to his, but he dipped lower to kiss her neck and collarbone. Amber sighed, the tension in her shoulders easing. Where his lips and occasionally his teeth met her skin, warmth spread in softly tingling trails, dancing from her throat down into her belly. The warmth pulsed in time with her quickening heartbeat, and Amber arched her back and hummed, her voice low and soft. He kissed from the side of her neck up to her ear, nibbling her lobe just sharply enough to draw a gasp from her lips. The warmth became a heat, desire pushing away the last of her irritation.

Amber wrapped her arms around Ben, ran her fingernails down his spine the way she knew he liked. He shifted against her and moaned, his breath hot in her ear and on her throat, sending a pleasant shiver down her spine. Amber closed her eyes, shutting out everything but the feeling of the mattress beneath her back, Ben above her, and her growing pleasure. She pressed her right knee against the inside of Ben's leg, signaling him to shift his weight, give her room to lift her legs and wrap them around his waist.

The world began in the warmth growing between them and ended in the circle of soft candlelight ringing the room. Amber let thoughts of anything beyond their bodies slip out of her mind, and she could feel that he was as ready as she was. When she pressed against Ben, he chuckled, his voice low and rich, his breath and his tone both sending another shiver down her back. She tightened her legs around his waist and, letting her need move her, lifted her hips. Rather than acquiesce to her impatience, he slid farther down and turned his attention to her breasts. His tongue and his fingers teased her. Amber dropped her head back into the pillows, breathing hard. Ben knew just how to build the rhythm; he knew when a gentle bite or a light pinch would send a spike of pleasure through her, from the soft warmth in her belly through the sweet tingling up her spine and in every breath. Amber bit her lip and raked her fingers through his hair, sliding against him. She opened her eyes and let her gaze drift to the right, to three of the candles flickering on shelves built into the corner of the room.

Ben's breath tickled her skin, and Amber held him more firmly, imagining the candles' warm glow in the feeling that sparked where he touched her. He moaned in response and she sighed and the light in the room dimmed and then brightened as if her soft breath had wavered every single little flame. Ben kissed lower, his lips warm and firm on her stomach.

A soft noise came from the direction of the dresser against the wall opposite the bed. Amber lifted her head and peered over Ben's back, accidentally catching a glimpse of the mirror above the dresser. From this angle the glass showed her mostly the headboard and the wall behind it, only the top half of her own face visible, eyes firmly closed though Amber didn't so much as blink.

She let out a soft cry, quickly stifled, dropping back onto the mattress and tilting her head back. No. Not this again, not right now. Amber needed the pleasure, needed the *comfort*, but she'd been drawn out of the moment. Ben murmured against her as his hands traced over her hips and down to her thighs, but Amber couldn't melt into the sensation again. Cold—cold like glass, like the mirror—tried to spread between her and this intimacy with her husband. She pulled herself tighter against him, but his touch failed to drive the cold away. She needed something hotter, something brighter.

Turning to her right again, she fixed her eyes on the candles—the glow, the warmth, these soothed her unease. The tiny fires suffused her with languid heat and drove away whatever she had been worrying about a moment ago.

When she pulled Ben closer to herself, he gave her a wolfish grin. His eyes, dark with lust, reflected the candlelight. Amber traced the shape of his face with her fingertips, watching the points of light in his eyes, then pulled him down so his chest touched hers. He moved his mouth to her ear again, and she reveled in his touch and the solid weight of him and the candles' slightly smoky scent.

She tightened her grip on him with her arms and her legs and tilted her head back, closing her eyes. His stubbled chin tickled her throat and his tongue flicked her ear, her fingernails slid over his skin. When he slid into her she arched her back, but as Ben built a rhythm Amber found her attention drifting like smoke, curling away from this moment. The warmth between them, steady and slow, failed to ignite into the kind of fire she craved. For Ben's sake she gasped, and her hands kept moving up and down his body in the ways she knew he liked, but the thing filling her mind was not the sweet tension of lovemaking.

It was the candles. Their glow and their heat, the steady flicker. It was the fire.

Amber opened her eyes, turned her head on the pillow, let her gaze wander over the collection of tiny flames, and the next gasp Ben's touch drew from her was unfeigned. Her gaze found one candle on her own bedside table, at the edge farthest from the bed, and a soft smile curled her lips. How had she missed that one before? Ben wouldn't normally put any of the candles near enough to bump accidentally, would he? But he must've figured it was safe there, on the far side of the table.

The flame flickered, it grew and it shrank. Amber moved in time with it, changing the pace, forcing the rhythm to shift and sending sparks of pleasure along her skin and in her very breath. Closer, she wanted the flame closer. Letting go of Ben with one arm she reached out, but the candle sat just a few inches too far away. If the candle could just rest nearer the bed, Amber knew the last of her distraction would flee like shadows before light.

"Amber," Ben's voice breathed in her ear, low and questioning, and with slow reluctance she turned away from the fire to meet his eyes. He didn't break her new rhythm, his hands didn't stop their teasing, even as he glanced from Amber's face to the candle just out of her reach. "Closer?" he asked, and she nodded, and he pulled away from her long enough to lean out and lift the candle, setting it right by their bed.

She cupped her hand, her palm curled around the low candle with only an inch or so between her skin and the flame. When Ben returned to her, she spared him a glance and smiled to see the way his own eyes fixed on the fire, the way its light danced in his gaze, the way he didn't need her prompting anymore to move in time with the sway of the flame.

With one hand, Amber raked her fingernails down Ben's back and he groaned. She curled her fingers nearer to the candle, the warmth growing on her hand feeding the fire building inside her. Ben pushed himself harder into her, leaned more heavily upon her, pressure and weight robbing her of breath.

Pleasure spiked in one near-perfect moment, electric and shivering, but not enough—not hot enough, not bright enough. Amber lowered one finger into the candle's flame, and as the heat flared on her skin she let out a long, soft moan. At the last second she pressed down on the flame, burning her fingertip and snuffing the fire in the instant that bliss coursed through her with a quiet, breathy cry. Her body pulled tight for a long, long moment and then gentled all at once, and in that instant the pain in her finger flared, hot and throbbing. At just that moment Ben climaxed as well, his arms squeezing her, forehead dipping to rest on hers, breath hot on her face.

When the tension drained out of Ben's body he slid down and out of her, then stopped. He rested half on her for a moment, her legs spread to either side of his. Amber held very still beneath him, the weight and sweat-dampened warmth of him pressing her into the mattress, grounding her as she stared at her right hand, raised over his shoulder. At the blister already forming on her pointer finger.

Disentangling her other hand from Ben's hair, she traced the reddening edges of the little injury, which blurred in her vision as she let her gaze slip out of focus. The rest of the candles in the bedroom swayed, lovely and enticing.

Ben shifted his weight at last and rolled off of her onto his back. He traced a hand up her right arm, leaving goosebumps in his wake, paused with his fingers at her wrist, and then traced one fingertip up to touch the red and shiny mark the candle had left on her, murmuring, "We should use candles more often."

"Mm," Amber hummed agreeably, shifting closer to him, pressing their sides together. If she asked him to, he would get up and bring the other candles, and she could lower her hand over the flames one by one, and keep the heat and the fire burning inside her. "Grab another one for me," she said, turning her head to give him a languid smile.

When he rolled off the bed and stood it left Amber chilly. She sat up and pulled the blankets around herself, draping them over her shoulder, and watched as Ben picked up the nearest candle, cupped the flame to keep it safe, and carried it back to her.

"We'll need a shower," Ben said, settling back onto the mattress and holding the candle out to her, and Amber nodded as she reached for it. "Maybe we can take one together?"

Amber's palm hovered over the flame. As she let her hand drift lower the gentle heat grew, and grew, and she lifted her eyes to her husband to tell him that a shower together seemed like a *very* nice idea—

Two knocks on the bedroom door interrupted the moment.

The sound startled Amber, she twitched, and her hand slapped down on the candle so fast the displaced air snuffed it before her palm could. She hissed at the sting of molten wax on her skin and jerked away, tucking her arm in close. Her pointer finger throbbed, a hot pain that flared with every beat of her thumping heart.

Marigold's voice called through the closed door, "Can I have more ice cream?"

But Ben was climbing back off the bed, his eyes wide and darting between Amber's hand cradled between her breasts and the candle still warm in his palm. "What . . . the *fuck* were we just doing?" he asked, his voice thick at first, like a man waking from a bad dream. Faster, clearer, he repeated, "What were we *doing*, Amber?"

"I—I . . ." Amber groped for some excuse, some reason, anything to make the way they'd been behaving just now make sense—they'd never even explored an idea like this before—but her thoughts moved slow and sluggish, turning away from the moments before.

The warmth of lovemaking was gone; all that remained was the burning in her hand and the sweat cooling on her skin and a shiver crawling up her spine.

"I *said*," Marigold repeated, her voice impatient, "can I have more ice cream?"

The question, the demand, shattered what little hope Amber had of bringing the last several minutes into focus in a way that she could rationalize. Irritation flared, uncomplicated and hard, and Amber clung to the unambiguity of that annoyance. "Absolutely not, Marigold, and you know better than to even ask," she snapped.

"But *please*!" Mari demanded. "Please, please, *pleeeease*!"

The whine made Amber want to grit her teeth, but a small part of her latched onto Mari's poor behavior as an excuse to entirely abandon the topic of whatever she and Ben had been doing.

She pushed herself off the bed and bent to grab her clothing. Mari was chanting for ice cream now, over and over, and as Amber yanked her clothing on she raised her voice to be heard over the little girl—raised her voice more than she needed to, shouted, really, but the strange tension in her chest needed out and this was as good a way as any—"Go to your room, young lady!"

It felt good to let out her ire, it drove everything else away for just one instant.

Marigold whined again, closer to crying now, and Amber stormed toward the door, her voice hard as she added, "If you're not in that room by the time I leave this one you'll be going to bed *right now*."

Yes. Yes, anger and discipline. Yes, taking control of the situation. This was what she needed, not to dwell on the strangeness but to banish it. She could forget the pain in her finger and the stinging in her palm, she could forget Ben's wide eyes on her and the smell of the two snuffed candles, she could forget the other candles ringing the room, still lit.

Until her hand touched the doorknob. The candles' flickering stilled at once and Amber froze. Ben took a sharp breath and the sound cut through everything else—did he see it? Had he noticed? She spun to face him, to search his face for the understanding, the fear, that she needed to see because if it was there, if he saw the strangeness and was afraid of it, she wouldn't be all alone with this anymore.

The moment her eyes found his, every last flame flared. The rush of heat stirred the air like a breath on the back of her neck and Amber let out a little cry, jerking forward as if to dodge a blow. Despite the blackout curtains, the room was as brightly lit as if full of sunlight, but sunlight had never felt so hostile.

"What's happening?" Ben shouted, and amid the fear and the confusion Amber could have sobbed for relief because he saw it, he saw it, none of it was in her head, it was *real.*

But Ben didn't understand, he didn't share the catharsis weakening Amber's knees, he saw only the flames, their violent light reflecting in his eyes and in the beads of sweat rolling down his body as the room grew hotter around them.

The *tink* of something striking glass was so quiet but so clear, a tiny noise that should not have filled her with a dread so cold she almost longed to burn herself again.

"Amber," Ben said, turning toward the sound.

"Don't," she said, her voice a dry rasp. "Ben, don't, don't look."

But he did, he turned, he looked dead on at the mirror, and when all the color drained out of his face she could not help herself. She looked, too.

There they stood, ringed by fire barely contained within the candles, her back to the door. That there was not enough space behind her for anyone else didn't matter to the thing hiding behind her reflection, almost a shadow, barely visible over her shoulders and behind the tangle of her postcoital bedhead, almost not even there until its hands slid around her face from behind, closing over her eyes. Amber cried out and scrabbled at her own face, ducking and lurching. She tripped over Ben's discarded boxers and staggered backward, still swiping at her tightly shut eyes. Her back struck the door and she fumbled with one hand, found the knob, and turned it.

The door swung open and in that instant the red glow of the candlelight through her closed eyelids and the suffocating heat both collapsed into nothing. Cool air from the hallway sighed in, along with Marigold's voice—still whining, but the sound was so blessedly, perfectly normal that it made Amber's heart ache.

Amber straightened and opened her eyes. The doorway framed her, and Amber leaned against it as she took in the bedroom before her. With the blackout curtains still drawn and the candles all snuffed now, twists of smoke rising from each one, the space was more shadow than room, and for several dizzy seconds Amber couldn't tell if this was her bedroom or her parents'. Then she blinked and there, of course, stood Ben, still next to the bed, his jaw hanging open even as he hastily grabbed the comforter to obscure his nudity. His eyes met hers, and Amber knew he was going to ask her what they'd seen. If it was real. What was going on.

She couldn't have that conversation, not yet, not until she figured out what to say and how to handle it. So, Amber turned from Ben's frightened eyes and scooped up Mari—in the throes of a tantrum now—and carried the little girl into her own room to calm her down.

For the rest of that evening she wouldn't meet her husband's gaze. She got the kids tucked in, and rather than risk having to talk about anything they had seen, she went straight to bed herself while Ben was still bidding Xander and Marigold goodnight. When he came into the room she pretended to sleep, and he knew she was faking it, and she knew that he knew, but she didn't stop.

All that night she lay in a state of fitful fear, the infrequent moments of sleep interrupted by nightmares that she told herself she could not remember when she woke—a fire; Hannah standing silhouetted before it, looking as she had the last time Amber could remember feeling close with her sister, maybe ten years old; Hannah going up in flames, too; Nathan laughing as she'd seen him laugh twenty-two years before. All at once *Amber* was the one burning instead of Hannah, burning and screaming and—*no*, no, better to not remember a dream like that.

When the sun rose in the morning it did not make her feel any better.

CHAPTER 9

EVERY WINDOW A MIRROR

SEPTEMBER 2020

"Rosie, sweetie," the tinny voice called from the cheap little laptop they'd bought for Xander. "You need to mute yourself. Rosie? Rosie McInnes, are you listening to me? The whole class can hear your brother. . . . Mute your— Okay, hang on, I can do this from my end. I'm going to mute you, Rosie. Okay?"

Amber glanced up from her work and over her shoulder, past Xander sitting with his back to her in the far corner of her home office, to his screen. She checked the mic icon for the little red slash running through it to show that he, at least, had his computer muted. He did. But as another round of indistinct background talk swamped what his first-grade teacher was trying to say, Amber fought the urge to cross the small room, unmute him herself, and let any parents listening in along with the other students have a piece of her mind. The teacher had been specific in asking the children to keep their mics off unless they were called on, she had clearly explained why, and still half these parents couldn't be bothered to make sure their kids were following the rules. It drove Amber up a wall.

The brand-new school year had started two weeks ago. During any other year this would usher in a period of daily quiet at the house. Marigold should have been all set to start preschool and Xander had entered first grade.

This wasn't any other year. This year it meant finding a place to set Xander up with a virtual classroom. Amber had spent a week dragging a small table and chair around the house, looking for an out-of-the-way corner he could use. Not his bedroom; she didn't want him distracted by his toys or too far away to help while she was working. Not the living room because of the television, not the kitchen because there was no room.

It had come down to her office or the laundry room, and Amber wouldn't admit even to Ben how seriously she'd considered the laundry room. But what if the teacher could tell? They'd get into some kind of trouble. At the very least, it would look just awful. School, then, meant the loss of her last private space.

"Sit back down, Xander," Amber admonished, taking her phone headset off her ears. Xander turned in the act of sliding from his chair onto the floor, twisting himself so he could see Amber. He shook his head. "I said get in your seat."

"No. I'm *bored*. This is *boring*."

"I don't care if it's boring," Amber hissed, shooting one quick glance at the work phone on her desktop, making sure she had no incoming calls. "You sit still and you pay attention!"

"I don't wanna," he whined.

"You'll get a time-out," Amber warned, "in front of all of your classmates." He pouted, and she raised one finger. "One . . . *two* . . . thr—"

"I'm *going*, I'm *going*!" Xander yelped and pulled himself back up into his seat in time to find that he'd missed the instructions the teacher had given them for their next activity. He unmuted himself and leaned too close to the laptop's screen, filling the window that showed his face with a close-up of his nose instead. "What are we doing?" he asked too loudly.

Amber's phone rang.

"Shh," she hissed at Xander.

The teacher said something about a scavenger hunt in the house, and Xander took off from his desk without waiting to hear what he was supposed to hunt for. Amber punched the button to answer the call. "ShieldWall Insurance, this is Amber speaking, how can I help you today?"

For the next fifteen minutes Amber dealt with one of those problem customers, the kind who didn't really want a homeowner's insurance quote but knew it was important and handled their internal conflict by creating a conflict with Amber instead, irritably resisting answering any of her questions. The combative attitude made the process all but impossible. Amber didn't land the sale, but she took down the phone number and the name and marked them as someone to call back in three days. By the time she finished the call her shoulders hurt and she'd been grinding her teeth until her jaw ached.

This would normally be a moment of downtime, but instead she had to get up and riffle through the huge binder of information and materials Xander's teacher had sent home the week before, trying to find the worksheet for the next lesson, trying to manage the situation. If she got another free moment, maybe she'd take a break or maybe she'd spend the time trying harder to make this corner of her office feel like a classroom for Xander. She clung to the ill-defined hope that if it looked more normal to him, more engaging, he'd stay in his seat longer instead of getting up to follow her every time she went to check on Marigold, or trying to sneak away whenever he got bored.

Amber put the worksheet on Xander's table and dropped into her chair again, leaned back, and pushed her hair away from her face with both hands, her cheeks puffing with a sigh.

After slogging through to the end of Xander's classes, Amber still had three more hours of her workday remaining, then finally she could go see what Ben had planned for dinner.

If only that could have been the end of her day. Unfortunately, playing catch-up all the time meant Amber had to work late, too, after the kids were in bed.

After she got the kids settled and collected her end of the baby monitor she'd had to find for Marigold after the last round of nighttime sneaking, she grabbed her personal laptop and returned to her office. She stood in the center of it for a moment, trying to find some semblance of motivation despite the exhaustion from months of the worst sleep of her life, trying to understand how it was that everything was happening all at once.

The passing of summer had taken with it a strange limbo Amber hadn't realized she and her family had been in. The murder of her parents was a small thing on the global scale but had changed so much about her life—the move, obviously, and funeral arrangements, but also navigating the unclear waters of all the legal business of their estate. And of course, there was the house itself. . . .

The *house*. The shadows and the voices. The sleepless nights and the stretches of time lost to an unfocused daze. The mirrors. Amber pushed the thoughts away, trying not to let her face pull back into a grimace. Never show the fear. One certainty, rock solid and unquestionable, drove her—to show fear, to present anything other than the right face, would bring calamity down on them. On her.

Between that and the distance of the terrible stories on the news, sanitizer shortages and riots and wildfires being problems for places other than her own neighborhood, it had been easy to move the greater concerns of the year as a whole into a back corner of her mind.

Amber already worked from home, had for the past three years, Ben's job was unchanged—they didn't furlough firefighters—and the kids had no school in the summer anyway. September arrived cool and cloudy and pushed aside her complacence with a barrage of meetings and paperwork and errands and emails, all revolving around two main themes.

One was school, with the new remote learning setup, and that would have been challenging all on its own. But on top of that, there loomed the second topic of all those messages and e-meetings.

Her employers cut more jobs, expecting the sales teams to lift twice the workload. Amber held a license in personal property insurance, and while she'd always specialized in homeowner's insurance and its subcategories, the license broadly applied to personal vehicle insurance, too. She already ended every day by stepping out of her home office with a tension headache and knots in her back. Preparing for this change in advance of actually starting the new workload made her grind her teeth.

It had only been two weeks since the work announcement and the start of school, and Amber wanted to tear her hair out or scream.

Twilight's increasingly early arrival didn't help. The changing times of sunrise and sunset were eternally gradual, but by the first month of fall, night's early advance always took Amber by surprise. At a little past eight the darkness made staying at work late to catch up all the harder. She kept her back to the window in her office; she hated the way night outside turned every window into a mirror. She'd hung curtains, of course, but she couldn't stand the thought of catching a glimpse of herself in the crack between those curtains. A glimpse of herself, and of whatever else might—

No. No. If she let herself think about it, she'd crumble. And she didn't have time for that. Amber cracked her knuckles, focusing on the pop and following relief, telling herself that she'd put the idea of reflections out of her mind even though the back of her neck still crawled. The extra project and the increased work it created for her recaptured her attention.

Amber sat down and pushed her work computer's keyboard to one side of her desk to make room for her laptop. She returned to the search she had been browsing through the evening before.

The screen filled with an image depicting the aftermath of a terrible car accident. Below the image waited thumbnails for more of the same, row after row of smashed up cars, burned-out trucks, twisted motorcycles.

She set the baby monitor next to the laptop with an irritated sigh. It had taken Amber some searching to find it, months after the move. Back when Marigold was two or three, Amber had packed it away with other outgrown baby things—blankies, toys, clothing—to save for the day she and Ben might start trying again, but the time had never been right. Occasionally Amber had thought she should give the box to the first friend to have kids, or donate it to a secondhand shop or charity, but could never quite bring herself to do it. When the move happened, the box came with them, and might have remained forgotten if not for Marigold's continued nighttime wanderings.

Just now, Amber listened as the monitor transmitted the quiet sounds of Marigold in the throes of a nightmare. She mostly ignored the soft whimpers and muffled cries—if Marigold woke up and called for her, Amber would judge then whether the girl needed an adult or if it would be best for her to practice soothing herself back to sleep. In the meantime, the rustling sound of a small body rolling restlessly beneath the covers and the periodic sniffling breaths went ignored. Amber had research to do.

"Knock, knock," Ben said from the door in lieu of actually knocking, stepping in without waiting for permission.

Ever since the night the candles had . . . no, best not to think of it like that. Ever since the night in their bedroom, Ben had been jumpy, his nerves straining hers more with every quick glance or hasty breath.

Worse, he still wanted to talk. The morning following that frightening night, Amber had asked Ben into her office and had explained the things she had been seeing and hearing, the things she had been feeling. Talking about her feelings, being vulnerable and guileless, made Amber feel ill at ease, less with Ben than anyone else she'd ever known, but still, she'd kept her explanation brief and to the point. She only needed to know that someone else knew, that someone else believed her. She should've realized that after experiencing only one of the incidents that had been haunting—no, she wouldn't use that word, *no*—after only one of the incidents that had been *troubling* Amber for weeks, Ben would be the one wanting to talk and talk about it.

At least after so long together, he understood when Amber would not speak about a subject anymore. He never tried to force it. He just lingered more in her presence than normal, vacillating between smothering overattentiveness and silent watchfulness. Maybe he hoped she would change her mind and have a real heart-to-heart about the grasping darkness and the reflections and the whispers and . . . she wrenched her mind back on track.

Amber tried not to be annoyed by the sound of his voice, deliberately light; he used this falsely cheerful tone when he wanted to hover around under the pretense of checking up on her, and she was starting to hate it. Amber looked over her shoulder to tell him she was fine—busy, but *fine*—but as she did, his eyes flicked to the images on her computer monitor. She tabbed over to a social media site instead.

"Rear impact crashes?" he asked.

She shrugged, and though the screen now showed a scrolling feed of selfies, personal reflections, and political memes, she still reached out and shut the laptop without bothering to put it into sleep mode first.

"Research for the big switch at work."

"Right," Ben agreed, his voice mild.

"Having concrete examples of the worst that can happen helps people decide to buy the best policy they can," Amber went on. The words sounded rehearsed, but that was good to know now. Better to get that out before they needed to sound smooth and convincing. This was work she should have been doing already, but she'd kept finding little reasons not to get it taken care of. It never felt like the right time. *The right time.* That was the problem, time: Amber was clinging to the past and she knew it, and it was going to spoil their future. She didn't want to discuss any of that with Ben right now, however, so instead she added, "Customers are more likely to buy better policies if they know what can happen to them."

"For sure," Ben said, nodding, pleasant. He leaned with his back against the door frame and asked, "Find anything interesting?"

Amber picked up her phone and fiddled with it, trying to put together an answer that would make sense to him, but before she could, Marigold's nightmare noises from the monitor stopped sounding soft and vague.

"Huhh . . . what . . . ?" The girl's voice came clearly, no hint of drowsiness slurring the words, capturing Ben and Amber's attention. "Hey . . ."

Five minutes ago, the interruption would have irritated Amber, but now she masked her relief behind an apologetic face and raised her hands as if to say she didn't have a choice but to be taken out of this conversation. She stood and reached for the monitor.

"What?" Marigold's voice asked again.

Something answered her.

Amber's hand froze. She turned and locked her gaze on Ben, her lips pressed tight together. A low voice murmured, too indistinct to make out anything other than a repeated *shushing*. Ben's eyes widened, his mouth open as if he'd been about to speak and the words had been stolen.

"No," Marigold said, hesitant. "No, no." The words dissolved into crying, muffled, as if the little girl covered her mouth.

Goosebumps swept Amber's skin and her face went numb. Ben pushed himself away from the wall, his body stiff. He shut his mouth with a snap, the muscles in his jaw jumping as he clenched his teeth. He heard it, too.

The whisper that was not Marigold grew louder but no more intelligible. Amber finally snatched up the baby monitor, but then she stood in the center of her office, mouth dry, clutching it and staring as if she could peer through the speaker and into Marigold's room.

We have to go to Mari's room.

The thought floated, hazy and disconnected, across her mind, barely registered as it skimmed along the surface of her growing fear and then drifted away.

"Why are you in my closet?" the little girl asked, her voice pitched high, the words clear. In Amber's office the only sound was Ben's breathing, increasingly ragged. Another muffled wave of crying followed from the monitor before Mari's voice came back, exclaiming, "That's not where people *live*!" She paused. "It *isn't*!"

"Amber," Ben said, the word breaking out of him as if with terrible effort. Amber nearly jumped out of her skin at the sound of it. She wrenched her gaze from the monitor in her hand, back to her husband. He licked his lips and went on, "Should we . . . we should check on her. Right?" Amber didn't like the tension in his voice, something more than simple fear, something like internal conflict, but this was absolutely not the time to pick it apart.

The whispers that answered Marigold were vague, and as Marigold's voice grew louder and higher, the whispers seemed to be trying to quiet the little girl.

Amber's skin went cold, her hands clammy. As her stomach twisted into a knot, a dozen reasons why a strange voice would want to hush a little girl flashed through her mind. None of them were good.

The monitor creaked, a door in Mari's room opening.

"Amber," Ben's voice was a cracked whisper. Amber fought to suck in a breath, pulling against the weight in her chest.

Marigold's cry rang out two-toned, tinny through the monitor and muffled through the walls.

That cry broke the paralysis. Ben shouted. Amber dropped

the monitor. They ran together through the house. On the stairs Amber fell behind, her bad knee slowing her. By the time she reached the landing, Ben already stood at Marigold's door.

He hesitated, frozen, shadows painted upward on his face by the night-light below, the blue glow casting him in a greenish pallor. When he turned to Amber, his eyes were wide and baffled, gleaming from shadowed pits. The familiar lines of his body were rigid, tense.

Amber drew nearer, opened her mouth to ask him in a whisper what he was doing. Why wasn't he going in? Couldn't he hear that Mari was still crying out? The sound from the other side of Marigold's bedroom door stopped her. Mari's voice was raised, but not in a scream or a sob.

She giggled, high-pitched and loud.

Amber's throat constricted. The laughter was bright and clear. Joyful. Amber's stomach heaved. She put a hand over her mouth.

When Marigold stopped laughing the voice murmured again. A swooning horror seized Amber. Her head felt light, knees rubbery. Without taking her eyes from that door she groped for Ben, grabbing his arm to keep from stumbling.

The darkness in the hallway hung thick and cloying. Marigold laughed again at whatever the voice said. The laughter rang healthy and pure, but it crawled in Amber's ears and reverberated in her skull. Tears slid down her cheeks, wetting her fingers where they clasped over her mouth. Why was she weeping? Her breath shuddered in her lungs.

"Amber," Ben's whisper was low and hoarse, rough. Her fingers tightened on his arm as she turned to him, pulling her gaze from the door with difficulty. His eyes shone with tears, his face drawn. Was he sick? "What *is* it?" he whispered.

Amber shook her head, struck mute. On the other side of that door someone murmured to Marigold, and Marigold was delighted, and Amber had never heard anything as horrifying in her entire life.

Even so, she could not bring herself to set a hand to the doorknob.

Her stomach churned. She couldn't breathe.

"Is Marigold all right?"

Xander's voice spoke into the uneasy quiet with no warning. Amber nearly screamed, whirling on him so fast she had to tighten her grip on Ben's arm to steady herself. Xander's wide, concerned eyes broke the queasy, clutching terror. At that moment, Ben shook off her grip. Amber heard him open Marigold's door.

"She's fine," Amber said, certain as she said it that it was true. Cold struck her down to her bones, illogical but powerful. "Go back to bed," Amber forced the words out in a shivering whisper.

"Who's in her room?" Xander asked, holding on to his own bedroom door as if ready to retreat back in and slam it behind him.

"No one's in her room. I said go back to bed."

"I heard—"

"Bed!"

Though she knew he disobeyed, Amber didn't linger in the hallway to handle it. She forced herself to turn and follow Ben into Mari's room.

He stood in the dark in the center of the room, his hands at his sides, shoulders slumped. His gaze was locked on Marigold's bed. When Amber came up behind him and put her hands on his arm again, he jumped but didn't look away.

The bedcovers hid the little girl from view, her body a small lump underneath. Amber strained to hear the voice, the laughter. Silence filled the room. The shape of Mari beneath the blanket rose and fell with rhythmic breaths. She couldn't really be sleeping, it was impossible.

Had it been a trick? Did Marigold think this was a joke?

"How dare you scare us like that, Marigold," Amber said, pushing herself to speak. The way her voice fell into the room, heavy in the quiet, made her tighten her grip on her husband's arm. Ben tried to pull away but she didn't let go, shaking her head. "Careful," she whispered, and then immediately wished she hadn't, because that one single word of warning brought the sour taste of fear back into her mouth. *Careful of what?* Her heart stuttered, and she inhaled sharply. But she didn't take it back, because she did not want Ben—what? Going too near the sleeping child? Entering too far into the room itself?

He only patted her hands and then pulled his arm free. A cold, wriggling discomfort twisted in her belly as Ben sidestepped her and approached the child's bed. She wanted to stop him, to pull him away, but forced herself to be still. She watched as Ben flipped down the blanket, desperate to see Marigold lying there with her eyes open, stifling more laughter with her hands.

For one instant, in the dim light from the hall, Mari's sleeping face looked so much like Hannah that Amber's mind had to catch up to the present moment. *It's just because of the room*, she thought, realizing that Ben or the movers had put Mari's bed just where Hannah's had been when they were kids. The jarring confusion passed when Marigold murmured in her sleep, stirred and groped clumsily until she found a teddy bear, and settled again.

In place of the sense of dislocation came another wave of nauseous fear. Marigold was not awake. She had not been awake.

No. She was *faking* it. That was it.

That had to be it. So now Amber brushed past Ben and knelt, taking the girl's shoulders to shake her, to sit her up and make her admit that she'd been faking. The moment her hands touched Marigold, the closet door banged open. Mari's eyelids parted a second after that. At the same time, Amber jerked backward. She landed gracelessly, sitting on her own heels, knees bent, hands splayed behind her. Her eyes snapped between the open closet door and Marigold's slowly waking face. The air squeezed out of Amber, the cold deepened. It took her two tries to get back up onto her knees by the bed, her mouth dry and her hands shaking.

Marigold had been asleep. True, deep sleep. Amber's head buzzed, couldn't settle on a concrete thought.

"Hmm . . ." the little girl mumbled, and the tired slur of a child abruptly woken in the middle of the night only deepened the pit of unease in Amber's stomach. "Whass th'matter?" Mari blinked slowly and looked at Amber. For a breathless moment there was no recognition in her gaze, until she blinked again and murmured, "Mommy? What . . . is it time to get up?"

Amber licked her lips, swallowed hard. She tried to find her voice, wheezed, "It was . . ." but trailed away. She glanced up at Ben, but he stared in the direction of the closet, still as a statue. Amber turned back to Mari, stretching her lips into a smile, and tried again. "You were having a bad dream, baby," she lied. "We were just waking you up out of it. You can go back to sleep now."

Marigold nodded and settled back down onto her pillow. Amber pulled the blanket up. She stood, her mind already spinning to find some way to convince Ben that they didn't need to *talk* about this, ever. But he didn't look like a man who wanted to talk. His gaze never strayed toward her. His jaw was set and his lips were thin. He pointed at the closet door.

It was closed again.

PART FOUR

CHAPTER 10

NOTHING TO FEEL GUILTY FOR

OCTOBER 1998

Amber kicked a pile of autumn leaves, scattering them with a crunchy rustle. She stuffed her hands into the pockets of her light jacket, zipped up to hide the ghost-patterned Halloween sweater Nathan and the other kids made fun of her for earlier at school. Hood pulled up, head ducked low, she let her dark blond hair hang in waves on either side of her face. The patch of grass and leaves under her feet held no particular interest for her, but Amber kept her gaze there rather than on the nearby fence. Nathan stood on the other side, in the nearest corner of his yard, with his arms draped over into the yard behind Amber's house. If she looked at him he might see the redness of her eyes and guess that she'd been crying, and she knew better than to let the other kids see her cry. When that happened, when they sensed weakness, they always turned more vicious.

"Come on," Nathan said, his voice soft and beseeching. Amber's chest hurt. "I said I was sorry."

"Would you say that if Glenn and Luke were here?" she asked. "Or Claire?" Not the popular kids, no. It was the mean kids whom Nathan had fallen in with. More than that, he had them all following him around already. "Would you say sorry in front of them?"

He didn't answer. Which was all the answer Amber needed. She took a breath to say something else, but the breath caught with a hitch. If she tried to talk now she would start crying again. She let it out in a huff instead and turned back toward her house. She waited until her back was to him to raise a hand and wipe at her eyes.

"Wait—hang on," Nathan said, and the metal of the chain-link fence rattled. Amber didn't need to look back to know he was climbing over into the Nowaks' yard. She thought about being stubborn, running back to her house and slamming the door in his face before he could catch up. But he might catch her first, which would feel like losing, and that'd be more than she could handle right now. Or, worse, he might not try to catch up at all. Simply give up and go back to his house and not apologize anymore. The thought made her wince, so she didn't speed up . . . but she didn't slow down, either.

She listened for the squeak of the gate hinge and the clatter of it swinging back into place, but Nathan must not have bothered with that, instead clambering over the wooden fence right there at the corner. His feet hit the ground in her yard with a thump, but she kept walking until he grabbed her wrist.

"Hey, I *said* I'm sorry."

"I thought you were my friend," she answered, trying to shake his grip off.

He didn't let go, insisting, "I am your friend! I just . . ."

"You just didn't realize what a big loser I am?" She didn't need to look at him to know she was right, and she added, "But somebody who won't be my friend at school isn't really my friend at all."

It wasn't the first time this had happened. There'd been the Johnson brothers, whose mom was friends with her mom and who were happy to hang out with her as long as no one else knew about it; there'd been her entire former soccer team, before her mom had let her quit, who ignored her at school but were forced to act nice when the coach was watching during practice; and there'd been Cecelia Jasmer, Amber's classmate, who really only wanted to be friends with *Hannah* but knew she was too cool to be seen with a kid two grades younger, so she pretended to be Amber's secret friend in order to hang out with her sister.

"I'm sick of it," she said, and saying it broke through the hurt and let the anger out instead. She turned on Nathan and shoved him, yanking her arm out of his grip as he fell back a step. The cold air stung as she widened her eyes, and her hard breaths puffed in a cloud between them, but she didn't feel like she was in danger of crying anymore. "People think I'm okay to hang around with as long as nobody else finds out, and it sucks. And *you* suck, too, if you're too scared to admit we're really friends."

"I'm not scared," Nathan snapped, frowning. "You take that back."

Amber made herself laugh. "You are too scared. You're scared if they all find out you're friends with me, you won't be cool enough to make them keep liking you."

"No, no, it's not like that."

Amber crossed her arms, as much because the breeze was cool as because she was angry.

"Prove it," she said.

"What?"

"Prove it. Go to school tomorrow and tell everyone you lied, and actually we *are* friends, and I was your friend all through the whole summer."

"I can't do that—"

"That's what I thought."

"Yet. I mean, I can't do that *yet*. Use your head, Amber." He stepped close again, and when she tried to turn away he shifted, his eyes staying on her face. "I just gotta wait 'til my reputation is set. Once everybody's my friend and they won't drop me for knowing the wrong people, then I can start being your friend at school, too."

Amber hesitated. None of the other kids had claimed to have any plans like that. She wanted to believe it. It would mean she could still hang out with Nathan after school and on the weekends, instead of going back to being bored and lonely all the time, especially now that Hannah was getting along with Steph again.

"I don't know," she murmured, and Nathan must have heard the wavering uncertainty in her voice, because his face brightened.

"Listen," he said, "once I'm set with the popular kids, I'll be your friend at school again, and that'll make *you* popular, too."

It doesn't work that way, she thought, but bit her lip and kept quiet. She wanted it to work. She wanted to believe Nathan actually thought it could work. Amber brushed aside the fact that none of Nathan's friends were *popular*, only mean enough to make the other kids leave them alone. Even that was better than what she had.

Amber looked up at the gray sky, away from his dark eyes. She listened to the wind rattling the dry leaves against one another and a distant birdcall. The quiet stretched on. A lawnmower started up in another yard. Finally, the righteous anger blew out of her in a sigh that left her drained, weary. Her defensive stiffness dropped, her shoulders slumped, and when she spoke, she didn't look at Nathan.

"You promise? You promise you're still my friend, for real?"

"I promise," he said, putting both hands on her shoulders. She dropped her gaze to his. His smile was relieved, eyes concerned, but there was a tension in his grip that she couldn't place. Maybe he was trying to convince her, the way he'd convinced her parents after the wine. . . . No. Amber wouldn't entertain that thought. One more chance couldn't hurt, and she was probably imagining the buzz of anger underneath his soothing voice.

"All right. But for now, I gotta go do homework," she said. Homework, and maybe some time alone to make sure she truly was calm.

Hannah stepped out into the crisp air then, and unless she'd been eavesdropping before, all she could've heard was their last sentence or two. Since school had begun and Amber and Hannah had gone back to their different social circles—or lack thereof—nearly all the tension between Hannah and Nathan seemed to have eased. Sure, there were odd moments when Amber thought the way the boy looked at her sister was particularly intense, but they always passed, and Hannah had been almost comfortable.

"I can hang out a bit," Hannah said. "Mrs. Grayson didn't give us any homework today, and Steph's grounded. Wanna play catch?"

Nathan gave Hannah one of those penetrating looks again, but when he saw Amber watching him, he blinked and the expression vanished.

"Sounds cool," he said. "My yard, though. Dad wants me to stay close to home today."

They split up, but Amber paused before she went in. With one foot through the doorway, she turned to watch over her shoulder as her sister followed Nathan back to his house. He didn't walk next to her but stalked ahead, and Amber's brow furrowed. An urge to go bring her sister back home swept her. She opened her mouth to call out, but hesitated. Still wrung out from the confrontation with Nathan and with no good reason to ask Hannah not to go with him, anyway, Amber shrugged and went to tackle her math.

The homework should probably have taken her no more than half an hour, maybe a little longer, but nearly an hour and a half passed before she finally put down her pencil and leaned back in her chair. She let her arms hang down at her sides and closed her eyes for a moment. The problems weren't hard. Keeping her mind on task was the issue. Still, she'd finished. She ought to go back over her work and double-check it, but if she tried, her eyes would unfocus and her mind would wander and she'd sit there staring blankly for who knows how long.

She stuffed the page into a folder and stood from her desk, bringing her backyard into view through the second bedroom window, the one Nathan had never thrown rocks at because there wasn't a good place to hide from view of the living room below. Not that being seen would be an issue at this moment, with Mom at the grocery store and Dad in the garage. Amber was the only person in the right part of the house to look out and see into Nathan's backyard.

Nathan was nowhere to be seen, but Hannah was. She sat on the ground in Nathan's yard with her back to their own house, leaning against the chain-link fence, kicking her legs, her hands at her throat.

"What . . . ?" Amber muttered, leaning over her desk to press her face against the window. She squinted, blinked, and rubbed her eyes hard.

Her sister was tied to the fence by her neck, knotted on the other side of the chain links where she couldn't reach it. Red jump rope handles dangled almost to the ground.

Amber's heart kicked into a panicky race, and she backed away from her desk. Stumbling, feet heavy, she dashed out of her room and nearly tumbled down the stairs. Halfway down she jumped and landed hard in the hallway, pain lancing up her shins. It didn't slow her. Amber raced through the house and across the backyard, the fastest she'd ever run in her life. She all but vaulted the fence into the Nowaks' backyard, skidding to a stop behind her sister.

"Hannah, oh my god," she gasped.

"Amber? Amber! Untie me!"

Hannah's words came smoothly, not like she was in danger of choking, but her voice was a little scratchy and trembled as if she'd been crying. Knowing her sister was all right didn't entirely calm her, and Amber worked on the knot with clumsy, fumbling fingers.

"What happened?" she asked as the jump rope finally began to loosen. "Where's Nathan?"

"He tied me up and left! He said he was hungry and went in for a snack. I've been *screaming* for help!"

The knot unraveled all at once, and Hannah yanked it off. The smooth jump rope went back through the chain-link fence with a long *ziiip*. Amber climbed over to the other side and took Hannah's hands, helping her up. Both girls breathed in shaky gasps, and Hannah had an angry red welt on her throat.

"We gotta get a turtleneck or something for you," Amber muttered, leading her sister toward the gate rather than back over the fence. "Hide that mark from Mom and Dad."

"What? Why?" Hannah demanded, drawing back from Amber.

"So nobody gets in trouble," Amber replied. She frowned, cocking her head. Why would Hannah need her to spell out such an obvious answer?

Hannah pulled farther away from her sister, shaking her head. "You and I aren't the ones getting in trouble. *Nathan* is. I'm not hiding this from Mom and Dad, I'm telling!"

"Hannah!" Amber exclaimed. She dropped her voice and took the younger girl's hand, pulling hard to hustle her all the way back to their own yard before rounding on her and whispering, "You *can't* tell, okay? Nathan and I just made up. If you tell Mom and Dad, they won't let me hang out with him anymore, either. It wouldn't be fair!"

"You don't need to hang out with someone like that," Hannah said, voice flat. Apprehension squeezed Amber's chest, and bitterness followed hard on its heels.

"Easy for you to say."

"What's that supposed to mean?"

Amber rubbed her eyes. "It means," she said, "that you have tons of friends, and you don't know what it's like."

"I don't—"

"You'll *never*," Amber interrupted, her voice rising into a shout as the sharp anger swelled in her chest, "*ever* know what it's like! And you're going to take away the *one* friendship I have, and . . . and if you tell Mom and Dad, I'll tell them I saw you put that rope burn on your neck yourself."

Hannah recoiled. Amber squared her shoulders and crossed her arms but avoided her sister's eyes. Never had Hannah looked at Amber with such stark lack of trust. Her sister's eyes glinted with tears, and Amber's heart squeezed. With a scowl she took a breath and pushed the guilty hurt aside, and when she made herself meet Hannah's gaze again, she tilted up her chin and froze herself off from her sister's betrayed expression.

"They won't believe that," Hannah said, her voice thick.

"It'll be your word against mine *and* Nathan's." Amber's words came out cool and smooth, and her lips twitched as she suppressed a satisfied smirk. Hannah couldn't manipulate her. "So, like I said, you should go put on a turtleneck or something."

The shaky terror that had coursed through her was buried now, crushed beneath the weight of hurt indignation at the idea that Hannah might deliberately try to sabotage her. Hannah burst into tears and ran for the house. Amber watched her go, refusing to feel the faint prickle of guilt.

Someone was watching her. The impression of a dark, unblinking gaze flickered in the corner of Amber's eyes, from the window of the house next door.

Amber spun, sucking in a startled breath. Then she scoffed.

In one of Mrs. Jones's windows, facing Amber's house rather than the street, a poster board skeleton Halloween decoration stared down with empty, black eye sockets and a goofy grin.

What had Amber been worried about? And, anyway, what did she care if anyone had been watching her? There was nothing to feel guilty *for.* She'd rescued Hannah, hadn't she? And her sister had *still* wanted to ruin everything for her. It wasn't Amber's fault if Hannah went and worked herself up over something so stupid as a prank that had hardly even gotten out of hand at all.

Satisfied, Amber shook her head and followed her sister inside.

CHAPTER 11

I'LL TELL THEM MORE

NOVEMBER 1998

Amber lounged on the couch, eating cheesy snacks and watching a rerun episode of *Are You Afraid of the Dark?*, reluctant to give up on Halloween and look toward Christmas just yet.

Both of her parents were still at work, and Mom had errands to run in Cleveland after that, which meant neither of them would be home for a few more hours. Hannah had pointedly *not* invited Amber to join as she and Steph played house in the Nowaks' backyard—not that Amber *cared*; the last time they played Hannah wouldn't give Amber a turn at being the mom, ending the game in a nasty fight after Amber bragged that being older meant in real life she'd get to be a real mom first. Whatever, she was too old to play those games anymore. And this way, for as long as Hannah stayed busy outside, Amber had the actual house all to herself. With the shades drawn, she watched wide-eyed as the high schoolers on the screen endured frightening scenario after frightening scenario. One of the teen girls let out a scream and at the same moment the back door slid open so hard that Amber echoed the TV with a quickly muffled shriek. She jerked straight up on the couch, scattering her snack.

She was still picking up cheesy bits and pieces when Hannah pounded into the family room from the kitchen. Amber turned to reprimand her, but one glance at her sister's face stifled the sharp comments before they could come out of her mouth.

"What happened?" she asked, jumping to her feet and crossing the room in an instant. Hannah breathed in shuddering gasps, her lip trembled, and her eyes were red. Had there been another problem Amber was going to have to smooth over before her folks could get involved? She grabbed her sister's shoulders and shook her, forcing herself to stay gentle. "Hannah? Tell me what happened?"

"I thought he was hurt so I went over—he fell out of the tree, he did it on *purpose*, who does that?" Hannah said between shaky breaths. She wiped her eyes with her hands, brushing away more tears before they could fall. "He was yelling for help and nobody else was outside—Steph went home early—I thought he was really hurt—"

"Who?"

"Nathan!"

Burning heat swept Amber's skin, followed by icy cold that left behind prickly goosebumps.

"I wasn't gonna hang out with him again but when I saw him fall—and he was lying there under the tree, just shouting and moaning—I went to help. And those guys from your class jumped out from around the far side of the house. You know the guys, the brothers? Those short, mean kids?"

"Glenn and Luke," Amber said, her voice hard.

"And Nathan jumped up, and he said it was just a joke. They were being really, really nice at first. But then, then the one kid—Glenn?—he said I should be Nathan's girlfriend." Hannah said the word with distaste and then sniffed and wiped her nose. She paid no mind when Amber sucked in a breath as if she'd been hit, only went on. "And Nathan, he, he made me kiss him."

"He did *what*?" Amber asked.

"He grabbed me and he made me kiss him. He tried to stick his *tongue* in my mouth." Frank disgust joined the frightened embarrassment in her sister's voice, and hot fury coiled in Amber's belly.

How could Nathan do something like that to someone? Especially to her sister? Amber bit her lip, hard, until she tasted blood and made herself unclench. Nathan's friends thought he should date her *sister*, did they, and he tried to force her to make out with him?

"No way," she snapped, tightening her grip on Hannah's shoulder. "I'm gonna beat the crap out of him."

"Amber, don't," Hannah said. "I'll just tell—"

"No!" Amber shouted. Why was Hannah always trying to *tattle*? Amber took a breath, made herself speak softly. "I mean, no, don't worry about it. Let me handle this. He won't bother you again. This is . . . it's way too far. I'm going over there right now. You go to your room and lock the door and don't come out 'til Mom and Dad get home, or me. Okay?"

Hannah sniffed and nodded, but still needed a push to send her in the direction of the stairs. Once Amber was sure her sister was in her room, she grabbed her jacket and stormed out into the cold afternoon.

Nathan lounged in his backyard, and as Hannah had said, Glenn and Luke were there, too, along with another kid Amber didn't know as well, a boy from the seventh grade who she was pretty sure was named Travis. Normally she would have hesitated to say anything at all in front of those boys, but any qualms had been burned away. She hopped the first fence without embarrassing herself by falling off or needing a second try, and started shouting before she was all the way over the second.

"Hey! You *asshole*"—it was the first time she had ever cussed and she wanted to bare her teeth at the surprise on the boys' faces—"what'd you do to my sister?"

She crossed half the yard before she finished speaking, reached him before he had a chance to formulate a response. He opened his mouth to speak but instead she slapped him full across the face, twisting her body with the blow so the *crack* resounded through the air. He stumbled back, his cheek reddening. Amber's palm stung and she shook it once but didn't wince. Glenn, Luke, and Travis stood frozen, staring with wide eyes. Amber stomped forward and shoved Nathan's chest, making him stumble again.

Nathan finally gathered himself and pushed her back. The action broke the surprised stillness of the others, and Travis jumped forward to grab the sleeve of Amber's jacket. Luke followed suit, and Glenn crowded close behind her. She tried to pull her arms away but couldn't, and her chest constricted with a sick fear that the rage couldn't keep at bay. Beneath that was a different kind of feeling in her gut and the fleeting thought, quickly buried—would Nathan try on her what he'd tried with Hannah?

Instead, he punched her in the stomach. Pain exploded, doubled her over. She gagged.

"What the *fuck*, Amber," Nathan yelled.

Her mouth hung open, gaping but unable to draw in a breath for several long moments. When she did, it came in a long wheeze that set the other guys to laughing. Nathan didn't laugh. His silence was not a relief. He radiated remote, cold fury.

The paralysis of sick pain faded and she struggled to straighten up. Before she could try to fight back or think of something to say, Nathan hit her again. This second blow was emotionless, and he didn't give her a second glance. He struck and turned away as her knees wobbled and her vision swam and she tried not to puke.

"Get outta my yard," Nathan said, his voice calm and empty, already having dismissed her importance. Travis and Luke dragged Amber to the gate, pushed it open, and shoved her through into the Nowaks' yard. They turned their backs on her with sneering laughter as she tripped over her own feet and fell on her butt in the cold grass.

"No," she said, scrambling to her feet. "No, no, no way. No *way.* You don't *treat me like that*! You—you apologize to me! Now!"

Now Nathan did join the laughter. They sauntered away, talking softly among themselves, chuckling. She heard her name muttered.

Pain and embarrassment collapsed into nothing, leaving in their place a hot, furious kind of focus. She didn't know where it came from, had no time to analyze it, but she leaned into the burning as it spread through her.

When she spoke again her voice did not quaver with embarrassing desperation. "If you don't apologize," she said, and the flat, hard tone drew Nathan back, made him turn around to watch her bend down and pick up a stick that had fallen off one of the trees in Steph's yard, "then I'll let Hannah tell my parents what you did. I'll back her up. *And* I'll tell them more. I'll say you did it to *me*, too. *And* beat me up."

"I didn't—"

Amber *thwacked* the stick across her shin.

"That's screwed up," Glenn muttered.

Amber didn't listen. She kept her eyes on Nathan. She smacked the stick into her shin again. And again. "I'll punch myself in the face. A black eye. Tell my mom and dad you did it." He scoffed. She hit herself with the stick again and smiled. "I'll tell *your* dad you did it. And what you did to Hannah."

Nathan paled. Amber's smile widened, showing her teeth.

"Be nice to me, Nathan. Leave my sister alone." She hit herself again. "Tell me you're sorry."

"You're outta your mind!" Nathan shouted. Was his anger dulled? Amber didn't think she imagined the way his lips twitched like he was hiding a smile. She had him, and he knew it. But it didn't look to her like he hated that.

She hit herself with the stick again.

"Fine! I'm sorry. I'll be nicer to you. And I won't tease Hannah anymore."

"And you'll apologize to Hannah, too. *If* I let her around you again."

Nathan's eyes widened. "Why wouldn't you let Hannah hang out with me?" he asked, and the confusion in his voice sounded genuine. "I didn't do anything *bad* to her."

Hannah's tear-streaked face came back to Amber with painful clarity. Nathan's expression shone with the belief that he *hadn't* done anything bad to Hannah. Amber didn't understand how he could believe that any more than she could understand why it didn't surprise her. Even so, she felt her own face twist into a snarl.

She hit her leg again, all but growling, "All you *ever* do to her is bad stuff. So, you'll say you're sorry to her, too, or *else*." She didn't let herself wince with the next blow of the stick, though it stung more each time.

"I'll apologize to her if she doesn't rat me out," Nathan said.

"Fine."

They both knew Amber couldn't actually guarantee that Hannah wouldn't say anything. Amber wasn't surprised a few hours later, over dinner, when a shadow shifted in the darkness outside the sliding glass door to the kitchen. She watched as carefully as she could, trying not to tip off anyone at the table. Trying, too, to keep Nathan from realizing that she knew he was out there, loitering in the backyard again, watching them eat. He never told her why he did it. Outright denied it, even. But there he was. Making sure Hannah didn't tattle.

Fortunately, she kept her mouth shut.

Nathan stayed out there as a light snow began to fall and all through the time she and Hannah spent cleaning the kitchen after dinner. For all Amber knew, he was still standing in the dark November night looking into their house after they were done, too, but to go and check would give away the fact that she'd known he was there all along.

The next morning when she and Hannah went out to catch the bus to school, Amber alone noticed the kid-sized shoe prints in the snow. They came from around the corner, between dormant shrubbery to the picture window at the front of the house, to the porch, on to the garage, and around the far corner. She stepped up onto the school bus, imagining Nathan sneaking around the outside of her house at night, trying to get in.

CHAPTER 12

EMBELLISH

NOVEMBER 1998

Amber stared at her homework. More accurately, she stared in the direction of her homework, her eyes unfocused, tapping her desk with the eraser of her pencil. With three whole weeks until the long weekend for Thanksgiving, preholiday distraction wasn't near enough to blame for her inattention. No, the events of the earlier school day ruined her concentration. Amber replayed it all over and over, varying between sickly sharp flashes of outrage and a teeth-gritting kind of satisfaction. She didn't know who had started the rumor—the other boys, or Nathan—that Nathan had kissed Hannah and made out with Amber as a prank. It didn't matter, really, who started it. Only two things mattered.

Hannah still went to the elementary school. So, at least the stories probably wouldn't reach her. They wouldn't hurt her, and she couldn't tell on anyone for anything that happened because of them.

And whoever the rumormonger was, they forgot to account for exactly *how* unpopular Amber was. When the truly popular kids started making fun of Nathan for kissing someone like Amber and her little sister, it dawned on Amber that the best way to get back at Nathan wasn't to deny the rumors.

It was to embellish them.

The stick had left a nasty bruise. It looked worse than it felt, but that was always the case with Amber. Mom said she bruised like a peach. When she got over the initial surprise of the whispers swirling around her all day, all she had to do was wait for someone to come at her about them directly. It had been one of the less unkind kids, which meant playing for sympathy was on the table, and Amber managed to make herself sniffle convincingly while she whispered that actually Nathan had made her kiss him—it was *almost* true, she told herself, except he'd done it to Hannah instead—and that he'd punched her in the stomach and kicked her. She pulled her pant leg up, not high, just to reveal the bruise on her shin. After *that* the rumors spreading around the school took on a different tone entirely.

Satisfaction won out. Nathan had tried to do something bad to her sister and Amber had slapped him right in front of his friends. They'd tried to do something bad to her and she'd turned it right around on him. She'd finally won.

Settling on feeling pleased with herself gave Amber the space in her brain to finish her homework, and gave her something to smile about during private moments for the rest of the night. She went to bed still full of warm contentment.

As she sank toward sleep, she wondered how mad Nathan might be with her. Well, tough. Amber finally understood that, whatever he said at school or in front of the others, she could talk him into staying her friend. He always hung around, hiding out in their yard, trying to get in their house. He needed something from her—she wasn't sure what—as much as she needed a friendship.

So, when a fistful of pebbles struck her window in the middle of the night, scattering off it with more force than other times he'd tried to get her attention this way, the sound pulled Amber out of sleep without particularly surprising her.

Amber tiptoed to the window and cracked it so they could talk but didn't open the window all the way. The light snow had melted away during the day, but with sunset long past the air had a bite.

"What do you want?" she called down in a low voice, pitched soft to avoid waking her family.

Shadows concealed his face, hid his eyes except for a dull gleam, but Amber knew the flat expression well by now, in spite of the darkness. He answered her in a voice devoid of emotion, "Come down."

Amber squinted at her alarm clock. "It's like two in the morning, are you crazy?"

"We gotta talk about what happened."

"You mean talk about how I stopped you from making everybody laugh at me? Or about you spreading lies about me? I know, let's talk about how you promised once you had friends, you'd start acting like *my* friend at school, too. Wanna talk about that stuff?"

"Just . . . come down."

He didn't shout, the anger didn't flash across his half-seen face. He simply pivoted and made his way back to his own yard, careful to stay out of sight of the windows in the other bedrooms. Amber turned away, and once her back was to the window, she allowed herself a grin.

She'd been right. There was nothing to worry about. He still came to talk to her.

Though she *wanted* to run downstairs and out the door, go get the whole talk over with and get back to normal, she made herself wait two or three minutes. Sneaking out at night would get her in more trouble than she'd ever been in, true, but the delay was just as much to let him wonder if she was going to come. Make sure he knew she didn't answer to him.

Once she'd waited long enough to make her point, she crept down the stairs, forcing herself to keep to a walk. She snatched a jacket from the coat closet and put it on in the hall, but carried her shoes with her until she stepped out the back door, sneaking more easily in her socks.

Her yard was empty, and for a moment an embarrassed blush crawled up her cheeks. She'd miscalculated, she'd made it worse instead of playing it cool, and Nathan had gotten mad and gone inside—

A soft whistle caught her attention. She turned toward the sound and there was Nathan, on the far side of his own yard. In the darkness Amber barely discerned him waving at her to come over. In the interest of continuing to show him that she wasn't eager to chase him around, Amber took the time to go through the gate into Steph's backyard rather than hop fences. Finally, she made her way into Nathan's yard. He still stood on the other side of the lawn, his hands stuffed in his jacket pockets. He jerked his head for her to follow him and disappeared around the far side of the house.

Amber followed. Nathan waited a little down the walk, leaning on the vinyl siding and watching her with sharp eyes. A streetlight shone on the curb, and though its yellow beams didn't reach far, the illumination at least gave Amber some better visibility. Nathan wore a hard expression, and she tried to make hers match it.

The moment she stepped out of sight of her own house, he stood up straight and came at her. Before she knew what he was going to do, he'd shoved her hard against the wall, the blankness leaving his face, replaced by betrayed anger.

"How could you do that to me?" he said, his voice a quiet snarl. She regained her balance but he shoved her again. "You embarrassed me in front of the whole school!"

Amber shoved him back. She couldn't shout for a grown-up to help her, she'd get in as much trouble for being out of bed as Nathan would for pushing her around. But this time he had no backup holding her still and she had no naive misconception about whether or not Nathan would hit a girl. When he swung for her, she pulled back. The blow caught her elbow instead of her belly. She kicked out, then jumped at him. He tried to kick her back but their legs tangled, and they fell hard.

His fist connected with her mouth and Amber tasted blood, and she reared back and punched Nathan as hard as she could. She didn't have much strength, but he shifted at the wrong moment and her knuckles slammed into his neck instead of his chest. He gagged, and she jerked away. When she got some distance, she kicked him again, but he grabbed her leg and pulled her back down. The two of them scrambled in the cold, muddy grass, grunting and huffing, trying to keep quiet amid the violence.

It was Amber's first fight, and when they broke apart several minutes later, she wasn't sure how long exactly they'd been scuffling or how well she'd done, although Nathan looked as disheveled as she felt. They both panted, breath clouding in the cold air, and Amber pulled herself around to lean back against the wall of Nathan's house. After a moment he joined her, and they sat with their legs out in front of them, muddy and grass-stained, neither looking at the other. Their shoulders touched.

Heavy breathing slowed, evened, and Nathan sounded normal when he finally said, "I didn't start that rumor. Glenn did."

"Did you tell him not to?" Amber asked. The fire in her voice burned out.

"No."

"Did you correct everybody when you heard it?"

"No."

"So, I think we're even."

Now Nathan turned to her. A smear of mud itched on her cheek, her hair hung in clumps thick with more mud, and a warm drop of blood beaded under the stinging split on her lower lip. Nathan touched an abrasion on his own forehead gingerly, then rubbed his throat.

"Yeah, I guess we are even," he said, and his eyes, always distant, grew . . . not warm, but less cold. Did he mean they'd come off even in the fight, too? Had she managed to impress him by holding her own? Warm pride blossomed in her chest, but she played it cool.

She shrugged. "Almost. You still have to apologize to my sister."

Nathan laughed, and she shushed him. "Fine," he said. "Go back to bed. Bring her over tomorrow. There's something in the garage I wanna show you guys anyway, something I discovered, so meet me in there after school."

"All right." Amber got stiffly to her feet, careful not to grunt at the twinges. She took greater care returning home than she had leaving. Both her parents should have still been asleep, but if one of them woke up and saw her coming back from Nathan's yard muddy and roughed up, there'd be big problems. She crept through the house, the air indoors almost too warm after her exertions in the crisp cold, and cleaned herself up as quietly as she could manage before changing her pajamas and slipping back into bed. Though she imagined she'd stay awake well into the rest of the night, the buzzing adrenaline drained out of her, and she fell into a sound sleep.

Over breakfast the following morning, choosing a moment alone with her sister to deliver the news, Amber murmured to Hannah, "Hey, Nathan says he's ready to apologize for the other day."

Hannah looked up from her scrambled eggs, lowering her fork back onto her plate. "Really?" she asked, raising her eyebrows.

"I told him he has to, or else," Amber said, leaving the exact threatened consequences vague. "He said he also wants to show us something cool in his garage after school."

Hannah's expression remained dubious, but she nodded before she went back to her breakfast. Mom bustled back into the room, adjusting one of her earrings, and paused as her eyes passed over her daughters.

"Are you feeling all right, Amber? You look pale."

"I just didn't sleep well," Amber lied, then shoved a forkful of eggs into her own mouth to avoid any further conversation.

After school that day, Hannah and Amber popped into the house to drop their backpacks in the front hall, and with Amber in the lead the sisters went straight on to Nathan's house. There hadn't been any reason before to hang out in anyone's garage. The space was bare, the car gone with Nathan's dad at work. In the far corner, near a coiled-up green garden hose, Amber glimpsed the now-empty mouse trap lying askew next to a match box and a pile of burned matchsticks. She looked away. Along the back wall stood a worktable.

Nathan stood tiptoe on the bench that went with it, which he'd dragged to the right, to the high shelves holding bottles of weed-killers and fertilizers, engine oils, grease, and cleaners. With his back to Amber and Hannah, he inspected labels and selected specific bottles, bending down to put them carefully on the worktable next to an empty bowl and a stained cleaning rag.

At the sound of their footsteps, he turned with a grin, saying, "Hi, girls. Gimme one second." He went back to the shelves, still talking over his shoulder. "I figured out something real cool. Can't wait to show you."

A moment later he jumped off the bench. He landed hard, stumbled, and rubbed the knee Amber had kicked during the fight. Guilt tugged at her gut at the same time as satisfaction warmed her.

"Amber says you wanted to say sorry to me," Hannah said, crossing her arms.

"Yeah, sure, I'm sorry," Nathan said, turning to the bottles he'd selected and the empty bowl. "How 'bout this? I'll let you try my invention first."

"Invention?" Amber asked.

"Yeah . . ." His voice turned distracted as he worked the child-proof caps off the bottles. "I figured out a way to keep warm even when it's cold out. Better than just a jacket. Watch . . ." He poured a dollop from one of the bottles out into the bowl, then leaned back from the table and worked at arm's length as he added splashes of the rest. A sharp, stinging kind of smell tickled her nose, grew stronger. Amber coughed.

"It reeks," she said.

"Yeah, got a few kinks to work out," Nathan said, his voice rough as he strained not to cough, too. "Done!" He turned with the bowl and nodded his head from Hannah to the center of the garage, where there was a drain in the concrete floor. "Go over there and roll up your sleeve."

Hannah hesitated, huffed a sigh, and did as instructed. Amber crowded close, though the fumes from the bowl stung her eyes until they watered. Nathan folded up the rag and dipped a corner in the bowl, then held it out and let the liquid soak and spread in a bit. He gave Hannah another grin, and Amber frowned.

"Wait," she said, reaching out to grab Hannah's arm.

Nathan swiped the cloth over Hannah's forearm and Amber jerked her hand back.

For a moment silence filled the garage. Hannah glanced from the growing smugness on Nathan's face to the worried frown on Amber's.

"Nothing's happening. It doesn't do any—" She cut herself off, eyes widening. "Wait, it *does* feel warm. It's . . . no, no, wait, it's burning. It burns!"

"Gotcha!" Nathan exclaimed with a wild laugh. "I gotcha, you brat!"

"Amber! Amber!" Hannah's voice rose, grew shrill. "Amber, it *burns*!" A red mark spread across her skin where Nathan had rubbed the cloth on her, and Hannah's next breath came in a hitching gasp as she started to cry, clutching her arm above the elbow with her other hand, shaking. "It burns, it burns, help, Amber, help!"

Amber elbowed past Nathan, catching him hard in the chest, interrupting his laughter. She grabbed the hose and the knob, twisted it the wrong way at first, then corrected herself. She ran back to Hannah as the water hissed through the length of the hose and aimed the nozzle at her sister's arm at the same moment it started spraying.

Hannah's cries escalated to a brief, sharp scream, before subsiding to low, hitching sobs that dwindled away under the rush of cold water. When her sister calmed, Amber turned on Nathan.

He took one look at her eyes and stepped back a pace, raising his hands and putting on a disarming smile. "Hey, calm down, it was a mistake. I don't know what happened, it worked befo—"

Amber twisted the nozzle of the hose until the water came out in a concentrated blast and aimed it directly at Nathan's face. He spluttered and forced out the word "accident" before gasping in a mouthful of water and succumbing to a fit of coughing and choking. Amber advanced on him, keeping the spray on his face as well as she could in spite of his attempts to dodge. Behind her, Hannah's cries slowed, breath coming in great, sniffling gasps. Amber's hot fury did not similarly abate.

Finally, Nathan turned his back on her, letting the stream of water hit the back of his head harmlessly. Amber's lip curled and her jaw clenched. She was not done with him yet.

"That was not an accident!" she meant to shout, but it came out as a scream. "You don't say '*gotcha*' after an accident!"

She shifted her grip and swung the hose like a weapon.

"What's all this commotio— *Augh!*" The hose swung and water slashed through the air, dousing Nathan's mother as she opened the door from the house to the garage. The metal nozzle struck Nathan on the side of the head. He looked over his shoulder to give Amber a split-second smirk before clutching his temple and letting out a wail.

He fell dramatically to the floor, writhing, and Amber didn't have the energy to feel surprised as she watched him summon real tears. She didn't wait around for his mom to gather herself to respond to the situation; she grabbed her sister by the arm that hadn't been chemically burned and dragged her back home as fast as she could.

Nathan had hurt Hannah instead of properly apologizing. He'd tricked Amber into bringing her sister into danger. He'd lied to her and he'd broken their deal! Her chest filled up with burning, hard-edged outrage and her palms itched to slap him like she had the other day. Hannah still whimpered softly, and this time Amber had no intention of convincing her sister not to tell on their neighbor.

He had told her he'd stick to their deal, and he'd lied to her. She was done with him.

"Mom!" Amber shouted as she pulled Hannah into the house. "Nathan hurt Hannah!"

She spilled the whole story, downplaying her part in bringing Hannah to Nathan's house and framing the hose-hitting as an accident. Everything was going fine until Hannah pulled away from Amber and gave her a dirty look.

"It's all your fault," she sniffled, and sick betrayal rushed through Amber with an intensity that left her lightheaded. It was Amber who'd pulled Hannah out of there, Amber's quick thinking with the hose that had stopped the burning, and now here she stood telling Mom things that would end her friendship with Nathan . . . and Hannah turned on her.

Hannah told Mom everything. *Everything.* About being tied to the fence with a jump rope, about the kiss, about the way Amber had covered up for Nathan and helped him get away with his dangerous behavior over and over again. By the time Dad came home, Amber was already locked in her room and threatened with being grounded until the New Year.

She listened through the door as Dad called Nathan's house, listened to the shouting and the cussing. Resentment consumed her, prickling and total. She'd thrown in with Hannah, given up on Nathan for good, and burned to the ground months of work on establishing a friendship—for what?

Hannah wasn't grateful. Her parents weren't proud of her for getting Hannah out of the Teldegardos' garage safely. In fact, she was probably facing the longest punishment of her life.

Never again. She would never take their side in anything again.

"From now on," she told herself in a growling whisper as she listened to Hannah and Mom go around the house locking every door and checking every window, "it's me against them. Against everybody. I'm done trying."

PART FIVE

CHAPTER 13

ALL GRAY

SEPTEMBER 2020

Amber sat sideways on the couch, resting her back against its arm, her legs stretched along the length of it. Balancing a bowl of some overly frosted cereal on her lap—living dangerously, risking a cold milk spill down her thighs—she ate with a spoon in one hand and her phone in the other. She bounced back and forth between a cartoonish color-matching game and social media scrolling, her coffee within reach on the end table. She wanted nothing more than to spend all of this Saturday lounging with her hair in its messy ponytail and wearing her oldest, rattiest, comfiest sweatpants and T-shirt. Marigold sat cross-legged on the floor less than a foot away from the television, eating her own bowl of cereal, sans milk, with her fingers.

Xander would come down almost silently whenever he woke up. By comparison, Ben's footsteps on the stairs always sounded heavier in the mornings than any other time of day, particularly the morning between two overnights at the fire station.

He came around the corner from the front hallway, rubbing

his face with one hand, the other on the small of his back. "Hey, Mari-berry," he yawned without looking into the room.

"Good morning! Look! I'm putting my cereal between my toes!"

"That's nice," Ben mumbled. He paused, frowned, and said, "Wait . . ." Amber stifled a chuckle. He moved his hand away from his eyes and opened his mouth, almost certainly to tell Marigold not to do that, but saw Amber sitting in the living room as well and did a visible double take.

"Morning," she said.

"Were you just upstairs?" he asked, then shook his head. "No, you're wearing blue."

"What?"

"I just saw someone walk from Marigold's room into Xander's room. Tall like you, but in all gray . . ."

"That's not funny," Amber said, the smile slipping off her face as she straightened and set her cereal on the coffee table. Ben knew exactly how unnerved she'd been lately. She wouldn't have told him about the mirrors and the whispers if she knew he'd turn around and make jokes about it.

"I'm not trying to be funny," Ben said, and what convinced Amber was the way he didn't waste time trying to convince her at all. He'd already backed out of the room. The glimpse of his face as he turned away—pasty, no trace of sleep left—made Amber's heart pick up speed. Over his shoulder, voice strident, he added, "I saw someone upstairs. I saw someone going into Xander's room!"

He ran.

Ben's frantic exit catapulted Amber to her feet, her pulse leaping. As his footsteps flew up the stairs, Amber's stomach plummeted. She followed him without thinking, scrambling for the doorway, dragged by Ben's urgency.

"Can I come upstairs, too?" Marigold asked as Amber rounded the corner out of the room.

"Stay here, watch your show," Amber called back, voice sharp.

Her heart thudded as she ran up the steps. A chill worked its way through her veins, and she took a deep, shuddering breath, trying to push it back. They'd get to Xander's room and there'd be nothing. They wouldn't find anything wrong. It would be like the other night with the monitor, nothing there. Everything would be totally normal.

Ben must have been remembering that night as well, because when Amber climbed up and peered into the hallway, he stood outside Xander's door with one hand hovering a hair shy of touching the knob, watching over his shoulder for her. He waited for her to step all the way up off the last stair before he turned the knob, and she crossed the hall in a hurry. Ben eased the door open and they peered into the six-year-old's room together.

Nothing jumped out at them. Ben moved quietly as he stepped farther into the room, turning a slow circle. Amber followed him in, eyes sharp.

By nine o'clock in the morning the sunlight outside shone bright and strong; even with Xander's green curtains pulled, the light in the room was not dim so much as diffuse. With no distinct illumination there were no sharp shadows, and the indirect reflection off the warm cream walls created a sort of glow. It wasn't a big room, but the mirror over Xander's dresser gave the illusion of some depth. Toys lay scattered around the floor and a pile of clothing had been half shoved under the bed. A cardboard box left over from the move stuck partway into the closet, scrawled with the word FORT in marker. Inside the box sat a pair of loose batteries that Amber would have to remember to throw away. Xander sprawled sideways across his mattress, one foot sticking out from beneath the covers and hanging over the far side, snoring softly.

Nothing out of the ordinary.

The tension eased out of Amber's shoulders, the knot in her gut loosened. In fact, the scene held such peace, represented the picture of a drowsy Saturday morning with such perfection, that

Amber felt herself inclined to yawn. She turned to Ben and patted his arm. He shook his head, the muscles in his jaw softening as his expression shifted from alarmed to bemused.

Although Xander could sleep through a drum solo, Ben kept his voice down as he muttered, "This house is starting to get to me." He headed for the door.

Amber took a deep breath, the somnolent calm of her old bedroom settling over her and soothing the last of the apprehension. With a small, almost indulgent smile, she gave the familiar space a last glance before she turned to go.

Her eyes skimmed over the mirror above Xander's dresser with the full intention of not letting her gaze stop on the glass surface at all. But behind her, in the reflected recesses of the closet, something moved. She couldn't help it. She looked. Not at her own face, no, not even to see if her mirror-self's eyes were still shut as tight as last time. She focused just beyond herself.

The hangers rattled softly. When the shadow materialized into a figure, it did so almost out of sight, almost fully hidden behind Amber's own body in the reflection.

It shifted and a little more of it became visible, just a little, and pins and needles swept over Amber when she realized what that shifting meant. It was drawing nearer, coming up behind her. She tried to draw a breath and could not. Her throat constricted.

She spun to face the closet. From this angle she could not see the figure hiding within.

"Ben." Amber meant to shout her husband's name, but it came out in a strangled whisper.

Her hands went to her throat, she sucked in a wheezing breath. To her right, the doorway stood empty. Her husband thumped down the steps.

"Ben," she tried again, her voice a weak rasp, the word hardly recognizable as his name.

She couldn't make him hear her. Alone. She was alone in the

room with only a sleeping boy and a looming presence in the closet. Every second, Ben moved farther away from her.

"Ben." This time she didn't manage even a whisper, her lips numb, tongue clumsy.

She couldn't make herself shout for him, for the one person who knew something was *wrong* in this house.

He might as well have been gone entirely.

The air in the room dried out, hot and thick in her throat, heavy and stifling in her lungs. She fought to breathe it, staring into the closet. Was it empty now? Xander's good shirts swayed gently, barely perceptibly. Amber's eyes stung—no, they *burned.* Her breath came in shallow whistles.

With feet of lead, her knees wobbly, she forced herself to step closer to the closet. For the first time she wished Xander had gotten into sports, despite the hassle it would have been. Her palms itched to have a baseball bat or a hockey stick, even a tennis racket, anything to wield. She took another step. A bead of sweat trickled down her back. Her eyes itched, dry and gritty, but she dared not blink.

The closer she drew to the closet the more of the room loomed behind her. Especially the mirror. The mirror over the dresser. Over her shoulder. Behind her, against the far wall. Watching her, watching her and reflecting god knew what. Anything. Her skin crawled in waves, pinpricks running from her spine up to her scalp. She had to check the closet, had to be fast, then she could get the hell out of this room and away from that mirror.

With a hiss she jerked forward at last and peered around the half-open closet door.

The thing inside was made of shadows and ember-flecked smoke and hate.

Amber opened her mouth to scream but it shoved her right in the center of her chest, pushing her back and knocking the air out of her. Its mouth opened and a thick, acrid stink crept into the room. Burning cold radiated from where it struck her, and Amber's voice stuck in her throat. The whispers began, drifting from the thing that shuffled nearer to her. The lips did not move, the tongue lay flat and dead within the reeking cavern of the mouth, but the whispers came nevertheless. Hate-filled. Hissing. Indistinct, until eyes like smoldering coals met Amber's and the whispers filled with her name.

She stumbled back, tripped over her feet, and fell on her ass. One of her hands landed hard on some small toy, the pain sharp but distant. Amber flinched, shut her eyes. The smell overpowered her, choked her, the whispers wormed into her ears.

"Stop," she managed to gasp. Ragged and harsh, her voice wasn't loud, but it broke the deathly quiet of the hissing voice. From the bed somewhere to her right, Xander shifted and let out a tiny sigh. The whispers fell silent in an instant.

"Who's there?" His voice was small and sleepy. "Mom?"

Amber opened her eyes. The figure was in the closet again, fading, receding. The fire in its eyes flared once, dimmed, and vanished.

The little pain in her hand made her wince as she pushed herself stiffly to her feet, her eyes wide in spite of her attempt at regaining composure. Her gaze jumped around the room, and she forced her panicked breathing to slow.

"What're you doing?" Xander asked, drawing her attention to him.

She arranged her face into a smile that hardly trembled at all as she answered, "Nothing, buddy. Just came to check in on you and, ah, tripped."

She stepped toward the closet again. It stood open and empty, no whispers or hate creatures or deathly stench lurked in the shadows. The quivering tension drained out of Amber in a rush, leaving her wilted and limp. The constriction drawn tight around her lungs loosened, and she managed a deep, calming breath.

When she turned back to Xander, he sat up in bed, rubbing his eyes. She didn't mean to look into the mirror again, in fact she meant *never* to look into that mirror again, but it pulled her eyes.

From where she stood now, the mirror no longer reflected Amber, showing her Xander's toy box and only half of the closet, empty of anything but clothes and the cardboard box fort. Amber sighed, closed her eyes. Everything was as it should be. Relief coursed through her, made her shoulders sag. For a moment she thought she might keep sagging, might sink all the way to the floor and sit in a heap and try to get her trembling under control. She rubbed a hand over her face and then opened her eyes again.

Her reflection stood within the mirror.

She hadn't moved, not an inch, not at all, how could her reflection have gotten into the mirror? The shock of seeing herself where she could not be overrode her caution and Amber looked full in the face of her own reflection. Her stomach clenched, and she groped behind her for the wall.

Within the mirror she did not merely stand with her eyes closed. Her eyes were *gone*. Smooth skin stretched across her face, eyebrows and cheekbones framing nothing but a scatter of freckles. Amber jammed her hands against her mouth to keep in a cry and her reflection did the same.

Fingertips first, a pair of hands reached around from the back of the reflection's head. The hands closed over that eyeless face at the same time as the rotting breath washed over the back of her neck and filled her nose with the smell of death. Amber shouted, shuddering forward and whirling in a tight circle.

There was no one there. Every corner of the room, though empty, seethed with menace. Where was the shadow-thing now? Where would it be when she closed her eyes? Turned her back? Shifted her gaze? Her heart climbed up into her throat, her stomach sank so fast that she thought she'd puke, and she bit the inside of her cheek to keep from screaming. Fear tightened heavily around her, a crushing pressure that did not leave room for breath or thought.

Amber's eyes landed on the boy, sitting straight up in bed. He was a stranger to her, a small intruder in her bedroom. He didn't belong, he was *wrong*. She winced, stepping back from him. Her heel landed on the same small toy and she stumbled.

When she glanced up again the strangeness hanging around Xander had passed. He sat silent in the bed, his bed, his bedroom now. The covers pooled around his waist and his dark blond hair stuck up at strange angles, but no trace of sleep remained in his unusually pale face.

He stared at Amber with wide, unblinking eyes. No emotion at all marred his smooth, still features.

If he opened his mouth and began to hiss decaying whispers at her she would lose her mind.

Amber ran from the room.

CHAPTER 14

EMPTY AND MENACING

SEPTEMBER 2020

Xander and Marigold played outside, Amber having chased them out to work off their energy after their third fight over who would be in charge of the remote control. The last time she checked, Xander had been leading his sister around the yard, referring to her as his "first mate" and declaring different areas to be full of various kinds of sea monsters. Though she knew Ben's schedule, she glanced at the calendar hanging on the wall again anyway. It was the fifteenth. Ben would be home on the sixteenth. Her father's birthday would have been the day after that, but Amber squeezed her eyes shut and pushed the unpleasant thought out of her mind.

With Ben away working the last overnight at the firehouse in his twenty-four-on, twenty-four-off three-shift cycle, Amber decided on corned beef for dinner. She and the kids loved it, but Ben didn't care for the dish, and he flat-out hated the smell of it permeating the house while it cooked. He had the next four days off, and she didn't want to have to spend all of their downtime undoing whatever stupid attitude problems he'd come home with. She could always tell who he'd been scheduled with based on how he behaved when he got back—especially when he came home with an attitude and caused friction between them, at least until she managed to remind him that at his core he was a reasonable person.

So, for now she'd cook the corned beef with the kitchen window open, and tomorrow she'd make his favorite dishes, and that would go a long way toward making sure he'd be her Ben during the off days, and not the firehouse's Ben.

Having the window open also let her listen for the kids as she prepared the side dishes, handy for keeping them out of trouble, but helpful also because being able to hear them kept the strangeness—the hateful whispers and rot and menacing reflections—at bay.

Amber let her attention sink into the small, repetitive task of washing the potatoes and carrots to go with the beef. Xander shouted something about a mermaid. Amber peeled the potatoes, her hands moving into and out of the stream of water. The breeze blowing through the window still smelled more like summer than fall. Somewhere in the neighborhood, someone else's kid shouted and laughed. Amber set each peeled potato in a bowl, reached for the carrots. Her eyes slid a little out of focus. Curls of orange carrot peel fell into the sink, formed a little pile. Marigold yelled something at Xander, but Amber couldn't make it out. She turned off the faucet before picking up a knife to cut the potatoes into wedges. Xander said something quiet, maybe from the other side of the yard. Amber cut the carrots. She scraped them off the cutting board into a shallow pan. The blade scratched along the wood, loud. Too loud. Silence stretched out. Why couldn't she hear the kids playing, shouting about sea serpents and sharks?

Setting the knife and cutting board down, Amber rested her palms on the counter and leaned over it, bringing her face close to the window. She peered from one side to the other, craning her neck, nose almost brushing the screen, but Xander and Mari were nowhere to be seen. Her heartbeat quickened and the pit of her stomach twisted up.

What if something had happened to the kids?

The scene painted itself vividly before her eyes. She would walk into the backyard and call their names, calmly, just checking up on what they were doing.

Then more loudly.

And again, this time fearfully. She would circle the yard and not see them. She would repeat the circuit and still not see them, looking in stupid places like behind a rock too small to hide behind. Maybe a neighbor would step outside, call out to see if everything was okay, and she'd ask them in a quavering voice if they'd seen Xander and Marigold.

Amber imagined calling Ben, then the police. Her breath quickened.

She imagined waiting outside when the cops arrived, wondered if any of them would be the same who had been at the house at the beginning of the year when her parents were murdered. The thought of all the questions the cops would have for her, the way they'd look at her, made her hunch her shoulders. Imagining how terrible she'd feel for having to say that the kids had disappeared while she was inside making dinner, that she hadn't been outside watching them play, sent a crawling shiver over her skin. She could think of few things worse.

Her heart raced now as she pictured the long weeks during which nothing would be found. The vultures of society would circle over what was supposed to be a time for grieving. There would be bills and legal complications to compound the loss, though she imagined them only vaguely. What she pictured in greater detail was the neighborhood gossips, who would pretend to be horrified when they heard about it, but eventually they'd say what the rest would only think. They'd call Amber and Ben terrible parents, they'd lay blame, they'd pass judgment. None of them would be surprised, in fact horrible old Mrs. Jones would be delighted, when Amber and Ben packed up and moved away, out of the neighborhood, escaping this awful house.

Then, somewhere new and untainted by the past, would come the gradual acceptance, the eventual healing. Maybe she and Ben would find it in their hearts to try again, to start over. With enough time she could see herself feeling ready, could picture convincing Ben.

Amber shook herself and crossed the kitchen in a hurry. The sliding glass door wobbled on its track as she opened it too fast.

"Kids?" she called.

Silence.

Maybe she really wouldn't find them.

She swallowed hard, put a hand to her chest as if to stop the fluttering inside.

"Kids?" Louder this time.

"We're over here." Xander's voice drifted from around the far side of the house, from around the corner where the back fence enclosed a sort of dead end of the yard. Her dad had kept a scrap woodpile there, along with some old spare tires. Amber thought about telling them not to play with the broken plywood and worn-out rubber, then let the idea go.

She went back into the house. The tightness in her chest unraveled and dropped, so fast she had to take a steadying breath. Relief, that's all. The feeling in her heart and in her lungs was nothing but powerful relief.

Standing in the dining half of the kitchen, Amber looked into the front hall and the entry to the living room. Her nose wrinkled and her eyes stung before she consciously registered a sharp stink underlying the richer scent of the corned beef and the spices she had prepared for the potatoes. Once she noticed it, it struck her hard. How had it not bothered her before? The powerful smell clung to her throat and even her lungs when she breathed, acrid and eye-watering. It burned her nose, familiar in a dim, distant way; it didn't trigger a memory so much as the sensation of one, a warning in the pit of her stomach.

"What *now*," she muttered, stepping into the hallway. The smell came from the living room, and the farther she followed it into the house the more her eyes stung. She blinked against the shimmer of tears, tried to inhale, and coughed instead. Shaking her head, Amber retreated back to the front hall and took a few shaky breaths of relatively fresh air. Once steadied, she sucked in as much air as she could, pulled the collar of her shirt up over her nose, and hurried back into the living room, holding her breath.

All normal. Nothing there could cause such an astringent, painful reek. Her eyes stung and she blinked hard. A tear dripped down her cheek, another, more, wetting her shirt. Amber moved into the hallway, testing the locked door to her office and peeking in the laundry room. Nothing obviously wrong there.

The door at the end of the hall, the one leading to the garage, stood ajar, hardly a crack. It hadn't been visible from the living room. Old dread—the long hallway in the dark, empty and menacing—welled up, dousing her in cold.

Spots danced in front of her eyes. Her chest first tingled and then burned with the need to inhale. Amber shook herself and tried to make her feet take her quickly to the door, but all she managed was an unsteady shuffle.

By the time she reached it her chest spasmed, her vision swimming and gray, and she couldn't stop herself anymore. Clutching the fabric of her shirt more tightly over the lower half of her face, she inhaled and immediately choked on the sharp, bitter stink. Coughing, eyes streaming, Amber pulled the door the rest of the way open.

Ben had taken the car to work and in its absence the garage seemed big and empty, a dim, gray shadow space lit by a small window high along the garage door. Amber slapped the button to raise that door and hurried for the bright light and fresh air flooding in. As she went, a darkness and a small shape caught her eye.

Old rags plugged the drain in the garage floor, sodden in the center of a wide pool of liquid from which streams of foggy mist rose. Scattered around the garage lay every single bottle and tub of detergent, lubricant, bleach, chemicals, and rat poison. All open, all emptied into the noxious pool on the floor.

Amber stumbled to the driveway and dropped her shirt, bending over to rest her hands on her knees. Her head floated and she felt that at any moment she might pass out. Little by little the fog lifted and her thinking cleared. She blinked. Why was she still standing, bent double like this? It would be wiser to sit down. She sat, right there on the concrete.

When the vertigo passed and her eyes and nose stopped dripping, Amber scooted around in place to stare at the garage. The back hall, the office and laundry room, and the living room would all be totally unlivable. When she found out which of the kids had done this, she'd ground them for so long they'd forget what the sun felt like.

Except they'd been in the backyard all afternoon. And Ben sure as shit would have mentioned if the garage had been like this when he'd left.

Amber thought about calling him, but what could he do? He couldn't come home unless there was an emergency. Well, a real emergency, not some dumb joke gone too far. How would it look if she called Ben home over something like this, something easy for her to take care of herself? No.

Her eyes sought out and found the rake, leaning against the wall of the garage, where she could reach it without having to step in the noxious pool. She gathered her nerves, took and held another deep breath, and hurried in to grab the rake. Holding the handle as close to the end as she could, Amber used the tines to scrape the rags away from the drain without stepping into the mess. Once done, she stood back and let herself breathe again, watching the liquid go down, listening to it gurgle as it ran through the pipes, and trying not to think of where the drain let out. Hopefully the sewer and not the nearby creek, but either way it wasn't her problem.

In the confined space of the garage the air still burned her lungs when she inhaled, but not as terribly. Once the spill had all seeped away except for a damp oval on the floor, Amber stepped back in and turned on the hose.

Her gaze followed the arc of water, the stream of it moving along the floor to the drain. Tears still filled her eyes. She kept her focus on the water. Putting her thumb over half the nozzle concentrated the flow, turned it into a blasting spray. She tried to keep her mind from wandering, but a memory pushed to the surface—spraying a hose right into her old neighbor's face, swinging it like a flail and smacking the end into the side of his head.

A thread of unease crept up her spine. Was someone watching her? She glanced over her shoulder, into the corners of the garage, then snorted at herself and scowled. Yes, the smell was overpowering and familiar. But it was just a coincidence. It didn't mean Amber had to let herself follow the rest of the memory the reek conjured up in her mind. No. No, there were enough problems.

This was a prank. Maybe not Mari and Xander. But some neighborhood teens or something. A prank, nothing more. Not related to anything at all. Not related to memories she didn't want to examine.

It didn't mean anything.

She took care to wash down the entire floor, standing always by the walls and aiming the spray directly toward the drain, wincing at the stink every time she breathed in, but never having to take a break and step back outside. Amber made three circuits and deemed it finished, but when she went in she left the garage door wide open to allow it to keep airing out.

She checked the rest of the house. The master bedroom was above the garage, and the smell reached up there, but not the suffocating fumes. The upstairs hall, the kids' rooms, and the bathroom were fine. So at least she wouldn't have to try to get them to camp out in the kitchen all night.

When Amber called the kids in for dinner, she planned to tell them about the spill in the garage and warn them that certain parts of the house were temporarily unlivable.

Xander came into the house first, and he stopped short in the doorway. Marigold, unprepared for her brother's abrupt halt, ran into the back of him. They stumbled forward together, Xander's nose wrinkling and Marigold's face pulling into an exaggerated grimace. She slapped her hands over her nose and mouth and shouted, "Stinky!"

"What *is* that?" Xander asked, pinching his own nose. His little voice was scornful. He turned to Amber. "What'd you *do*?"

Was he blaming *Amber* for the smell?

"Excuse me?" she said, raising her eyebrows and crossing her arms. "What did *you* do? You know you're not supposed to play in the garage!" They'd been in the backyard the whole time, though, hadn't they? Or had they snuck around, into the garage from the side door? Amber shook her head. The quiet, earlier. When she hadn't been able to hear them. What *had* they been up to, then?

"The garage?" Marigold repeated. "We didn't go in the garage. It's *boring* in there."

Amber scowled. "Well, either way," she said, "the TV is in the living room and we can't *use* the living room right now, so I guess no shows for anybody until probably tomorrow. Maybe later." Her voice, laden with blame and sanctimony, made a punishment out of the precaution.

"What!" Xander yelled.

"That's not fair!" Marigold whined.

The rest of the meal passed in sullen silence, broken by occasional bouts of argumentative whining.

Before Marigold and Xander's bedtime finally rolled around, Amber had to stop herself from telling them to go ahead and sit in the living room, watch their cartoons, and choke. Instead, she let herself out the front door and stood on the porch, shivering a little in the cool night air, rubbing her arms and looking up at the cloudy sky. She counted to ten, didn't feel any better, but took control of her temper and went back in to get bedtime sorted.

The kids were both already upstairs playing in their rooms, with nothing else to do, and Amber turned in that direction. One hand on the banister, one foot raised to the first step, a flicker of light from the living room glinted in the corner of Amber's eye. Frowning, she stepped away from the stairs and turned to the living room entry instead.

A fire burned in the fireplace.

Amber tilted her head. Had there been any logs there before? How could Xander and Marigold have gotten it going this fast? Amber glanced at the ceiling. Their voices still drifted down, muffled and distant but unmistakable from above her.

A sour taste flooded up from the back of her throat. The skin on the back of her neck tightened. Her gaze was drawn, slow and unwilling, back to the fireplace. To the flames. To the eyes watching her from the smoldering coals behind the flames.

Amber blinked and the eyes were gone.

No, she told herself, clenching her hands into fists, letting them loose again. Not gone. They'd never been there. And she couldn't let it burn all night.

Bedtime for the kids would have to wait.

She hesitated.

The fire could wait until after bedtime, couldn't it? People left fires burning in their fireplaces for a little while all the time, and usually it was fine. Besides, this had been a long day. Maybe tonight after Xander and Mari were in bed, Amber could get herself a bowl of ice cream and read a book for a while. She didn't want to prolong the wait for that peaceful, calm time. Putting the fire out now would only push that back further. Did she have to go to it right away? Reluctance tugged her; she wanted to draw away and go up the stairs. But was that safe? Ben wouldn't want her to leave it like that. Especially since she didn't know who had lit it—*no*, it was one of the kids, that was all, and she'd have a *serious* talk with them both about it.

Amber shook her head, one sharp jerk, but her thoughts stayed scattered. Except one.

No, the fire couldn't wait.

She moved into the living room. But shouldn't she have something? A bucket of water, or maybe sand, to put out the fire? The condo hadn't had a fireplace. She wasn't sure how to safely put it out. The fire crackled merrily at her. Amber kept walking, her eyes filling and filling with the flames. The flicker was somehow soothing. A concern had been troubling her, hadn't it? Amber couldn't quite recall. Somewhere behind her the fourth stair creaked. Amber knelt before the hearth. The fire was a touch too big to be safe. Warmth washed over her face, over her hand as she reached out. Not for the poker next to the fireplace. Toward the flames. Her fingers grew hot. Hotter, almost too hot. She leaned forward—

"Hey! You said the living room's not safe!" Marigold's voice, accusing and petulant, rang out. Amber turned, the words on the tip of her tongue to tell Marigold everything was fine and to go back to her room, but as soon as she stopped looking at the fire the heat on her hand flared at last.

Yelping, she snatched her hand back. The lingering, suffocating reek of the chemicals hit her as she scuttled backward in an undignified crab walk. She coughed, gagged. How had she forgotten that smell? The choking rasp in her throat?

She scrambled farther away and said, "It *isn't* safe, Mari, back up."

Marigold moved forward instead, until a whiff of the chemical stink made her sneeze. She backed away again as Amber reached her.

Glancing over her shoulder, Amber watched the flames gutter and die.

"Why'd you start a fire?" Marigold asked, taking Amber's hand.

Amber shrugged, leading the little girl back up the stairs. "I don't know," she said, unwilling to admit that she hadn't done it and risk scaring Marigold right at bedtime. After the day she'd had between work and the mess, she wanted nothing more than an easy end to the evening.

Leaving Xander's room and heading into her own thirty minutes later, she was cautiously pleased it had indeed gone easily, though weariness pressed down on her. She opened the drawer to pick out her pajamas and stifled a yawn, eyeing the book on her nightstand and considering whether she should stay up late or try to sleep. Getting the kids down was always harder on nights when Ben wasn't home. As she pulled her pajama shirt over her head, she caught sight of the mirror in her peripheral vision.

Her reflection faced her head-on. It still had no eyes.

Amber shouted and recoiled, bumping the nightstand and stumbling. If she fell and looked up and saw that reflection still standing there facing her without her eyes she'd scream, and if she screamed, if she lost control, something worse would happen, she just knew it. When she regained her balance she hurried for the door, but the total lack of movement from the corner of her eye stopped her in her tracks.

Her mirror-self hadn't moved when she moved.

Forcing herself through a reluctance so profound it almost hurt, Amber made herself check the mirror one more time.

It showed an empty room.

Amber's hands jumped to her mouth, the gasp she sucked in thin and labored.

Where was her reflection? Before she could think better of it, Amber stepped closer to the mirror, revealing more of the space around her.

There, there she was. Her reflection, eyeless and motionless and standing with its back pressed into the far corner of the room.

Terror pinned Amber in place. Her throat constricted—a thin, keening whine came out of her. Her back tingled.

What would happen if she turned her back on the mirror again? What was happening in the room behind her? In the corner her reflection hid in?

She fixed her gaze on where her reflection's eyes should be, gritted her teeth, and *willed* the mirror to go back to normal.

Nothing changed. Nothing happened. The fear swelled, flooded and filled her until it bore her thoughts away. She couldn't breathe. She couldn't break her gaze from the silvered surface.

Amber lifted a hand to touch the glass, her fingers almost brushing it. At the last moment she yanked her hand away and stumbled back with a hiss. She'd almost touched it! Her scattered thoughts were difficult to pull back in. What was she doing? Stop, *stop*, she had to stop looking at the room reflected like that, with the shadow-shape, the not-person, coming into focus almost completely overlapped by mirror-Amber, peeking around the edge of her face, and *it* got to have eyes, it had eyes like fire and hatred, and they stared and stared and—

Sucking in a sharp breath, Amber slapped her hands over her own eyes, but no, that was wrong, that was just like the shadow-figure had done before the mirrors took her eyes. Amber let her breath back out in a noisy rush as she snatched her hands away from her face again, half afraid that she wouldn't be able to even as she did.

Skin crawling, Amber forced herself to turn toward her bed. Her hands trembled as she untucked the comforter and pulled it all the way down to drape off the end. Movements fast and jerky, she grabbed the top sheet in both fists and yanked it off the bed entirely, pulling it out from beneath the end of the comforter.

Clutching the white sheet as if it could protect her, she turned back toward the mirror. Her reflection had returned to its proper place, holding the sheet, the skin where its eyes should be shadowed now, as if sinking into her face. Amber could see the shape of the eye sockets—growing more defined by the moment and very obviously empty of eyeballs—beneath that skin, and her stomach turned.

Stepping closer to the mirror felt impossible, her heart hammering so hard she imagined it was trying to knock her away from the glass. Her limbs shook, her mouth tasted sour and sharp. The reflected Amber—lips pressed together and face white and eyes gone—stood similarly frozen.

The sheet, however, did not. Though it remained limp and unmoving in her grip, the folds of fabric in the mirror twitched. Amber's breath caught in her throat as it twitched again, and then bulged, a shape forming beneath it, leaning out: an obscured face, a head, shoulders. Spectral fingertips, smoky-gray and rot-black, appeared at the edges of the sheet and curled around the fabric, and *now* Amber felt a tug of resistance in the real-life sheet.

She cried out and let go and it billowed as it fluttered down—but not far enough down. Amber skittered backward until the backs of her legs bumped the foot of her bed. She lost her balance and sat gracelessly.

The sheet settled gently over a shape—a figure—hunched and huddled on the floor, but only for a moment until it stood, it straightened, the sheet outlining the shape of a person, the reflection matching it perfectly now as the form's arms raised beneath the draping white. As it reached for her.

"No," Amber gasped, yanking her feet up off the floor and scrambling backward across the mattress. The sheeted figure drifted with terrible silence toward her bed and her heart raced so fast she could hardly tell one beat from the next. Amber lashed out, grasping for anything she might use to defend herself, her eyes locked on the white fabric. The back of her hand knocked into her bedside lamp and it fell askew, tilted against the wall. She grabbed it and yanked the cord free, and the figure drew nearer still as Amber sat straight up in the bed and hurled the lamp at the sheet with all her might.

The second the lamp left her hand, the sheet collapsed, falling in a fluttering heap onto the floor as if nothing had ever been holding it up. The lamp flew through the space where the figure had been and smashed into the mirror behind it, the high, bright tinkle of breaking glass filling the room, and silvered shards scattering atop the dresser and onto the floor around it.

Amber sat still in her bed, trembling arm outstretched, wide eyes unblinking, and stared. Her breathing slowed but did not steady, still shaking with every exhale. Her heart continued to thunder in her chest. Swallowing made her dry throat rasp, and moving took every drop of Amber's will. She crawled to the foot of the bed and looked down at that sheet.

It lay, innocent and inert, on the floor.

She glanced at the broken mirror. Only a few jagged pieces remained within the frame. Gone. The mirror was gone. She'd won this one. Amber tried to feel the rush of victory, but fear still chilled her spine and made her eyes sting. When she grabbed her phone from the bedside table, it took her three tries to unlock it, her fingers shaking so badly she could hardly touch the right numbers on the screen.

She paused, finger hovering over the call icon, and then curled her hand into a fist instead. Ben knew what was going on now, yes. He believed her now, yes. But could he admit that out loud in front of the other firefighters?

And how would he get the go-ahead to come home a night early, anyway? Would he say, *Sorry, chief, my wife's being haunted and I have to go now, hope there are no fires while you're short-handed*?

The crushing mundanity of having to worry about Ben's job, about their financial stability and their livelihoods, while surrounded by the wreckage of a mirror she'd smashed while fighting a *fucking ghost*, made Amber want to scream almost as much as the fear had. She chewed her lip and stared at her phone and almost called him anyway, then shoved it in her pocket instead. This was no time to shake things up, to invite scrutiny.

She had to get the hell out of this room, though. Victory over that mirror or not, she would never be able to sleep in here alone—or maybe at all—ever again. Cleaning up the glass could wait until morning. Hastily, Amber grabbed the comforter and a pillow and stood, edging around the shards toward the door.

As she went she watched her step, wary of slicing her feet, so she was looking right at the silvery surfaces of the jagged mirror pieces when each and every one of them filled with her own face, miniature but still clearly eyeless, staring out at her, a multitude of mirror mouths opening as if to—

Amber fled the room, slamming the door behind her and leaning against it as if to barricade herself away. The night-light-blue hallway stretched cool and quiet to either side of her, the children's doors shut.

Whispering filled the air, an overlapping and unceasing subvocal murmur. A high whine escaped Amber and she clamped the pillow over the lower half of her face, breathing hard through her nose, eyes watering.

Beneath the fear was a kind of desperate despair. Where could she go? She couldn't afford to take the kids to a hotel—and would it even be safer there, or would she only be trading uncanny menace for the very real chance of catching Covid? God, she needed sleep, she could hardly think, and the whispers followed her as she stumbled downstairs with a vague idea of lying down on the couch, covering her head with the pillow, and blocking everything out to try to get even one moment of real rest.

Instead, she rounded the corner into the living room and stopped.

Hadn't she put out the fire in the fireplace? It crackled there, bright and too alluring, and though the chimney had been cleaned before they'd moved in, smoke drifted in a haze through the room. It was the television that knocked the breath out of Amber, though. Turned off, the screen reflected the living room back at her, darker than in life but no less clear. Before it could do anything it shouldn't, Amber turned on her heel and fled.

She found herself in the kitchen, curtains drawn over the window above the sink and the sliding glass back door. Slumping into a seat at the table, she plopped her pillow down in front of her and draped the blanket over her shoulders. It would be hell on her back, but there were no reflective surfaces staring at her here. No fireplaces, no candles. Amber leaned down onto the table, head turned sideways and resting awkwardly on the pillow, but the moment she closed her eyes the whispers grew louder. As if something had come closer to her. She bolted upright, eyes wide, but the whispers didn't fade back into a malevolent background murmur. As unintelligible as ever, they remained louder, nearer.

And so it went every time she started to fall asleep all through that long night. Like a terrible game of Red Light, Green Light, every time Amber closed her eyes the indistinct voice came a little closer, grew a little louder, the hatred in its hissing clear even if the words never were. Only vigilance, all night, would keep her safe.

Dawn broke, weak and gray and lacking any relief.

By the paltry light of day, the hideous unreality of the night did not bear thinking of—to examine it would be to risk her sanity. But she had not imagined it, this wasn't her fault. Turning her mind from what had happened left Amber with only the hollow, scraped-out feeling of utter exhaustion.

Only when the children woke and wandered downstairs wanting breakfast, only when she was no longer all alone, did any of the terror fade, giving Amber a chance to think clearly. Something must be done. Ignoring it was not working, just as it hadn't worked on bullies in her childhood. She needed a plan, and she knew what the first step would be.

When Ben got home, they'd remove every mirror from the entire house, and she could not bring herself to care even the littlest bit if he still had a problem with that.

CHAPTER 15

STONE STILL AND SILENT

OCTOBER 2020

"You're back late."

Amber stood in the kitchen, peering through the entry toward the front door. She kept her voice level, kept the words a statement and not an accusation. Ben should have been home nearly two hours before. It was a Thursday morning, the first day of his four in a row off. Xander was on a five-minute break from remote class, hiding in Mari's room as if that would save him from going back to his school desk when the break was up. Amber hated bouncing between both kids during Xander's school hours; she could've used some help.

"Grabbed the mail on my way in," he said. Did his smile look forced? He tossed a pile of envelopes onto the counter. "Did we remember to request mail-in ballots? I think it's too late, if we didn't. We might be screwed."

"You've been home late a lot lately," Amber went on, picking up the mail and riffling through it as she talked. If he thought he could change the subject and slip past her, she'd show him otherwise. "For at least a month now."

Ben shrugged.

"Chief keeping you extra? Will you get overtime? That would be nice."

"No, Amber," he said, the forced lightness in his voice fracturing. "Chief Hardy isn't keeping me late. I just . . ." He ran his hands through his hair, cheeks puffing out in a sigh. "I just need a break before I come home sometimes, is all."

"A break."

"Yes."

"From coming home?"

"Don't say it like that." Ben sounded tired.

"How am I supposed to say it?" Amber asked. "What do you need a break *from*?" She did not ask *from me?* but it hung between them.

Ben's jaw tightened, and Amber put down the mail and turned to face him fully, her fists on her hips.

"Tell me," she said.

Ben took a breath as if to speak, but held it for a moment before exhaling in a rush. "I don't know, Amber." His gaze grew distant, as if he were looking not at Amber but through her. "Look, I know you don't want to talk about it, okay? So . . . what do you want me to say?"

Amber didn't answer right away, too busy trying to keep the surprise off her face. She'd expected Ben to be a little standoffish, a little difficult, as he often was after spending too much time with the other firefighters. She knew the shape of how that conversation should go, knew the ways to respond. To be confronted instead by a weariness that would seem almost vulnerable if not for the tinge of caution in his gaze threw her off.

She frowned. "Don't put words in my mouth; I just asked you to talk to me."

Ben's eyes sharpened then, his focus coming back to Amber. "Okay," he said, and was there a note of challenge in his tone? That, at least, was closer to what she'd been expecting, until he glanced around as if to be sure they were alone and said, "Something's wrong with this place, and you knew it and you never told me until I saw it for myself—and don't look at me like that, okay? I get why you didn't tell me." Amber crossed her arms, and Ben closed the distance between them, putting his hands on her shoulders. "Hey. I really do understand why you didn't say anything. I keep wishing I could—" Ben stopped himself, sighed, and dropped his hands from Amber's shoulders. His gaze went a little distant again. "I get that talking about things is hard for you. But it's making me feel . . . alone, I guess. I leave work and it feels like I'm driving into this storm cloud the closer I get to the house. And I can't even *talk* about it. So, sometimes I go to a Metro Park first, and take a walk to get my head on straight. That's all."

Amber had made a mistake. Ever since childhood she'd struggled to trust people with her heart, her truth, but Ben had always accepted her silences. He'd been there for her anyway. Over the past months, Amber's closemouthed ways had become less a well-worn habit and more an active defense again—except this time it was against, not bullies or misunderstanding family, but a terrible presence in her home. But along the way she'd messed up—she'd failed.

She had to fix it.

After a deep breath to steel herself, Amber said, "I'm sorry." The surprise in Ben's eyes encouraged her. "I felt so alone with all this for such a long time, when you finally saw it and I could tell you everything, I was still so freaked out that all I could think about was how relieved I was that you knew what was going on, and how relieved I was that I hadn't lost my mind, you know? Talking about it more after that was so hard . . . I just didn't even realize you might need to, too. But I'll try harder, okay? For you." Ben's whole demeanor softened, and relief coursed through Amber in a heady rush. She moved closer to him, put a hand on his chest. "When you stay away from the house later and later, I . . . I just need you here. Please?"

Ben put his arms around her and said, "All right."

After a moment, Amber broke out of the embrace with a smile she hoped looked less forced than it felt, and said, "I'm gonna go get Xander back to class. You grab some breakfast." She pointed to the table, where a plate of eggs goldenrod, his favorite, waited at his place. It was cold by now; if he'd been home on time it would've been hot and perfect, but Amber trusted that to speak for itself.

Two days later, Amber shooed everyone out to spend the afternoon in the yard. The weather was unseasonably pleasant for late October, and she and Ben had yard work they'd neglected the previous day in favor of getting pumpkins for Halloween.

Yard work and the beautiful weather, Amber told herself, were the only reasons she had chosen to spend the whole day outside. She dug along one fence, harder work than she'd imagined. Still, there was something satisfying, deep in her bones, about the sharp sound of the shovel's blade cutting into the earth.

Marigold let out a laughing scream as she ran in a wide loop around the perimeter of the yard, Xander close behind her, brandishing a stick that still had a clump of leaves clinging to the end.

"Leaf monster!" he shouted, lunging forward to rub the leafy end on top of his sister's head. "Leaf monster attack!"

Marigold ducked and threw her hands up, letting out another shriek as she put on an extra burst of speed.

Amber stepped on the shovel to drive it deeper into the soil. It was midafternoon on a Saturday; if any of the neighbors had a problem with the sound of children playing, they could take it up with her and Ben. Besides, Ben was in the backyard as well, piling stones in a ring to build up the fire pit she'd been pestering him to set up. If the kids got too out of hand, well, he could deal with them for a change.

She heaved back and down on the long handle of the shovel and scooped the dirt up, turned the shovel over and let it fall back to the yard. She probably should have dug the layer of grass off the top first and put it somewhere, but the point today was not really to do things the right way as much as to get started. If she began the task—even if she began it wrong—of setting up a vegetable garden, she'd build up the momentum to eventually do it right. Never starting was her weakness, not balking at fixing her own mistakes. She flattered herself to think that she was willing to go further than most people to fix mistakes.

Her eyes drifted toward the kids again. They'd fallen silent, which meant they'd either been scolded for being too noisy or they were getting into some trouble, and she hadn't heard Ben tell them off. He stood in the middle of the fire pit, turning in a slow rotation and eyeballing his stone circle.

"Have to get some mortar to slap between these stones," he said, "but I think it'll work for tonight."

Amber's eyes moved past him, picking out the small shapes of Xander and Marigold. The leafy stick lay forgotten behind them and they stood side by side, holding hands. They faced the far corner of the yard, Xander stooped slightly, his eye level matching Marigold's. They were peering under the small pine tree in that corner, the one Amber still thought of as Hannah's tree, with the shaded hiding place under the low branches. A chill seeped down Amber's spine, a memory of subtle motion and swelling dread surfacing in her mind. Squeezing her eyes shut, she pushed the image away. She'd been imagining things that day, nothing more.

Hadn't she?

The whispers and cold breaths, the shadows, the mirrors and candles . . .

No, she *hadn't* been imagining things.

Amber's eyes snapped open, locked on the kids.

They stood before the tree, stone still and silent. The friendly warmth bled out of the sunlight, the atmosphere in the yard turning stark and harsh. She drove the shovel into the dirt again and this time the sound held no pleasure for her; it was a gravedigger sound. When Amber let go of the handle the shovel stood up straight.

Marigold tugged on Xander's hand as Amber started across the yard, her gait stiff, legs wooden. Mari stooped down and Xander bent lower still, and in the shadows under the low-hanging, dark-needled branches Amber saw a shifting movement. Her heart leaped into her throat.

"Hey, kids," she called, voice tight, picking up her stride but not running. It wasn't time for running, running would mean something serious was happening, and this was just . . . was just what? Just a spot of nerves? A misunderstanding?

A neighbor, now gone, paying as unwelcome a visit as he had when Amber was a kid?

No. No.

"Hey. Kids!" She didn't shout, not yet, but her tone sharpened.

They didn't turn, didn't so much as hesitate. What was wrong with them? She knew they could hear her. Ben heard her, she could tell. He looked up from the stones of the fire pit, his eyes moving first to his wife, then to the children. Amber picked up her pace, still unwilling to run, shifting instead into a sort of tripping scurry.

Marigold pulled on Xander once more, and the two of them got down to crawl. Something about the way they moved, slow and vague, spiked Amber's fear. Ice flooded her veins, her knees weakened. The shadow shifted beneath the boughs again, leaned forward. It reached out from the dim shade, one hand held palm up. Fog crawled in at the edges of Amber's vision, her focus narrowing on that hand. Gray and cracked, stretching. Beckoning. Amber nearly stumbled to a stop at the sight of it, her stomach flipping.

"What the *hell*?" Ben's voice barely penetrated the fearful haze obscuring Amber's mind. His footsteps thumped in the grass behind her, faster and faster.

The children reached together for that hand. Amber sucked in a breath, fought against the pressure in her chest and her gut to get enough air.

"Stop!" Amber shouted, her voice cracking like a whip, splitting the pleasant autumn afternoon.

She snapped her jaw shut, swallowing hard. Now that she'd let out one shout, if she opened her mouth again the scream bubbling in her chest would follow.

Finally, Xander and Marigold flinched. The hand faded like a shadow struck by sunlight, and Ben and Amber came upon the children at nearly the same moment. Amber grabbed Marigold's shoulders, pulling her to her feet and back from the tree with one strong yank. Ben pushed himself between Xander and the patch of shade under the pine tree and dropped to his knees, his back tense and fists raised.

His shoulders slumped and his hands drifted downward.

He'd found no one there.

Marigold stood with her arms limp at her sides, her head cocked. She turned, dreamy and slow, to look up over her shoulder at Amber with blank, unfocused eyes. The little girl blinked rapidly and shook her head, took a breath, and staggered a few steps away.

"Mommy . . . ?" she whispered.

"It's time to go inside for a couple minutes," Amber said, her voice soft and strained.

"Where were you?" Marigold asked.

Xander turned at the question. He met Amber's gaze and she found herself looking into the eyes of a stranger. She didn't know these children. Where had they come from?

"Where did you go to, Mom?" the boy asked.

Amber stood, her mouth open, her eyes locked on these small interlopers. Ben knelt next to them, and her gaze flicked to him.

"Ben, who—" she began, her voice floating and strange.

Ben's eyes turned grave, his expression concerned. He stood in a rush and snapped his fingers in front of her face. Amber recoiled, covering her eyes. When she dropped her hands again the strangeness had passed. Her glance skimmed off Ben's face, still creased with worry, to the children. Mari and Xander looked at her with the same familiarity they'd always had.

"I'm right here," Amber said. "But it's time for you two to go inside for a few minutes."

Marigold looked at Xander, waiting to see his nod before she agreed. He led her inside, her hand tucked into his. Amber watched them go, waited until the door was closed behind them, and sagged against the nearby fence.

"What just happened?" Ben asked, and though there was concern in his voice, beneath his words ran an undercurrent of fear. She turned toward him, and had he always looked so run-down? For the first time since they'd met in college, Amber had an idea of what he'd look like as an old man. The glimpse of her husband's mortality struck her, and she pushed it away with a frown.

Amber wanted to shrug him off and just get back to normal, or as normal as anything felt lately. But after the conversation they'd had the other morning, she couldn't deflect. Maybe, after some time, she'd be able to ease Ben back into the comfortable understanding that talking about these things would make everything worse, but this was not the time for that. She chewed her thumbnail as she searched for the right words, the right way to answer Ben's question without encouraging more.

"I've been kind of forgetful, lately," she said. His eyes flared with quickly hidden alarm and Amber hurried to amend, "Not about anything important. I'm not going to forget to pay the bills or get us into trouble or anything. I think . . . I think the stress, and the sleep deprivation, it's just making it hard to remember things, sometimes." Like the children's faces. Like the very fact that she and Ben had kids. The kinds of things it should never be hard to remember.

"Listen," he said, and his tone didn't sound like the precursor to an argument; it sounded reassuring and worried both at the same time, and almost relieved. "If the—I don't know, the weird stuff? If the weird stuff and the pressure are getting to you, I need to know. So I can step up. We're in this together."

Had he hesitated for a second before he said that last part? Was he doubting her, doubting her ability to take care of them, to handle things? Time to remind him that the real problem wasn't Amber, it was this house and everything in it.

"Getting to me," she repeated. "You know that's not what's important right now, right? I mean, you *saw* what was going on, didn't you? Can you imagine if something happened to them? Right here in the backyard? In broad daylight, right in front of us?" She shivered, and Ben stepped closer to her. "How could we ever explain that?"

"Amber . . ."

At the reproachful warning in his voice she stiffened and drew away. His eyes held hers, solemn and worried.

"Don't you be like that, Ben. You know what I *mean*."

He looked away. For a long time he didn't answer, staring at the tree, his eyes distant and his face unreadable. The longer his silence stretched the more her chest hurt, as if she was deflating, losing air and composure in equal measure. Her fingers hooked and she wanted to claw into him, clutch him close, and make him tell her what he was *thinking*.

"I know what you mean," he said at last. "Just be careful."

He moved to go inside and she grabbed his wrist. "Look, I'm sorry for worrying you. How about we have dinner out here tonight," she said. Her voice shook, but she forced a wooden smile and added, "It's such a nice night out, there's no reason to go inside."

The windows of the house stared at her, the dimness within contrasting the brightness outside and turning them all into blurry mirrors. Amber averted her eyes.

Ben turned back to her, rubbing her upper arms with his palms. "I'm worried about you," he said. "Listen, why don't we start talking about selling this house after all. I think you were right at first, when you said we should've sold it and bought a whole new place."

The very words *selling this house* sent a lightning bolt of excited relief through Amber's chest, but she tempered it immediately. Getting her hopes up would only make enduring everything all the harder. So, she nodded but said, "It'll be hard. I mean, aside from just the probate and legal stuff, we don't know what selling a house even looks like with social distancing and all that. And nobody's going to want to buy a place where people were murdered less than a year ago. It could take a long time. We might get pennies for the property. All the same reasons we moved in here in the first place, you know? But . . . but yeah. We should try. Can we talk about it more later?" Ben nodded. Amber hesitated. She wanted a favor, but making the request felt too much like admitting to her fears. They were already having this conversation, though, and a better time might not come. "First, could you take down the mirrors tomorrow morning? As early as you can? I know it's a pain, and I know it'd look weird, but it's not like anybody's having guests anymore anyway, right?" When Ben nodded Amber kissed his cheek, leaning against him for a long moment before adding, "But for now, I'll send the kids out and get stuff for a picnic."

"Nah," Ben said, gently turning Amber and aiming her at the picnic table. "You relax." He walked her to one of the wooden benches.

Was he being patronizing? Amber glanced at him over her shoulder, but much of his earlier tension had eased; his expression was all concern now, genuine and unmitigated. If this was the result, Amber thought, she should work on opening up more often. A little, anyway, and without leaving her comfort zone *too* much.

"Thank you," she said, sitting down and smiling up at him. "I love you."

"Love you, too," he said, and disappeared into the house. From the kitchen she heard him call, "Kids? You can go back outside now!"

As the kids barreled back out the door, Amber added, "But stay away from that tree!"

When Ben returned, he had sandwiches and chips balanced on a platter in one hand and a six-pack of cream soda in the other. He looked a little jumpy, his shoulders tight and his movements quick, his lips thin and his eyes wide, as if something had startled him recently. Amber silently promised herself that if, later, he needed to talk about whatever had made him uncomfortable in his brief time alone inside, she'd find a balance between having that conversation without hurting his feelings, and keeping as much of her own comfortable silence as she could.

In the meantime, Amber summoned the kids to the picnic table and rearranged the place settings so that she could eat with her back to the house. It was better than sitting there avoiding her own reflection in the windowpanes, but still, having it looming behind her left her feeling a malevolent regard.

Throughout dinner that watched feeling had Amber glancing again and again to the side, at the flower bed, as if expecting to see a figure staring at them while they ate, as Nathan had done when they were kids. With an adult's perspective, Amber understood that better, at least; Nathan hadn't been taking some perverse pleasure in spying on them. He'd been staring through the window at something he craved and didn't have, starving for the kind of togetherness her family had enjoyed.

Or had appeared to enjoy.

By the time dinner was over, Amber had hit upon a ready-made excuse to stay outside a little longer, and if any of the neighbors happened to be snooping there would be nothing more normal.

"Who wants to carve jack-o'-lanterns?" Amber asked the kids, who let out a raucous cheer.

The rest of the evening, sitting at the picnic table in the setting autumn sunlight, indulging in a comfortable sort of complaining with Ben—about work, about remote schooling, about the way Mrs. Jones looked at Amber—while the kids helped scoop pumpkin guts, separated out the seeds for roasting, and drew faces on for Ben and Amber to carve, almost made Amber feel normal again. When she carried Marigold into the house and up to bed at eight o'clock, Amber managed to stay calm right up until the moment she stepped out of the little girl's room.

The shadows leaned in then, and though she would not look at it, an insistent tapping came from the mirror at the end of the hall. Amber made her way back to the yard, not quite running, barely pausing to duck into the kitchen and snatch a lighter out of a cupboard too high for the kids to reach. She had to stop for a moment to catch her breath after she stepped out onto the patio.

"Hey, let's not go in just yet," she said to Xander and Ben, putting up her hands to stop them from heading for the door. "I thought we could celebrate the new fire pit"—she wiggled the lighter in the air before shoving it into her pocket—"with a bonfire!"

"Marshmallows?" Xander asked.

"Sure thing, buddy," Amber said. "You go get 'em while we get the fire started. Deal?"

"Deal!"

He ran inside, and Amber turned back to see Ben already moving toward the fire pit. They didn't have much wood, no more than a mediocre bundle of sticks and twigs he'd raked up out of the yard following the last couple storms, but he took care to stack them neatly in a cone shape. Amber dragged the patio furniture into the grass, settling three chairs near the stone circle. After she'd arranged them to her satisfaction, she glanced at Ben.

Was he carefully avoiding meeting her eyes?

"What?" she asked.

Ben did glance at her then, his eyes searching, and she suspected that the sheepish smile he gave her was forced. "I'm just in my head. Don't worry about it."

"About what?" Amber insisted.

For a few breaths, Ben didn't speak, just watched Amber with that same appraising look, his smile fading. At last he said, "I didn't like the way the kids were acting earlier."

"That's all?" Amber said, her voice lightening, her gaze dropping idly to the fire pit. "Yeah, I didn't like that either. It was weird." It wasn't just weird, it was scary, but admitting that felt dangerous.

From the corner of her eye she thought Ben made a face at her, disappointed and unhappy, but when she looked again he'd turned, crossing the yard to the shed. He came back carrying the canister of gasoline for the lawnmower, and poured a little of it over the sticks he'd laid down.

"Is that really it?" Amber asked.

"I guess," Ben answered as he turned, sloshing out more gasoline in a small arc. "I don't . . . I don't want to push it." He looked up at her and his rueful smile was genuine, this time. "Talking about the—" He paused, glanced at the neighboring homes, then nodded toward their own house. "You know." Amber gave a quick nod, mouth shut. "It helped. I mean, I felt better. I felt *closer* to you, Amber."

"Why is that a bad thing?" Amber asked.

"It's not."

If he'd been sullen or standoffish, Amber could have let herself get angry with him. But he spoke with gentle concern, much harder to dismiss. Amber pursed her lips, trying to think of how to ask him what his problem was without sounding combative as she leaned over to rearrange the sticks he'd put into the fire pit a moment before. The smell of gasoline was thick but not unpleasant as she gathered a double handful of them back out of the carefully constructed cone.

She settled on, "So, what's worrying you?"

Ben kept his eyes on the gas canister as he worked with it, not on his wife, but he spoke almost delicately. "So . . . I'm thinking it might be good for us to talk a little more. I don't want to push it, but do you realize since they died you've only spoken about Hannah and Greg one time, *ever*? When we went to meet with Greg's parents, and you had to bottle so much in for their sake. But you never talked through your honest feelings about your sister. Never. And Greg, I mean, he'd been my friend once, and you never asked how I felt, or how I handled all that, after—"

"After you were first on the scene," Amber interrupted, her voice sharper than she meant for it to be, her eyes hardening. "I'm sure it was very hard for you to be the first firefighter in the house when my little sister and her husband died." She paused, making sure her next words would carry weight. "I'm sorry you had to do that. But I thought you understood a long time ago that I will never talk about them. That hasn't changed." She dropped half of the gas-soaked sticks on the ground, nudging them with her foot until they were arranged how she wanted them, much better than how Ben had set them up.

"And now your parents," Ben said, liberally splashing one of the two lawn chairs Amber had brought over.

"I don't know why you care if I talk about my mom and dad or not," Amber said shortly. She arranged the rest of the sticks to match the first pile, trails leading from the fire pit to two of the three chairs. Her hands were damp with the gasoline Ben had already poured over the wood. She wiped them on her shorts.

"Because I love you," Ben said, deliberately dumping the last of the gas on the second chair. From somewhere behind them came the sound of the back door sliding open, but neither of them turned toward it, taking their seats instead. "And because you're stressing yourself out way too much. I think we should, hmm . . ." He paused as if searching for the right words, then went on. "We should take things easy, for a little while. And," he gave her a teasing smile, "practice talking stuff through better. As much as you're ready for. But mostly, try to take it easy."

Amber looked at her husband, at his worried eyes, and her irritation evaporated. This was Ben, after all. He was on her side. She reached out to squeeze his hand, the wet back of her tank top cool on her skin when exposed to the air. Ben returned the comforting pressure, and then she dropped his hand and leaned back in her lawn chair.

"I know," she said, her voice gentle and almost apologetic. "I know it's been rough. It's this *house.* Being here. Hard on both of us, I think. As soon as everything's settled we'll sell this place, like you said. Moving into it at all was our only mistake."

"Sounds good. I love you, Amber," Ben said. "You remembered to grab the lighter, right?"

"Love you, too," she said as she fished the lighter out of her pocket and handed it to him.

"What are you doing?" The voice came as if from a great distance.

"Don't interrupt, Xander," Amber said.

"The grown-ups are talking," Ben added.

He flicked the lighter on.

"What are you *doing*?" Xander shouted, and he appeared as if from nowhere, standing before them. The moment he passed into Amber's field of view the smell of gasoline—no, the *reek* of it—choked her. She coughed and surged to her feet. Ben let out a shout and took his thumb off the lighter, the flame winking out. They scrambled away from their chairs, away from the fire pit.

"What the hell?" There was nothing funny in hearing the swear word slip out in the boy's high, bright voice. Amber barely noticed it at all, her attention locked on her husband. Ben didn't offer a reprimand. He stared dully at the lighter in his hand, the horror growing in his eyes not translating to his shock-slackened face.

"Uh, ha-ha, ha-ha-ha," Amber shouted, trying to keep the hysterical edge out of her voice. "Boy we got you, ha-ha, good prank! Right, Ben? Good joke on Xander, right?"

Xander stared back and forth between the two of them. His

eyes widened, and he burst into tears. "That's not a funny joke," he wailed. "You scared me too bad!"

Guilt struck Amber with the same painful breathlessness as a punch to the gut.

"We weren't trying to scare you, buddy," she said, and that much at least was true. Her heart raced, her hands trembled, but she tried to make her voice warm as she added, "How about we forget all about this, huh?"

How far back could a kid remember a traumatic moment, anyway? Amber gritted her teeth against the guilty pang, forcing it away. She didn't need anyone making her feel bad, not right now, not after what she and Ben had almost done.

Xander's loud hysterics might draw the neighbors' attention, though. Amber's glance flicked away from him, over the fence into Mrs. Jones's yard. She forced guilt and irritation both down, buried them beneath as much concern as she could muster, and she tried to hug him as she said, "I'm really, *really* sorry you got scared, buddy."

"Don't touch me! You're all smelly!"

"Let's get you to bed," Ben said, his voice like brittle wood. "We'll get a shower after that, and we'll roast marshmallows tomorrow. Promise."

Xander sniffed, wiped his nose on the back of his hand. With his red eyes and his shuddering breaths, he looked how Amber felt.

She drifted in their wake as Ben led Xander back to the house, hovered outside the door as he tucked the boy into bed without making him change into pajamas first. Her eyes wouldn't focus.

What they had almost done—Amber flinched, squeezed her eyes shut for a moment, and turned her mind away from the fire pit with a wrench.

She groped for something else to think of, anything else.

Probably thanks to Ben, what rose to the surface first (like sparks floating above the fire, she thought, and rubbed the heels of her hands hard into her closed eyes to try to stop herself) was Greg's parents, Linda and Tim Edwards. The memory of meeting with them after Hannah and her husband's deaths made for an effective distraction, but not a pleasant one.

Now all Amber could think of was the pale face of her late brother-in-law's mother. They'd met before; Ben and Greg and Amber had all been close in college, after all, until Hannah had come in and broken everything up the way she always did. It had been natural to see Linda and Tim before the funeral. Amber remembered the conversation in disjointed flashes: red eyes, shocked expressions, her own hands trembling. "We'll take care of everything," she had said at one point. "You don't want to worry about—about extra burdens and responsibilities right now." Swallowing had been hard. She remembered watching Ben reach out to squeeze the older man's hand. He and Greg had been good friends well before Amber had met them both; he had known Mr. and Mrs. Edwards better and for a longer time. Amber had marveled at how calmly he could reassure them that after the funeral, when things settled down, they'd visit often, they'd all stay close, and everything would be okay.

It hadn't been true, but it had been the right thing to say at the time.

It wasn't the right thing to think of right now, though. The past was gone. Hannah and Greg were gone. It'd been such a long time since they'd seen the Edwardses, they might as well have been gone, too.

The unwelcome reminiscence at least pushed aside, for a moment, the terrible dazed actions they'd almost taken in the backyard. Until Ben stepped back out of Xander's room and closed the door behind him, with the smell of gasoline still hanging all around him. He met her gaze with troubled eyes, and she knew he wanted to talk about what happened. Dread flooded her as he opened his mouth as if to speak, but he merely stood there with his jaw hanging. Finally, he shut it, wordless.

Amber grabbed his hands. "Can we shower together?" Her voice quavered, not like a woman asking her husband for intimacy, but like a child begging to sleep between her parents after a nightmare. "Please?"

He nodded, and though they did not say another word for the rest of that night, Amber guessed—hoped—that his thoughts mirrored hers: If they didn't cut through the probate court tie-ups and find a way around the legal bullshit her parents had left behind so they could get the fuck out of this house soon, things would get worse.

No. The smell of smoke and gasoline still lingered in her nose. Not just worse. Deadly.

PART SIX

CHAPTER 16

ONE THING RIGHT

JANUARY 1999

Through the end of December and into January, following the fallout with Nathan and with her family, Amber tasted for the first time the bitterness the holidays would forever after leave in the back of her throat. She moved through the glitter and lights of Christmas with a fake smile—intentionally as insincere as a plastic doll's, she *wanted* her family to know it—and grim eyes. On New Year's Eve she went to bed at nine o'clock.

Two days later Amber picked at her breakfast and pretended not to see Nathan, wrapped in a scarf and a bulky coat, watching them from his hiding place in the backyard. Heaviness settled on her. Being at home, stuck with her family and their disapproving looks and forced cheerfulness, sucked. But going to school sucked, too. This day, the last day of winter break, hung balanced between them, bad on one side and bad on the other, with nothing good to remember or to look forward to.

At least at home she could shut herself in her room and ignore everybody. Avoidance didn't work at school, especially now that Nathan had been trying since the day before Thanksgiving to get back on her good side. If she'd figured out over the summer that ignoring him was the way to break him down, to make him try to win her affection, the knowledge would have made her feel powerful and smart. But now a strange, fawning menace overshadowed his constant lingering.

If he'd only stopped at finally admitting to their friendship in public, none of the problems that followed would've happened, but he was embarrassing her at school instead—over-the-top stuff like standing up for her too intensely when situations didn't call for it or trying to buy her piles of snacks every day at lunch. Before winter break started, he'd begun paying her loud compliments all the time. The flattery had a strangely possessive tone, though she could never put her finger on what made her feel that way.

She ignored it all, but Nathan acted like he thought the break from school would reset their friendship back to how it had been in the summer, before he ruined everything. He threw rocks at her window all night. He knocked at the door whenever her parents were at work and Hannah was at Steph's. He emerged from his house every time he saw her in her own backyard.

And he watched them eat at least once a day. Sometimes more.

School would start the next day. Amber shoved a forkful of pancake into her mouth, watching Nathan from the corner of her eye. He stood at an angle behind the nearest tree to the back door. Amber's view of him was clear, but not Hannah's or her parents'. Was he doing it on purpose?

Amber snorted. Of course he was.

"Did you say something, Amber?" her mom asked, looking up from her own breakfast.

"Nathan's watching us from the backyard again," she said, the words falling out of her mouth before she fully considered them. As soon as she said it, though, she knew it was right. This hovering, embarrassing neediness had to stop. Now. Before school started up again.

Hannah jerked her head up at the same time that her parents pushed themselves to their feet. Nathan must have seen it, must have known what happened, because he turned and tried to run.

He slipped clumsily through the heavy snow, got no farther than the corner of the yard before her parents caught up to him. Amber didn't bother listening to what they said to him. She left that to Hannah, who shamelessly stood shivering in the open doorway, letting the cold air blow in past her. Amber ate the last bite of her pancake, put her dishes in the dishwasher, and returned to her bedroom and her self-imposed isolation. She didn't so much as look through the window. If Nathan looked up while her folks scolded him, he wouldn't see her face, watching. He'd know, she told herself, that this was the end, and he shouldn't bother her or embarrass her anymore.

The next day at school, in a hallway full of kids shouting and shoving and laughing more boisterously than normal after the break, she learned that she'd miscalculated.

Glenn tripped Amber on her way to her locker. She stumbled, regained her balance, and turned to tell him to back off. "Go aw—"

Nathan crashed into Glenn from behind. Glenn reeled forward and both boys toppled together. Heart thundering, Amber skittered backward out of their path.

The boys tumbled across the scuffed linoleum, leaving a thin but bright red streak of blood behind them. Amber covered her mouth, turned, and pushed her way through the gathering crowd of middle schoolers. As she rounded the corner, a thud, a collective intake of breath, and a sudden quiet signaled the end of the brief fight.

"Amber?" Nathan called, his voice rough. He panted. "Amber! Where are you *going*?"

She didn't answer.

Maybe it was Glenn, or maybe someone from the watching crowd, who told the principal how Amber had been part of what started the fight. When he called her down to his office to explain what happened, she didn't hold back.

She probably should have kept her voice down when she told him everything, though—when she left the principal's office, Nathan stood lingering near the door. He slouched against the oversized, cream-painted bricks with his arms crossed. His head was down, but not too far for her to see his expression. He glared daggers at her as she hurried past, avoiding his gaze.

Nathan was suspended, and the next day Glenn, sporting a black eye and a healing cut on his lip, found her at her locker before first period. He caught her off guard, shoved her hard. She landed on her butt in the hallway, books and papers scattering around her. Passing students paused, ready to gather in a ring around Amber and Glenn as they had around Nathan and Glenn the day before.

Amber braced herself for further violence, but met his gaze head on, willing herself not to flinch.

"That was to make up for yesterday," Glenn said. He brushed past her, kicking her math book down the hall as he went. The rest of Amber's classmates drifted away, most wearing mildly disappointed expressions. Nobody offered to help her as she scrambled around, gathering her things. But nobody made fun of her, either. Without Nathan drawing extra attention to her, maybe she'd come out even.

Nathan stood waiting on their front step when Amber and Hannah stepped off the school bus that afternoon, while their parents were still at work. One look at Nathan's blank stare made a coldness tighten in Amber's chest.

"Get out of our way," she said, trying to sound tough, brushing past him to the door while she pulled her copy of the house key out of her coat pocket.

"Let me come in to talk," he countered. "You have to talk to me, Amber."

Amber unlocked the front door, darted her hand past Nathan to grab Hannah, and pulled her inside. When Nathan tried to follow her in, she stiff-armed him backward. If he overcame her, though, if he bulled his way in, what then? Instead, his foot hit a clump of snow and he slipped, windmilling his arms to keep his balance. That one second gave Amber time to back inside and slam the door, twisting the lock on the doorknob and the deadbolt both.

He recovered a moment after the bolt shot home and pounded on the door, shouting through it, "Let me in, Amber!"

Amber watched him, wavy and discolored, through the stained-glass hummingbird window that ran down the center of the door. Her brows furrowed into a frown. She'd spent half a year trying to get this boy to be her friend? She scoffed and pressed her lips together. Months wasted trying to make him like her, when he'd been following her around as much as she'd tagged after him, the whole time.

Well, no more.

"I'm over this," she whispered, then raised her voice to yell back, "Go home, Nathan!" Over her shoulder she said to Hannah, "Go make sure all the other doors are locked. Windows, too."

Nathan pounded again, yelled something else, but Amber shook her head at him through the multicolored window, carefully schooling her expression into one of exasperation. Let him see that instead of the intimidation she was pretty sure he wanted.

Nathan's eyes widened, his face flushed red. He screamed once, a wordless cry of fury, and pounded the window hard. The blow cracked the glass in the biggest panel, a pale blue background piece.

From another room Hannah called, "The doors are locked! Should I call Mom and Dad?"

Amber didn't answer, backing away from the door and keeping her eyes on Nathan. Putting that long crack in the glass must have used up some of his temper; he locked his gaze on hers for another moment, and though he breathed hard the anger drained out of his face. He gave her a sneer before he turned away.

"Amber?"

"What?"

"I said, should I call Mom and Dad?"

"No . . . no. He's going away. They won't wanna be bothered at work. I know you and Steph wanted to build a snowman today, but you should wait 'til after they get home."

"It'll be dark by then," Hannah whined.

Amber turned, looking her sister up and down. The last time she'd tried to protect her, to make Nathan apologize and get him in trouble for hurting her, Hannah had turned on Amber. Although a whisper in her mind insisted the best, safest thing to do would be to keep Hannah indoors, she shrugged instead.

"Do what you want," she said. "I don't care."

She couldn't help feeling a twinge of disappointment in her sister when, instead of rethinking her priorities, Hannah's eyes lit up as if Amber had given her permission. Amber shook her head and pushed the twinge away. Hannah could make her own choices, and if anything happened now it wouldn't be Amber's fault.

With a quiet huff, Amber pushed past Hannah to the coat closet, dropping everything in a pile at the bottom instead of putting it away neatly, and took her backpack up to her room. She settled down at her desk and spread out her English homework, but she didn't get any further than touching the tip of her pencil to the paper.

Every time she tried to read the first grammar question, she thought she heard something from outside. No pebbles struck her window, but the image her mind conjured was as detailed as if she had already seen it—Nathan, standing in the snow, his face muffled by scarves, nothing more than his eyes showing, locked on her window, hands in his pockets. Silent, staring.

If she stood up to look through her window and he wasn't there she'd feel silly and immature, like a kid afraid of their closet. Worse, if he wasn't there and she still suffered a sinking little letdown (the soft flutter in her chest told her it was possible, though she didn't want to admit that even in her own mind), she'd be disappointed in herself.

And if she stood up to look and he *was* there, he'd see her and know she was looking for him. Any crumb of encouragement would make him even worse.

So, for the better part of an hour, Amber sat at her desk, waiting for *something* to happen and trying to bring her mind to focus on grammar exercises. She managed only to draw a series of various-sized snowflakes down the left margin of the page, adding more complexity every time she tried to read the first question and failed. Along the bottom of the worksheet Amber was adding snowmen having a snowball fight when, finally, something did happen.

A small, repeating noise intruded on her concentration. Someone shouting.

How long had that been going on, muffled by walls and distance? Now the yelling caught her attention, though, and she had little trouble identifying the voices of her sister and Steph. She wouldn't have been able to make out any of the words, except she'd been preoccupied with the idea of Nathan all afternoon; she easily picked his voice out of the shouting.

Amber didn't waste time checking the window. She ran downstairs and out into the snow without bothering with boots or a coat. Even though her father had shoveled the back patio the night before, her socks soaked through in a moment, her feet so cold they hurt. The shivering began an instant after that, violent enough to rattle her teeth.

Steph and Hannah huddled in Steph's backyard, ducking behind a half-finished snow castle. In his own yard, Nathan pelted them with snowballs. The coiled tension in her muscles eased—she'd overreacted. Ignoring this situation wouldn't get her in any trouble; Nathan was being merely obnoxious, not dangerous, and she could go back to her homework before anyone noticed she'd come outside. She turned to go.

One of the snowballs flew wide and struck the side of Steph's family's backyard shed. It hit it with a solid *bang*, and Amber looked more closely.

Those weren't snowballs. Those were rocks.

Hannah and the others still hadn't seen her. They focused on one another, on the unfolding violence. She could still go back inside. Maybe now that she knew, for sure, that Nathan wasn't under her window, she could focus on her work at last. After all, she'd *told* Hannah not to go out and play with Steph until after their parents were home. Duty done, responsibility fulfilled. She'd understood months ago that her family didn't care about her. Well, fine, she didn't have to care anymore about what happened to them.

Although . . . Nathan had done one thing right, hadn't he? Outside of her own family and now probably Steph's, nobody actually knew what he was like. The kids at school were happy to help spread a nasty rumor about him, but if she told them he tortured mice they'd laugh in her face. When she'd hit him with the hose, he'd cried real tears on command as soon as his mom opened the garage door. The way he'd apologized to her parents after the wine had been perfect, protective camouflage.

It let him get away with more.

If he'd been smarter about what he did and not just how he covered it up, he'd have gotten away with everything. Maybe all the time. Everyone would have thought he was a good, nice boy forever.

With a little more care, he could've done anything he felt like.

Amber wanted that.

Which meant she had to play the right part, starting now.

"Hey!" she yelled, in as big a voice as she could muster.

The chaotic shouting from the other yard stopped. Steph and Hannah turned to Amber, and the relief in her sister's face hardly brought any warmth to Amber at all. She stooped down to grab the snow shovel her dad had left out the previous day, then marched out into the deeper snow, bootless feet swallowed to her ankle, carrying the shovel like a weapon.

Nathan turned to her and let another rock fly, but that was why she'd grabbed the snow shovel. She managed to hold it up in time for the wide, flat yellow blade to deflect the rock. She shoved the gate open, digging a groove through the snow Hannah had already disturbed on her way through earlier, and let herself into Steph's yard.

"Go home, Amber, this isn't about you," Nathan said, his voice as cold as the January air. "You'll get yours later."

She blocked another rock, and a third. The shovel couldn't protect her whole body—the next stone zinged off of her right knee. Amber bit her lip to keep herself from crying out and kept marching toward the gate to Nathan's yard. It took a moment longer, but going over the fence would mean dropping her shovel. Making herself vulnerable. No. Amber was done with that sort of mistake. Especially when it came to Nathan.

"Fine!" Nathan snapped as she managed to push her way into his yard, grunting as she leaned into the gate to get it to open in spite of the snow. She continued holding the shovel up like a shield. "Come on, then!"

He threw another rock and she deflected it. He wound up for his next throw. Mustering as much force as her cold-numbed body could manage, she jumped forward. She held the shovel blade flat, parallel to the ground to keep it from catching the air, and she swung. It caught him in the ribs.

The blow didn't land with much force; it didn't even wind Nathan. Still, he backed up and dropped the rock with a sneer. Amber guessed it must've shown him that—whether she meant it or not—she was committed to the act. Here, in his own yard, she saw the cairn-like stockpile of stones he must have spent all day digging out of the snow and readying specifically for this. This was no spontaneous act of violence, but one he'd thought through in advance. She turned her eyes from the pile to Nathan and shook her head.

"You're sick," she said. "Leave my sister alone."

He didn't argue with her pronouncement. With a shrug, he stuck his hands into his pockets as if nothing had happened at all. She snorted and walked away, though she went at an angle that allowed her to keep an eye on Nathan all the while.

Back in Steph's yard Amber stopped by the snow castle and held out a hand to help her sister up.

"Told you," she said.

Steph stood as well, brushing snow off her pants. "Thanks," she said, shooting Nathan a dark glare.

"How come your parents didn't come out? Isn't your mom home?"

"Mom usually takes a nap during Luke's naptime," Steph answered. "She should be awake now, though." She jerked her thumb at her patio, at Lacey visible through the Nowaks' back door, barking her head off, definitely spoiling anyone's nap. Pitching her voice to carry and giving a sideways glance at Nathan's yard, Steph added, "And I'm telling my mom about this!"

Steph set off without a goodbye, her arms crossed as she tried to stomp angrily through the snow but managed little better than a stumbling gait.

"Come on, I gotta get inside," Amber said, grabbing Hannah's hand. Her teeth chattered, and her feet had hit the kind of cold that feels almost the same as burning. She pulled her sister with one hand, wrapping her other arm around herself.

They made it no more than two steps before a loud *crack* caught their attention.

"What are you doing?" Steph shouted.

Amber and Hannah turned together to see Nathan winding up for another throw. He took careful aim at a window on Steph's house, the second-floor window closest to his own yard.

"Stop that!" Steph cried, trying to run toward him through the snow. "That's Luke's room! Stop!"

The next rock crashed right through the glass, the sharp tinkling audible all the way across the yard. Hannah gasped, and Steph let out a cry. She rushed into her own house. Hannah tried to follow, but Amber's grip on her wrist pulled her back.

"Her mom isn't going to want you barging in right now," she said.

"Luke's *crib* is under that window, Amber!" Hannah's voice was breathless.

Amber imagined the rock smashing through the glass, raining shards down on a sleeping toddler, cold stone striking him, and she shuddered.

"Then their mom *definitely* won't want us there right now," she said, "and we don't wanna *be* there. Let's go in and you can call and see if everyone's okay. Mom and Dad won't be mad if you invite Steph over here if her mom needs her out of the house to . . . to take care of anything."

Hannah didn't look convinced, but Amber was done talking. She dragged her sister all the way back to the door. Pausing at the threshold, Amber looked over her shoulder. Nathan had vanished.

Inside, Amber and Hannah double-checked all the doors and windows, making sure everything was locked. This time when Hannah said she thought they should call their parents, Amber agreed.

Their dad's office was closer than the daycare where their mom worked, so he left early as soon as he heard what had happened.

The moment he walked through the door he rounded on Amber and demanded, "What were *you* doing when all this was going on?" His hard tone held more accusation than concern or curiosity.

"Homework! And then stopping him," she exclaimed, and fought not to sneer as she added, "Why? What do you *think*?"

"Watch your tone with me, Amber Marie Walker."

"She was helping, Dad," Hannah interjected.

"Well, did you finish your homework?" he asked. The sisters

exchanged a glance and shook their heads at the same time. "Then go do that while I make some phone calls."

Amber ran upstairs ahead of Hannah, fuming. So much for helping anybody out! All she got out of it was being sent to her room! Oh, sure, her dad hadn't *said* "go to your room," but he'd meant it, and the end result was the same. Amber alone again, shut out of everything, and everyone mad.

It wasn't fair.

Scowling at her homework, bitter realization struck her: She should've known better than to hope for anything different. It was no different than the day Nathan had put those chemicals on Hannah's arm.

Well . . . except this time Hannah had told their dad that Amber helped her. They believed Amber had helped because she really wanted to. They bought the act. A twist of smugness pushed aside some of the bitter sting. All she had to do now was hide out in her room, force herself to finish her homework, and keep her cool. If Nathan could pull this sort of thing off, Amber could, too. And she'd do it better than he did.

So, Amber kept to herself, didn't cause a scene, not even when her mom got home from work and asked her dad and Hannah what had happened, but not Amber.

By dinnertime her dad's mood had softened, at least. Her mom asked him, "So what made him stop? Did that mother of his finally exert some control over her son?"

He put a hand on Amber's shoulder, gave it a little squeeze, and answered, "Amber's the one who got the whole situation under control, from what I hear."

"Really?" her mom said, turning to Amber with surprise and pride warring in her eyes. "Well, good job, sweetie." Was there skepticism in her voice?

Understanding dawned on Amber.

Deep down, grown-ups must all be like Nathan—always lying, fake smiling, figuring out how to keep up appearances. Even her mom and dad. Well, of course. After all, she'd found out *their* secrets way back when she got grounded over the summer. So, pretending to care in order to get her own way didn't set her apart; she was simply turning into a grown-up exactly the same as all the rest of them.

Amber shrugged at her parents, smiled, and in as sincere a voice as possible, she answered, "Well, what else could I do?" Her mom and dad exchanged a look she didn't understand, and an uneasy silence stretched out after that.

The family remained subdued through the meal, and after it. She caught her mom double-checking all the locks, though Amber had told her they'd done that already.

The thought of sitting around in the living room pretending to watch *Full House* reruns while trying to ignore the unspoken tension in her sister and parents gave Amber a headache. She went upstairs after dinner and shut herself in her room again. It felt different when it was voluntary, not a lonely exile but a private retreat.

Only once that evening did she come out, to brush her teeth and her hair before bed, meeting her gaze in the mirror with a small, toothpaste-foamy smile. The moment before she closed her eyes in bed, a last thought crossed her mind: She'd figured it all out, at last.

When she woke up again, darkness still pressed against the window, and she didn't know at first what had pulled her out of sleep. Lying in bed, Amber listened to the nighttime stillness, trying to hear whatever hushed voice or furtive step had woken her. There was nothing happening in the house.

A high, muffled sound came from outside.

Amber pushed the blankets away and crept across her room, peering out the window facing where she thought the sound had come from.

In the light of the nearly full moon, the neighborhood had a pale, eerie glow to it. The trees cast shadows almost as clearly defined as by daylight, the whole world painted in shades of black and blue and silver. Amber felt that in a world lit like this, anything might be possible, and for a moment she forgot the sound she'd heard and the troubles of the previous day.

Then a flare of orange intruded into all that cool darkness, drawing Amber's eyes. Her stomach clenched before she knew what she was looking at. Flames, small but growing, in Steph's backyard. A shadow moved near them, and the high noise came again, and this time it didn't stop—a dog, yelping and whining, the sounds escalating toward a howl.

Amber slid her window up and pressed her nose against the screen.

Nathan lurked in Steph's backyard. Steph's bullmastiff, Lacey, stood tied to the fence in between their two yards, and Amber recognized the bindings as a jump rope only because she'd seen it before. The big dumb dog, trusting and friendly, must have simply let Nathan tie it up, or he'd never have managed. Lacey's tail looked bushier than normal. Amber squinted. Sticks. There was a bundle of sticks tied to the dog's tail. And those sticks were burning.

Nathan was trying to light Steph's dog on fire.

Amber's eyes widened, and she sucked in a breath. With the window open, Lacey's whining cries were increasingly loud. Incredible that no one else had woken up yet. Beneath the yips and yelps, Nathan's voice laughed softly, as if trying not to be heard.

She should go get someone, but she didn't move. She imagined going into her parents' bedroom and being told off for barging in and waking them in the middle of the night. And after that? In the morning would her dad ask her *What were you doing when all this was going on?* and dismiss her to her bedroom?

No. She wasn't going to get pulled into the blame for this somehow. She wasn't the one lighting a dog's tail on fire—whatever happened next wouldn't be her fault either way. And if everyone thought she just slept through the whole thing, she wouldn't lose face, either.

The whining yelps grew louder, higher, and Amber pushed away the twinge in her chest at the sound. Not her problem. Helping did nothing but get her in trouble. What she should do was go back to bed, but she couldn't take her eyes off the scene.

The chain links rattled, the dog's cries crescendoed in a terrible howl, and a second later it broke free and raced away across Steph's yard toward the house. Amber watched as a light snapped on through a second-floor window and Nathan ran.

He didn't run for his own yard. Maybe he thought that would be too obvious, too likely to get him caught. Instead, he bolted and vaulted the fence into her yard. Lacey kept howling, and distant, muffled adult shouts joined the sound. Amber expected Nathan to lie low, hide out until the hubbub died down. More windows lit up in Steph's house, and one in Nathan's house, and Amber finally heard her own parents' sleepy voices murmuring from across the hall.

Nathan crossed out of the moonlight and into the shadow of her dad's shed and Amber took half a step away from the window, ready to dive back into bed and pretend she'd slept through the whole commotion. She began to turn away, her back to the window, when a second flare of bright firelight painted her shadow in black and orange on the opposite wall. She turned back to the window.

Nathan wasn't hiding in her yard. He wasn't hiding at all.

Her father's shed burned. Nathan stood to the side, visible in profile, his features cast in the harsh contrast of violent firelight and stark shadow. At his feet lay a jumble of boxy red shapes. The lawnmower gas cans from inside the shed.

Nathan couldn't have heard her gasp through the window, over the sound of the growing fire and his own laughter, over the sound of Steph's dad throwing open their back door and bellowing in furious shock, over the sound of the dog's continued cries as its tail was put out at last. No, he almost certainly hadn't heard her. But he turned toward her window anyway. Looking for her. She met his gaze, his eyes a cold contrast to the orange reflection in them. When he smiled at her, Amber reached up to shut the window. She barely remembered not to let it slam. She threw herself into bed and pulled the covers all the way up to her chin, squeezing her eyes shut, waiting for her parents or her sister to burst in at any moment and accuse her of somehow being part of what Nathan had done.

They never did. The shouts from outside grew louder, the voices more varied, and at some point either a fire truck or a police car arrived with its flashing lights.

After the commotion peaked and died down, after quiet returned to the night, Amber still did not sleep. She lay awake, uneasy, until gray dawn light crept into the room. Then she got up and changed out of her pajamas. After that she sat at her desk, quiet, listening to the sounds in her house. She had nothing to do in her bedroom, but she didn't want to be the first one to go downstairs. Something changed last night—she wasn't sure what, but she knew it had. It was only when she heard her mom emerge from her parents' room and go down to start making breakfast that Amber went out as well.

She'd barely sat down at the table when Hannah appeared too, but breakfast was almost over before their dad finally joined them. His eyes were bleary and baggy, and after a quick glance Amber turned her attention away from him. Better not to catch anyone's eye this morning. If they guessed she knew what had happened and didn't tell anybody, she'd definitely be in for it.

Being in this family is a no-win situation, she thought, pursing her lips.

"Girls," her mom said as she sat down to join them. "There's something we need to talk about."

Hannah looked up with a puzzled frown. Amber copied the expression.

"Something happened last night," her mom began, "with that boy, Nathan, and—"

A knock on the front door interrupted her. She stood to go answer it, and her father pushed himself to his feet as well. He followed her, hovering nearby as she opened the door.

Steph's father stood on their front porch.

"Did you walk all the way around the block?" Amber's mom asked instead of greeting him.

"I just needed the extra moment to keep my head cool," Mr. Nowak answered, and from the undercurrent of anger in his voice that was possible, but Amber suspected he actually wanted to make himself feel more serious and important by coming to the front door rather than tapping on the back door like one of the neighborhood kids. He went on with no preamble, "How long has that boy been terrorizing our children, Theresa? Dave?"

He obviously meant Nathan, but if he was counting his kids in his question, the answer was for no longer than the previous day.

Still, her dad nodded and hitched up his belt in a way that reminded her of an actor in a cowboy movie, and the only reason she didn't roll her eyes at him was because she wanted to stay in the foyer and keep listening in. She imagined torches and pitchforks and tried to picture what the modern-day equivalent would be.

"We need to go and talk to his parents," Steph's dad said, using the kind of hard and unyielding tone Amber thought should be reserved for saying *interesting* things like "We need to run them out of town" instead of the unutterably boring thing he had actually said. Her dad's expression wasn't bored, though. He grabbed his coat and stomped into his shoes and followed Steph's dad out.

Her father came home from the "talk" with a bloody nose and in a towering temper. Amber hid around a corner and listened as her dad recounted the confrontation to her mom.

"It was four of us who went over there," he said. "Nick and Max"—two of the neighbors across the street from Steph's house—"came with us. And, Theresa, the *minute* that boy's father opened the door, the smell—barely past sunrise and the man already stinks like a whole bar. We hardly started talking before he was bellowing at us. Well, John lost it, started shouting how Nathan almost killed Luke and if Luke's nap hadn't ended a second earlier, they'd be suing the pants off of the Teldegardos for medical costs, and he expected Nathan to pay them back for the window and the siding, and that's when Dan swung at us." It took Amber a moment to figure out that Dan must be Nathan's dad. She'd never heard his first name before. "And John went at him, and—where's the phone book?"

"Cabinet next to the calendar."

"Good. Anyway, John went right back at him, and you know he and Nick are close, so Nick jumped in. Max and I were trying to break them up when Mary came flying out of the house in a bathrobe and slippers, and she's crying and screaming at us, and she grabs Max's hair in her fists and starts yanking him backward. He pushed her off and she slipped in those damn slippers and landed on her ass, and Dan clocked me with his elbow and grabbed her by the front of her robe, and he was screaming at her then—he all but threw the poor woman into the house. And the whole time that boy was standing in the hallway, watching it all happen with the deadest eyes I've ever seen."

"What do we do now?"

"First, call the girls out of school. Maybe get 'em out of the neighborhood for the day."

"What?" Amber's mother's voice sharpened with anxiety. "Why? What do you think is going to happen?"

"Nothing, Theresa," Amber's dad said, soothing her. "Nothing. But better safe than sorry. Do something fun with the kids, maybe take 'em into Cleveland, to Tower City Center or Dick's Last Resort, they'll like that."

Amber frowned at the thought of being banished from the house right when things were getting interesting, but didn't protest. Her parents never listened to what she wanted, anyway, and she did at least enjoy both the big mall with its cool fountains downtown and the rude service restaurant in the Flats.

Her mom asked, "What will you do?"

"I'm going to call city hall—and a lawyer—and maybe the local paper—I don't know! I'm calling everyone. I *do* know we can't have people like that around the girls."

Amber crept up the stairs to her room then, thinking that while she still didn't know what the modern version of torches and pitchforks might be, she'd learned "We need to go and talk to his parents" in the right context absolutely could be just as interesting as "We need to run them out of town."

A little over a month later, Nathan moved out. Amber lingered in her backyard, watching the process. As the moving truck pulled out and Nathan's father honked the horn on their sedan in long, blaring intervals, Nathan's mom drifted over to the same corner of the fence where Amber and Hannah had first seen her son.

"I don't know why this keeps happening," she said to Amber's mom, who stopped breaking icicles off the back gutter to watch the woman's approach. Amber had rarely heard Nathan's mother speak. Normally she moved quietly and saved her words for privacy.

Theresa pulled off her thick mittens and pushed some hair behind her ears. Amber looked back and forth between them and thought if her mother pursed her lips and blew hard, Nathan's mother might drift away into the sky.

Nathan's mom sniffed, and tears glimmered in her eyes as she continued, her soft voice wobbling, petulant, "Everywhere we go, nobody treats us right. Nobody welcomes us. I don't know why you people keep doing this to us."

"I think you do know why, Mary," Amber's mom answered evenly. "And if not, I hope you can figure it out."

Nathan's dad laid on the horn again. Amber caught a glimpse

of the car waiting on the curb, visible between Steph's house and what was about to be Nathan's old house. Nathan sat in the back seat, the window rolled down in spite of the cold, leaning with his chin resting on his arms, which were crossed halfway out of the window. His mom hurried off then, as much as if to flee from Amber's mother's words as to get on the way with her family. The car pulled away, and Nathan held Amber's eyes for the few seconds before he slid out of sight on the other side of Steph's house. With no reason to linger out there anymore, Amber headed indoors, passing her father on the way as he stepped outside to check on her mother.

She paused within, leaning close to the door to listen to whatever it was they were going to say. "Now that the Teldegardo boy's gone, Amber'll get back to normal," her mom said.

Amber moved closer to the door, keeping out of sight and taking shallow breaths.

Her mom continued, "She's a good girl. The trouble we've had this year only started because of that family."

Amber blinked hard and frowned. The casual, unthinking assumption that Nathan—or *anybody*—was responsible for Amber's decisions, instead of acknowledging that she was fully in control of herself, stung. Still, her mother was saying something nice about her—purely nice, not a backhanded comment about how she was too smart to be getting Cs and Bs, or an ignorant wish for Amber to just *try* to get along with the other kids, as if she hadn't been *trying* her whole life. This hit Amber different, deeper. *She's a good girl.* It had been said without qualifiers, praise of who Amber *was*, unconcerned with what she did, or what she failed to do. Amber could not remember the last time she had heard her mother say something like that, and she pressed her ear to the door, still and silent, hoping for more.

Her father gave voice instead to a skeptical grunt that struck Amber in the chest with unexpected force.

"I don't know, Theresa," he said, his voice heavy with a weariness that sounded a lot more like expressing a long-considered worry rather than an off-the-cuff remark. "Amber's . . . well, she's always been difficult."

He didn't say it, but Amber knew he was thinking *not like Hannah.* The anger coursing up from her gut hit all the harder because it shattered the fragile hope of understanding that had barely begun to crystallize at her mother's words.

Oblivious, her father went on, "Her grades were already slipping before he got here, she never could get along with the other kids—I don't *get* it. When I was her age"—Amber knew what came next, had heard it verbatim over and over since elementary school, and she moved her lips along with her father as he continued—"I was friends with the jocks *and* the chess club."

"Amber isn't you, Dave," Theresa said, and for all it was an empty platitude, Amber seized it, allowing herself for one moment to think her mother might stand up for her. Until she added, "She's just missing some social skills or something, it's not her fault."

The tears stinging her eyes infuriated Amber as much as her parents' casual cruelty. Why should she care what they thought of her? They'd never love her as much as they loved Hannah, no matter what she did. Why should she let them—or anyone—make her feel bad about herself, ever again?

Hurrying to her room, Amber tried to forget the eavesdropped conversation.

She couldn't.

Amber didn't tell them she'd heard anything; she didn't want to listen to them pretend they never said it or insist she'd misunderstood, or suffer their half apologies and clumsy attempts to convince her they hadn't meant any of it. She didn't want them to try to convince her that her memories were wrong, that *she* was wrong, and win her back over.

Like a colored lens, the knowledge that they felt this way overlaid every interaction she had with them.

It festered.

Winter thawed, a new family moved into the Teldegardos' old house, school went back to normal without Nathan always making a scene, and in quiet moments the words replayed themselves again and again. Her mother's unthinking assertion that Amber had such a weak personality that Nathan had changed her on some fundamental level. Her father's conviction that there was something deeply wrong with her.

As weeks turned into years, Amber never forgot the insight she had grasped the day Nathan left; if she let her parents talk her around, she would open herself up to letting them hurt her again. She drew away from them, a little at a time. They didn't seem to notice it at all at first. Amber didn't mind. They couldn't try to corner her about the growing distance if they didn't see it until it was too far to bridge.

At first after they discovered, too late, that she had pulled away from them, Amber enjoyed watching them struggle to reel her back in. Until, that is, they tried to pull the gap closed with grappling hooks and ropes, spending her teenage years binding her with more and more rules and restrictions until she could hardly breathe inside their home.

She got a job at sixteen as much to get time away from them as to start saving her own money. When she turned eighteen she moved out, finding a third-floor efficiency apartment that, even counting the comically tiny balcony, was smaller than her childhood bedroom, but felt like plenty of space to grow in.

As if Theresa sensed that this was the last chance to bring her daughter back into something like a close relationship, she spent the first year of Amber's independence trying to guilt her into spending time with her parents and her sister. The more the nagging piled up, the further Amber withdrew, until the guilt turned to threats.

It was over the day Dave and Theresa tried to take Amber and Hannah out for dinner at Amber's favorite sushi restaurant.

Amber bailed at the last minute, and the in-person family conversation her parents had planned took place instead as a scanned photo sent to her email. Dave and Theresa had rewritten their will, not writing Amber out entirely but putting her distinctly behind her sister. Amber knew, remotely, that this was meant to scare her back into their arms.

Did they not understand that if it had worked, they would have known it was their money and property she loved and not her parents themselves?

Instead, Amber burned the bridge.

CHAPTER 17

NONE OF THE RISK

SEPTEMBER 2013

I don't know why you stay on myspace, Hannah texted Amber, another in a long line of unsubtle attempts to get her to join the newer, more popular Facebook instead. It's been basically dead for like five years.

Amber typed back, What's it matter to you?

They'd been having a conversation—well, actually, Hannah had been nagging Amber—about their dad's birthday in a week, on the seventeenth. As soon as Hannah had convinced Amber to at least join the family for dinner, her sister had jumped back to this topic again.

I just want to be able to keep up with you better, that's all, Hannah replied.

Amber snorted at her phone, didn't text back, and muttered out loud, "Yeah, sure. You got Mom and Dad on it, too. I'm not falling for it."

Amber knew a weak attempt to trick her into tying herself back to her sister and her parents when she saw one, and over the years she'd grown practiced at resisting that exact kind of manipulation. She liked being able to choose when to answer the phone, when to text back, who to talk to or see. Publicly posting her thoughts and putting up pictures of herself, on display to her family at all times, ran counter to that.

After a long moment in which her phone was quiet, another message buzzed through.

> You don't want to wait until your ten-year reunion to see if all your old classmates are working at gas stations yet, do you?

Her parents had said that to her over and over, too. Someday, they claimed, her intelligence would pay off (eventually adding, *if only you would start putting in some effort again*). They said she'd find success and all the jocks and cheerleaders would wind up pumping gas. They kept telling her that what she lacked in social skills wouldn't matter.

It hadn't been until college that Amber had started to figure out how to make friends. She thought of Ben and his buddy Greg, and grinned. They never tried to make her feel small and last and forgotten, like her family did.

Still, Hannah had a point. It'd be awfully nice if all the old bullies and popular kids were toiling or ugly or unhappy now.

Fine, she texted back. But I'm not going to be friends or whatever with Mom and Dad.

You'll come around, Hannah answered, with a winking emoji. She never had been subtle, but that was the reason Amber still talked to her at all. Hannah could never manipulate Amber. And, of course, being on speaking terms with her sister made her look as normal as everybody else always pretended to be.

Amber set up her account on the new site that night, writing her bio, choosing her profile pictures. Hannah had been right for once; she should've done this a long time ago. There was no better place to build an image of herself the way she wanted everyone to see her. The thought drove her to spend hours on the details of her profile.

By the time she finished it was a few minutes past ten in the evening, and on a whim, Amber searched for Claire Ellis, one of the girls who had been mean in middle school and glamorous in high school and who had hopefully peaked at sixteen and never regained the dazzle she'd had when they were teens.

Amber frowned at the profile picture that popped up. Claire was as beautiful as ever. She posed in her picture with a baby that Amber grudgingly admitted was adorable. Her "about" info listed her as having some executive-type job Amber didn't fully understand.

She searched for more of her old classmates. Each new profile, each new picture of well-dressed, smiling adult versions of the kids she'd slogged through school with—kindergarten through graduation, over a decade of friendlessness and grades that deteriorated no matter how hard she worked to keep up appearances—hit her like a blow. In spite of her care to say and do all the right things, in spite of the empty reassurances of her parents (who pretended to worry about how she felt but only really worried about how she made them look), Amber was still working in a café, while the kids who had been popular in school used their own social skills—certainly not lacking—to win better and better jobs and positions.

Ignoring a growing headache, Amber kept at it for hours. She stayed awake typing names into the search bar well into the night, long after she admitted to herself that looking up former schoolmates felt more like picking at a scab over and over again than like a catharsis. They were as well dressed and impressive as they'd always been. It wasn't helpful or healthy, but she couldn't stop. She ran out of people to look up, until finally she thought of a boy she hadn't seen for fourteen years.

She typed "Nathan Teldegardo" into the search bar and scrolled through suggested people with the same name until she saw a profile picture thumbnail of an adult face that might have been the boy she had known for a short but intense time in her youth. She clicked it, and there he was.

Amber scrolled through his profile pictures, starting with the most recent and going backward. It was like watching him age in reverse, looking more and more like the kid she'd known. She remembered how charming he could be when he wanted to, the special attention he'd paid to her. Waiting up at night for the sound of a pebble tapping her window. There had been blank stares sometimes, too, bouts of anger, but Amber told herself she remembered those only dimly. Looking through his profile, what came back the strongest was the way he'd followed her around at the end.

At twelve years old, Amber hadn't seen the value in that. Now, though, she didn't think she'd mind having someone hanging around, desperate to prove himself to her.

Unlike the other former classmates she'd looked up, whose profiles she'd clicked through and backspaced away from without interacting, she found herself returning to Nathan's over and over.

A couple afternoons later, seized by impulse and acting on it before she could think of a reason not to, Amber sent Nathan a friend request and the simple message, Hi, do you remember me?

She expected to be left hanging, at least for a few days and maybe forever. She thought if he did message her back it would be to ask who she was, or to say the year they knew each other never mattered to him.

A few minutes later her computer dinged with a new message.

The message read, Haha of course I remember u Amber! She pushed down her initial impulse to correct his grammar as a second message popped up. I been thinking about u alot lately what are u up to these days?

The notification bell lit up a few seconds after that to show he had accepted her friend request, and a minute after that he posted a GIF of a glittering rose on her account's public page. She laughed when she saw it and clicked to like the image. She turned her attention back to the messages. In that short amount of time three more had rolled in, one after the other.

> Hows Hannah and Steph?
> Luke must be a big kid by now whats he like 14? Hows the old neighborhood?
> U still live in the same house?

The mention of Hannah drew Amber's eyebrows together in a frown. All the problems back when Nathan had lived in the neighborhood had been because of her sister, and here Nathan was asking after her within mere moments of messaging Amber. Still, it might be nice to continue reconnecting with her old friend. She kept that in mind and, rather than allow irritation to dictate her behavior, sent back a smiling emoji before typing a response message.

> They're all good. Hannah's in college. Luke's big now, yeah. I don't see him and Steph anymore. The neighborhood is probably as good as it can be, probably as boring and stuck in time as it ever was. I don't live in the house anymore, but Mom and Dad do.

She debated mentioning Ben, but he hadn't asked if she was seeing anyone, and she didn't volunteer the information. She hit send, paused, then gave him a little dig, in case his mentioning Hannah had been intentional to make her feel annoyed.

> How are your parents? Your mom didn't look too good last time I saw her.

Right after she sent it, she regretted it, physically flinching as she reread the words on the screen. They'd barely gotten back in touch, and now she was spoiling it.

"Goddamn stupid," she whispered to herself, and at that moment there was the ding of another incoming message. She looked at the chat window, but the italicized text there still read *Someone is typing . . .*

Along the bottom of the screen a new message icon blinked. It was Hannah. Amber opened the message to see a screenshot of the sparkly flower GIF Nathan had sent her a mere handful of moments before, and a message below it that read, wtf, Amber? Really?? Nathan Teldegardo? What does Ben think of this?

She tapped out a quick reply. It's none of Ben's business, he's not even my boyfriend. And besides, I'm just looking up old friends, like YOU suggested.

Once sent, Amber minimized the chat window.

No, whether or not she liked Ben's easygoing company, whether or not they were moving in a serious direction—after all, they had talked about their dreams, their career goals, even whether he'd want kids someday, too—Ben wasn't officially her boyfriend *yet*, and that was the important part: Who she talked to wasn't any concern of his. Besides that, her relationship with Ben *certainly* wasn't any business of Hannah's. Amber ground her teeth. She and Ben and Greg had had a good thing going, they'd been damn near inseparable, until Amber had made the incredibly stupid mistake of letting Hannah tag along on one of their nights out. Now she and Greg were all over each other. It was stomach-churning, really, and Amber and Ben had hardly seen Greg in the past few weeks. Amber knew Hannah talked about her to Greg—she pictured them lying in bed together, Greg listening like a credulous asshole while Hannah whispered all the old lies about Amber to him. So while Amber did plan to move things along with Ben (only *partially* to stop Hannah from one-upping her yet again), her sister had no right to try to bring Ben up now. Especially since what Hannah really wanted was to stop Amber from talking to someone else who'd remember how full of crap she was.

Amber turned her attention back to Nathan's flashing chat

window. Her breath hitched, the surprising intensity of her nerves making her queasy for an instant. Had she pushed too hard, bringing up his mom and the day they'd left?

Pulling up the chat didn't answer that question. He ignored the last message she'd sent as if it had not existed, only asking, Where u living now then?

The message notification from Hannah was dinging again, and her phone buzzed. A glance at the screen told her it was her mother calling. Amber hit ignore and looked back at her computer screen. Remembering how her family saw Nathan was like remembering their opinion of a television character. It didn't matter.

Another message had come through. Fine don't tell me, accompanied by an angry face followed by a laughing face.

It was easy to remember the time he'd brought her down into his basement, the way the fine hairs on her arms and the back of her neck had stood up from how near he was when he followed too close behind her. It was easy to remember the sharp way he grinned and her own breathlessness. Harder to remember exactly the sound that mouse had made, or the blankness of his eyes. She gave him the address for her building, but not the apartment number.

Still, she wasn't surprised when a pebble bounced off the glass door to her little balcony a week later. Amber looked up from the fantasy novel she'd been reading, waiting to see if the soft clatter would come again. It did. Her computer was in the other corner of the room, turned on, and she glanced over at it. Increasingly urgent messages from Hannah, all ignored, still made up her only unread communications. Her phone lay on her bedside table, turned off; she'd gotten sick of listening to it ring over and over.

Three days before, she'd dropped any pretense at communicating with her family when her father had asked over his birthday dinner, "What's Nathan up to these days? Escaped from prison? Skinning live cats?"

Her silence since had resulted in a frenzy. They claimed to be worried, but Amber knew the truth. If she stopped talking to them, the last hope they had of bringing her back under their collective thumb vanished.

Another rock bounced off the balcony door, and Amber marked her page and pushed the light blanket off her legs. She remembered abruptly that she was wearing nothing more than a long shirt and underwear. She hesitated, reached for a pair of sweatpants, then paused again. How much had he seen when he'd been spying out the building, finding her window? A third pebble struck the glass, and she took a trembling breath, dropping the sweatpants into a pile on the floor. Amber imagined the tingling in her arms and the bubbly jitter in her chest were similar to the sensation of absolute daring that skydivers felt before their jump as she slid the door open and stepped onto the balcony.

Nathan stood in the strip of grass between the building and the parking lot, a handful of pebbles held against his chest, his free hand drawn back to throw another. He saw her and froze like that, his eyes moving up and down. The intensity of his gaze made Amber's gut twist in an interesting way. She tried to hide the smile tugging at the corners of her lips as she leaned down, resting her forearms on the wrought iron railing of the balcony and crossing her bare legs at the ankles.

"How did you know this was my apartment, Nathan?" she asked by way of greeting.

He didn't answer, smiling wordlessly as he dropped the rest of his pebbles and brushed his shaggy hair out of his eyes. His grin didn't reach his eyes, which remained dark, but the charm was in his voice when he said, "Long time no see, beautiful."

Amber's smile faltered, but she plastered it back in place. Maybe it was the distance, the height she stood at above him on the third floor. Or maybe it was the cliché. But the curious flatness of his eyes didn't look secretive anymore. Just . . . dull. His posture, his smile, there was none of the risk his presence had seemed to exude when they were kids.

Fourteen years had passed, and Nathan had become nothing more than another boring adult, no different from every other old classmate she'd looked up. A little—okay, a lot—more ham-handed with the flattery, but otherwise disappointingly the same.

Before the silence could stretch too long, she answered, voice casual, "Yeah, same to you."

"Can I come up?"

His last few months in the neighborhood surfaced in her memory. The overattentive hovering that stifled at the time actually might not be all bad now. He didn't look like anything she couldn't handle anymore. And an image painted itself starkly before her, of the streak of blood on the linoleum after he'd beaten up that bully to try to defend her. Did he have any of that Nathan still in him? Amber had no trouble imagining how that side of him might come in handy, under the right circumstances. . . .

"Sure," she said at last. "Go around to the front and hit the button for number thirty-three. I'll buzz you in."

A guy like Nathan might be useful for a thing or two . . . if he was still what she thought he could be. Her computer dinged again, another message from Hannah. Rather than look at it, her eyes fell with a thoughtful pause on her phone, still turned off. It wouldn't be wise to move too fast, to make any rash decisions, but as the door buzzer sounded and she crossed the room to push the button that would let Nathan in, she thought she could probably keep him in line for a few years, if she was smart and careful.

CHAPTER 18

TOO DIM TO SEE

JANUARY 2020

Amber stood in the shadows on the front porch of her parents' house. Though a couple of her mom and dad's neighbors still had Christmas lights strung ten days into January, her parents didn't. Dave had always been prompt about that kind of thing when she was young, too. Amber knew from the last time she'd visited her childhood home, shortly after her sister's death, that her parents kept it almost the same as it had been when she was a kid.

For a short time in the wake of the house fire that killed Hannah and Greg nearly four years before, Amber's parents had made an effort to meet her on her terms. They wanted to feel whole, to stay connected with their remaining daughter, and be part of their grandchildren's lives.

But when Theresa slid slowly back into nagging and guilt-tripping, Amber finally forced a confrontation with her parents about the way they'd treated her as a kid. They denied everything, of course they did, accusing her of remembering wrong or lying. No catharsis there, but saying her piece at last still gave Amber a little thrill. And they'd confirmed the truth she'd always known—if they'd truly cared about mending the relationship, *truly*, they would have owned their part in making it crumble in the first place.

After that, Theresa's emails filled with heavy-handed threats about inheritance and the kids. Amber didn't do anything foolish like screenshot the emails, but it wasn't hard, in rare moments of weakness, to scroll down to reread the right one when she needed to. The way Theresa tried desperately to play the victim from the very start always bolstered Amber's resolve; that first message even said, right in the middle, "I just worry about what's going to happen to those kids when your dad and I are gone."

Standing in the cold dark, she didn't have her smartphone with her to check that email again. If she had she wouldn't have checked it, anyway. The light from the screen would draw attention to her if any of the sleepy suburbanites happened to glance out their windows. But remembering that email and the ones that followed was all she needed, tonight, to keep her nerve up.

If Theresa had simply stopped after the first clumsily dropped hint, things might not be moving forward the way they were. Amber had shown the email to Ben, pointed out the line in question, and her husband had been able to calm her down and soothe her worries. But the comments had grown more and more obvious over the last year, until eventually she had convinced Ben of the truth, helped him banish his reservations and agree with her. Her parents were trying to control her, and exactly as they'd done years before when they'd changed the estate to favor Hannah, they were trying to use the inheritance to do it.

Finally, three days ago, her mother had video called her when her father was out. "I . . . well, I would hate to see anything upsetting happen," Theresa had said. Amber suspected her mother was trying to look and sound as though she were simply giving a warning, but Amber knew better than that. She knew a threat when she heard it. "If you go on keeping Marigold and Xander away from us, your father's going to put everything in a trust instead of a will, and he's going to name your Aunt Allison his executor." Her mother paused, and when she continued, the words came out a little hastily: "We're looking into grandparents' rights, Amber. You can't do this to us, do you understand that?"

She went on, but nothing she said after that had mattered. Because none of it was what she meant. What she truly meant was "Do as we say or lose everything."

Thirty-three years old, married, raising children, holding down a good job and doing everything normal people did, and still Amber's parents tried to tie her to them no matter what she wanted. They thought they could hold threats over her head forever and keep her in line.

They thought it was safe to do that.

Now here she stood, shivering violently in the cold, her childhood home looming over her. She'd known that waiting outside for Nathan to arrive wouldn't be pleasant, but if the neighbors had home security systems, if there was any way she could be seen, her car had to stay away. Riding with Nathan was also out of the question; she couldn't leave any of herself—a fingerprint, a strand of hair—in his car by mistake. Even choosing to arrive when she'd told him to meet her instead of coming ten minutes early could've saved her this freezing discomfort, but there'd been too avid a gleam in his eyes when they'd finalized their plans. She remembered the broken windows of their childhood, and his eagerness. Amber didn't trust his impulse control. Coming early meant she risked being seen, but coming late meant the much greater risk of Nathan jumping the gun and spoiling everything.

Tires crunched through snow.

Amber glanced up. A beat-up old junker rolled toward her. It moved slowly, headlights turned off, no blinker as it turned into her parents' driveway. Amber's heart stuttered, dropping its rhythm before pounding back at twice its normal speed. When she drew in a breath it came in a shaky rush, and when she exhaled it felt as if the air would keep going and going out of her until her body collapsed on itself. Nathan got out of his car, shutting the door with quiet care. In one hand he carried the kind of flashlight strong enough to blind low-flying aircraft pilots, and in the other a baseball bat.

When he was near enough to Amber that she could speak to him in a hollow whisper, she said, "Do you have the shovels?"

He nodded once, eyes bright, face drawn in an expression that looked to her like lust.

"They're in the trunk," he said.

"Good," she whispered.

She didn't give a shit about the shovels, but if he thought she did it would help keep him . . . not calm, he was so keyed up he practically vibrated, not complacent . . . but under her control. He had wanted to bring gasoline and matches, to burn the house down once they were done, but no matter how much he liked fires, it would defeat the whole point. Reining him in on that idea had nearly cost her his complicity in the whole plan, and at this moment she needed him. When he insisted on shovels, she didn't argue. Easier to let him bring them even though she knew they wouldn't be needed. She took care not to touch the gun tucked into her waistband, although her palms itched to pat it, to reassure herself by its presence. Instead, she trailed her fingers over the hilt of the knife in a sheath strapped to her thigh, a self-defense gift from Ben. Nathan expected her to have that.

Trembling cold coiled in her belly.

It was time.

Amber found the key under the same large stone in the flower bed where her parents had always kept it. She plucked it out of the dirt and set the rock back down, then slid the key into the lock.

Or tried to. It wouldn't go in. She turned it upside down and tried, turned it back the other way again and jammed it at the doorknob. It still wouldn't go.

"Shit," she hissed. They must have forgotten to switch the key whenever they'd changed the locks.

Amber hardly had a chance to wonder *what next* before Nathan stooped and snatched the heavy stone up off the snowy dirt. He smashed the front door's window. Amber blinked, for a moment seeing double, watching the scene from inside the house. But, no, the hummingbird window had been replaced all those years ago and what Nathan shattered now was a single pane of clear, wavy glass.

Gasping, Amber yanked her black ski mask down over her face. With a bright grin, Nathan whispered, "Relax," before pulling his own mask into place. Amber put a gloved finger over her mask where it concealed her mouth, but he shrugged and reached through the now-empty window frame to unlock the door. He stepped aside and raised an arm to usher her through.

Everything about her parents' house was familiar still, even the smell, her mother's flowery air-freshener scent filtering through the wool covering Amber's mouth and nose.

Nathan brushed past her and made for the stairs, stepping confidently despite how dark the hall was, nearly too dim to see.

This house wasn't *his*. The familiarity he pretended to was mere bravado. A spike of anger in Amber's chest grew out of the fear in her gut. She reached out and snagged a fistful of his jacket sleeve. They'd talked about this—he was supposed to be following *her*, moving exactly in her footsteps. She shook her head at him once, sharply. She pointed from the stairs to herself, then raised one finger. *Me first.*

With a snort, Nathan shook her hand off his arm and started up the steps. Amber tried to grab the back of his jacket but she was still moving with too much caution. He outpaced her.

On the fourth step up, the wooden stair let out a tortuous creak.

"Son of a *bitch*," she hissed, hurrying up to him, stepping near the sides of the stairs to keep quiet. "I said to stay *behind me*."

Nathan started to roll his eyes, but stumbling footsteps from above interrupted him. Amber expected to see worry dawn in her coconspiritor's gaze. Instead his eyes crinkled with smile lines. Rather than gasping or cussing, his breath came hard and uneven.

He turned and ran up the stairs.

Amber raced after him. He followed the sound of the footsteps and threw her parents' bedroom door open. The door hit something with a *whack*. Someone fell with a heavy thud.

Her mother's voice called a concerned, "Dave?"

The first thread of doubt wrapped itself around Amber's heart.

"Fuck it!" Nathan shouted. He clicked on his flashlight and Amber blinked, her eyes too accustomed to darkness.

"Dave?"

The beam of the flashlight traced a wide semicircle around the room as Nathan reached back to hand it to Amber. He took the baseball bat in a two-handed grip and lunged toward the figure of her father, still disheveled from sleep but out of bed, probably alerted by Nathan's fucking impatience.

Amber didn't watch the blow land, but she knew by the sound that it hadn't hit the way he wanted it to. She turned the high-intensity beam on her mother's face.

Theresa cringed against the headboard, holding the covers up to her chin as if they could protect her. The childishness of it overwhelmed Amber. This was the woman trying to hold her future hostage? This weak nobody crying in her bed when the boogeyman came?

Amber ripped the blankets away from her mother, stripping her of false comfort, and grabbed her. Her hand easily encircled the thin wrist, and it took almost no effort to yank her mother out of the bed and onto the floor.

"Let go of her!" Amber's father shouted, and she instinctively flinched at the tone, one she had been forced to obey throughout her youth. Until Dave cried, "Theresa!" The desperation in his voice rang out like nothing she'd heard before.

He was terrified.

Power coursed through her in a rush, electric and sizzling. He was terrified of *her.*

The distraction nearly cost her. Dave dodged another swing of Nathan's bat, stumbled to his feet, and tried to tackle Amber. Nathan swung again. Her father ducked and raised his arms. The blow landed, hard but not lethal. Nathan leaned into the attack and dove on her father. He grabbed Dave by the throat. Dave tangled his legs with Nathan's. The two men grappled, clumsy but vicious. The violence mesmerized her; she forgot to focus on her mother.

Until her father shouted, "Get out of here, Theresa! Call the cops!"

Amber whirled. Her mother scrambled out into the hallway, breaking for the stairs.

"Shit," Amber gasped, her voice a hoarse whisper. She took off in pursuit. By now her mother had her second wind, and she reached the front hall as Amber gained the top step. Amber ran down three of the stairs and leapt down the last five. She landed hard on the scuffed oak floor, a jolt of pain lancing up her shins. One of her knees made a popping noise, and she gritted her teeth against a sharp ache.

In her panic, her mother made her last mistake.

She didn't flee into the night, didn't run outside screaming and drawing the neighbors' attention. No, she turned right instead, toward the kitchen and the painfully old-fashioned landline phone they still kept there. Amber slammed her hand down on the button to hang up the line and wrenched the receiver away from her mother's hand, swinging it in a tight arc and smashing it into the older woman's temple.

Her mother swayed, stumbled, and Amber grabbed the front of her nightgown in a double fistful. She swung her mother around and shoved her away from the phone, back into the foyer.

"Why are you doing this to us?" Theresa cried.

Amber drew her knife without answering.

Shuffling echoed from upstairs. Her father shouted, "Theresa! Theresa!"

A meaty thud followed, and Dave tumbled ass over teakettle down the stairs to land in a sprawled heap. Theresa started toward him. Amber kicked her feet out from under her.

Lying askew on the floor, Amber's mother lifted herself onto one elbow, raised the other hand, and gasped, "Please! Don't!"

Amber struck.

The knife sank into her mother with a sensation that sent an almost painful shiver crawling up Amber's spine. Theresa wailed, and Amber yanked the blade back out.

Near the foot of the stairs Amber glimpsed a commotion, but she couldn't hear it over the rushing roar filling her ears. Her knife rose and fell and rose and fell.

Finally, her mother lay still.

Amber stood over her, breath rasping in her throat and her body flashing between crackling heat and bone-chilling cold. The ringing in her ears dimmed. Hearing returned as if from a great distance. Behind her someone gasped, choked.

"Get over here and finish this fucker, will you?" Nathan growled.

Amber turned. Nathan had been unmasked. Her father, eyes bulging, clawed at a rope the younger man had yanked around his throat. Horror drew his mouth back into a terrible grimace as his eyes flashed between her masked face and her mother's body.

Amber changed her grip on the knife and swung it at Dave's midsection. In spite of the raging adrenaline, in spite of every muscle drawn taut until she vibrated with painful tension, slicing through his belly proved harder than it had been to stab her mother. More difficult than she'd imagined.

The knife came free at last with a sick, wet noise. Nathan gave the rope slack and let her father fall, clutching his stomach as the blood soaked down his pajamas. Amber and Nathan panted heavily. Nathan's face shone with satisfaction, with pleasure.

"Let's get outta here," he said, and was there a suggestion in his tone? Did he think they were going to go off somewhere together and bang, now? The mask hid her sneer, kept her disgust at the thought of being with anyone but Ben invisible to Nathan in this last, crucial moment.

As her accomplice fished in his pocket for his keys, Amber reached under her jacket and pulled out her gun. She aimed, watched his eyes as realization flooded him.

Nathan's expression hardened in an instant.

"Wait, hey, wait!"

There, the dead eyes and blank fury she remembered from her childhood.

It didn't scare her anymore. Beneath her mask, she bared her teeth.

"You'll be fucking sorry if you do this," Nathan snarled.

She fired one time, watched Nathan fall, and stood still for a long moment, her heart in her mouth. A sour taste rose up the back of her throat. Her breath whistled high and fast and her throat tightened. Clenching her fists, she willed it all away.

Her hands barely trembled when she took a burner phone out of her back pocket and called Ben. "Meet me around the corner at the east end of the block," she whispered, and hung up before he could answer. He'd be in position soon, after a quick drive from the parking lot of a nearby bar; her parents lived . . . *had* lived . . . in a small town.

Amber let herself out of the house quietly, closing the door with the shattered window carefully behind her.

The walk through the snow to the corner cooled her, and by the time she slid into the back of the minivan to change into the outfit the sitter had seen her wearing when she and Ben had left that evening, the hitching in her breath had nearly vanished. Still, as she fixed her hair and pulled a compact out of the purse she'd left in the back seat to check her makeup, she took care to avoid her husband's eyes. His presence soothed her more than she had expected, but she couldn't address the questions in his gaze yet.

When he drew in a breath, she knew he wanted to voice those questions, and she forestalled him with a flat, "It's done."

His shoulders stiffened—she must've hurt his feelings. He hadn't been this reticent with her after the fire four years before, but she had shut him down back then, too. She wouldn't ever want to talk about these things. But that didn't mean she wanted Ben to hurt. Or to start feeling resentful. Leaning forward, she put her hands on his shoulders and gave him a gentle massage over the back of the driver's seat. He relaxed under her touch, and she allowed herself a wan, grim smile as they drove farther and farther from the house.

"Everything will be ours, Ben," she told him. "Everything but the blame."

Let him continue to believe, forever, that this was why she'd done all of it. Let him think he understood her as well as she understood him. Things would always be easier this way. But her smile grew a little sharper and a little wider.

Who gave a shit about the house and all the rest? Amber had taught them both. No one put her fucking last in line.

PART SEVEN

CHAPTER 19

A NEEDLE OF DOUBT

NOVEMBER 2020

The filing cabinet drawer rattled as Amber yanked it open again. The documents wouldn't be there—they hadn't been the first three times she'd checked. Still empty. She slammed the drawer, and it rebounded and slid partway back out. Her right hand clenched into a fist, knuckles white and aching, around her car keys. The metal bit into her skin. Hot rage buzzed in her chest and she kicked the drawer shut again, denting the thin, cheap metal.

Okay. This was okay. Amber didn't really need her copies of the documents. Her parents' lawyers had them, too. All she'd wanted, really, was to double-check some of the wording before going ahead with her next steps. She didn't *need* the papers. But to find the drawer where they should've been empty, tonight of all nights, could not possibly mean anything good.

Ben stood in the hallway, a step away from the door, watching her with his arms crossed and his brow furrowed. "Slow down, okay?" he said, almost in his soothing voice but for a hint of tension in the words. "Let's go upstairs to our room, and talk about this calmly, okay?"

"Oh my god, Ben, this is not the time for talking," she snapped, not turning to look at him, grabbing the filing cabinet and pulling it away from the wall to check behind it. It was as heavy as it had been the day they moved in, but she vibrated with adrenaline and moved it without much difficulty.

Amber had been calm when she started looking for her paperwork, indulging Ben's suggestion of a last-minute check despite knowing everything was in order. That calm had worn entirely away by now.

"It doesn't have to be tonight. We never planned for a specific time. It can wait. And it's not like the lawyers don't have copies of their own," her husband offered, trying to de-escalate the situation.

Amber shook her head. The one person in the world she trusted other than herself was Ben, and here he was, trying to talk her out of doing what needed to be done. She shot him a furious, icy glance.

"You're under enough stress right now, is all I'm saying," Ben said. "We both are. I don't remember the last time you said you got a good night's sleep. You know?" Visibly ill at ease, he shifted his weight. "Things didn't even get better when we took down the mirrors. Now we've got blankets and towels over all the windows, too, and—"

"Ben, please," Amber said, the words clipped, her voice tight. "I don't want to think about *anything* with a reflection in it right now."

"Right. It's just that the kids are getting freaked out."

"The kids," Amber scoffed.

"Well, they might've been talking."

"To who?" Amber said with cold scorn. "They don't go anywhere. School's all here at home. They're not even allowed to have playdates."

"They see the neighbors, our own fear is scaring them, and they will *talk* about it. They're just kids." Amber straightened from moving the cabinet, staring at Ben for a long time. He shifted his weight from one foot to the other, finally asking, "What?"

"They're just kids, huh, Ben?"

He didn't answer, and she shook her head in growing disgust, bending back over the filing cabinet, muttering, "Pull yourself together. We wasted months—almost a whole year—hesitating over this. Shit!" The papers hadn't slipped behind the filing cabinet, either. Amber straightened and ran her hands through her hair, breathing hard. "Cringing and waiting and . . . and bullshit sentiment never served us in the past. Bold action. That's what's gotten us *everything* we have. And now we've waited too long! The election, the infection rates, the supply chain shortages, and we've got *nothing* solid to build on if everything falls apart, Ben! My family is *still* ruining my life—messing with my business. We have one chance to end all that bullshit. Don't fucking tell me you're getting cold feet?"

Ben raised his hands, protesting, "This is going way too fast, is all! I mean, we should wait, right? Until things settle down?" He talked too quickly, words tripping over themselves. "The timing—if the kids have told people it's been weird around here—and so soon, you know . . ."

Cold realization buzzing in her skull, Amber turned toward Ben with a hard enough stare to make the rest of his sentence trail away.

"Benjamin," she said slowly, "this isn't going fast *enough*. We should have acted weeks ago. No, *months*! It's too late to do this on time, so we gotta settle for doing it now. Did you fucking hide my papers?"

"What? Jesus! No, I didn't hide your inheritance shit. You need to get a grip," Ben snapped, defensive. Too defensive.

"You're the only other person with a spare key to this filing cabinet, and I *know* I put everything away right in here!"

For a long moment Ben didn't speak, and he didn't meet her eyes, and Amber's heart froze solid and sank to her guts. When he answered at last, the fumbling nervous energy in his voice wasn't gone, but it was reined in. "I didn't hide anything. I just . . . I put them away somewhere else. We need to think through all this again, and I wanted to make sure—"

Amber looked down at the dented drawer. The tense constriction around her lungs squeezed painfully, tighter and tighter, and released as if with a snap.

"Where are those papers?" she whispered, raising her gaze to her husband again.

Ben held his hands up, palms out, and said, "I'll tell you, I will. But first you have to promise—"

"I'm not promising *anything*."

"—that we'll talk this through better before we do anything else we'll regret!"

Amber stormed across the small space between her and her husband, slapping his hands out of her way and getting right in his face. "Tell me where you put my documents, Benjamin Hughes."

Ben recoiled, his composure giving way to his nerves. There was a flash of fear in his eyes, and it stung Amber that he would be afraid of her even as it gave her a tiny rush—she *would* get him to do what she wanted. She always managed.

"They're in a shoebox in the closet," Ben said. She started to brush past him but he stepped into her way again. "But we do need to think about this more, Amber. You're being way too impulsive."

She'd spent this year with her head buried in the sand already, hadn't wanted to think about what this cold and flu season would mean, or the issues making it tricky to sell the house, or how difficult it might be to escape the densely populated neighborhood if they needed to.

And if she stayed here much longer the house would get her before she could get away.

But, distracted and overwhelmed by fear, she'd dragged her

feet. Her inaction had screwed them, and had given time for Ben, *Ben* for god's sake, to doubt her. Amber's mind spun, whirling past the same thought over and over: Maybe she carried the blame for this moment, but the ultimate cause of the trouble went back to her fucking parents leaving everything in a trust for the kids first, before their own, only living daughter.

"*Impulsive*," Amber sneered. "We got complacent, got ourselves trapped in this fucking horrible house, and I'm *done* with it! Just . . . stay out of my way. Once I make sure everything is all right, all you gotta do is help me get them into the car." She glanced out the window and scowled. "It'd be better with snow, but I can make it plausible anyway."

Ben grabbed her arm from behind and she whirled on him, her belly sinking, heavy with a cold realization she'd held at bay until this moment: They were in too deep, and if he defied her now, if he was going to turn on her over those fucking kids, she'd have to handle *him*, too.

The thought alone made her eyes sting, but she bit her lip until she tasted blood and kept herself under control. She couldn't blow it now. They'd spent three years, since her parents had changed their trust, whispering around their plans without actually saying them outright. She'd spent months researching *exactly* the right kind of accident. It was almost over. Amber would have *everything*, and she would be rid of bullshit tedium and thankless responsibility. And she would finally, *finally* never be last, never again be shoved behind anyone else.

"I'm just worried. About all this. About you. You've been"—he paused, searching for the right word—"strained, *so* strained. Now, think. Really think. Can you honestly be okay after—" Ben swallowed, tried again. "After . . ."

He trailed away with an uncomfortable grimace.

Amber braced herself, pushed away the queasy discomfort, and said out loud the words both of them had been dancing silently around for three years.

"After I kill those kids?"

Ben recoiled, and Amber steeled herself.

She'd put it out in the open.

She expected . . . something. A thunderbolt of guilt, a spike of terror or fury. But having it said drew a cold calm down around her, stilled the frantic twisting in her.

Leaning closer to her husband, Amber went on, "I'll be *fine*, Benjamin. Will you?" She meant it to be a challenge, but to her surprise the words came out closer to a plea.

When Ben didn't answer right away something inside Amber broke, hot and much too sharp to even begin to let herself feel, not yet. She kept her face smooth—maybe too smooth, because Ben let go of her arm as if burned.

Then he swallowed hard and found his voice at last. "No." If the admission surprised Amber, it clearly shocked Ben as well; his eyes widened and his face lost color. He swallowed hastily and tried to correct himself. "I mean, I don't think so. This is different. You—you *get* that, don't you?"

Amber couldn't answer. She wanted to cry, to scream—why would he do this to them, to her, why would he force her hand like this, he *knew* she wouldn't let herself lose—and she didn't have time for it, didn't even have time to think about how she'd handle this, not right now.

Right now all she needed was to stage the accident and get through the time that would follow without Ben doing something incredibly stupid. Which meant right now she needed to find exactly the right thing to say.

So though she wanted to scream at him, though she wanted to run for the bedroom and the closet and the shoebox with her documents, she forced herself still and gave Ben the most sympathetic look she could muster. "Okay," she said.

The relief that spread over his face was like a blow to her gut. "Okay?" he asked. "We'll reconsider?"

"Ben. No. I mean, okay, I'll handle this alone. You don't have to be in the car. You don't even have to help me buckle them in. It won't be on you, not any of it, okay? And when it's done we'll have everything we need, and if there's anything left to figure out, I'll handle it."

Ben swallowed hard, the relief draining out of his eyes, but he shut his mouth and he nodded and that would have to be good enough for now. Amber took his hand and gave his limp fingers a squeeze, which he did not return. Then, as she'd wanted to all along, she turned and ran down the hallway, thinking only of the closet and her papers and the car and her plans.

When she skittered out into the living room, a scent of smoke and an incongruous chill penetrated her single-minded focus. Amber stopped moving, and when Ben drew in a breath behind her she raised her hand sharply, silencing him.

"Do you hear that?" she whispered.

Flames crackling.

Looking over her shoulder, she met Ben's widening eyes. They took off.

Amber skidded to a stop just inside the kitchen, eyes bulging. Marigold and Xander stood at the stove, their backs to the entrance, Xander on his tiptoes and Marigold on her little stool. On top of the stove sat Amber's stockpot, emanating a warm orange glow that rose and fell, casting leaping shadows. The occasional lick of flame reached above the rim, visible in tiny flashes. The window in the kitchen and the sliding back door stood wide open, letting in the cold November air, dispersing the smoke to almost nothing.

Two impulses rose in Amber, one after the other, each a powerful blow.

The first was to shout at them to stop, to ask them what they thought they were doing, to explain to the children how dangerous this was.

The second was to simply . . . leave them to it.

Walk away. Drag Ben out of the house and see what happened

next. The idea held a certain attraction. She reached up, extending a hand toward her husband, as if to grab his sleeve and pull him out to the garage. The scene painted itself in her mind. They'd go there and wait to see whether the orange glow grew. Linger in the garage until the last moment, give the impression of barely having escaped the blaze. She grabbed Ben's sleeve.

A needle of doubt worked its way through her certainty.

It left too much up to chance. And even if it worked, there would be too many questions. Ben was a firefighter, everyone would wonder why he hadn't done something. And the similarities . . . people would spread rumors.

No. She let go of her husband's sleeve, dropped her hand.

Beside her, Ben shook his head sharply.

"What's wrong with them?" he whispered.

"Does it matter?" Amber retorted, sparing her husband a quick, sharp look.

Which he ignored.

Amber stared at Ben as he sidled past her. He didn't even notice, only hurried across the kitchen to the children. They stood almost perfectly still, Marigold's head cocked to the left with a small backward tilt, one hand limp at her side and the other reaching slowly up toward the pot. Xander's body listed to the right, leaning toward his sister at an extreme angle. Amber couldn't guess how he avoided stumbling sideways into the smaller child.

Then Ben was in the way, skidding to a stop just behind them, his hands out as if to grab Marigold but hesitating.

"Mari-berry?" he said, his voice low and soothing, and Amber had never before hated that nickname but, oh, she did now.

Marigold didn't respond. Didn't even turn. Neither did Xander. Ben lifted Marigold down off the stool and her posture didn't change, and Amber's panic and anger faltered, unease flickering to life in their place.

It wasn't until Ben pivoted to Xander and then froze that the unease swelled into fear, and Amber didn't know why except that every line of Ben's figure grew tense, the shape of him more silhouette than not with the flaming stockpot beyond him. He audibly swallowed, and then reached out and took something from the unmoving, unresisting little boy.

"Amber?" he said, turning toward her, holding out for her the flat, white bundle he'd taken from Xander.

Papers.

Papers with the name of her parents' legal firm in elaborate script along the top. The air went out of her in a rush. She sucked it back in a wheezing gasp.

The children had been burning her documents.

"No!" Amber cried, as if she could prevent what they'd already done. She lunged forward and grabbed Xander, giving him a shake. His arms flopped and his head rolled forward, his body pliant. Amber snatched her hands back, then, slower, reached out for the boy again. She turned him to face her and recoiled.

Xander's head hung, hair drooping over his brow, not long enough to hide his slack lack of expression. Both kids breathed deeply and evenly, without a hint of excitement or nerves. Xander's eyes were mostly closed, mere slivers visible between his eyelids. Those slivers gleamed stark white. Cold dropped into the pit of Amber's stomach, and she took a sharp breath to try to push it away.

"What are you doing?" Amber said, taking Xander's shoulders again and giving him another, gentler shake. She clenched her jaw, hating the concern that bloomed in her chest when he didn't respond. Hating her parents and Hannah all the more for putting her in this situation. Why did they have to make everything so hard? Amber never wanted any of this! She used the hatred like a blanket, spread it over everything else, smothered the flicker of concern. Teeth grinding, Amber shook Xander again as if to erase the gentleness of a moment before.

"Answer me! How did you get those papers?"

Ben's touch on her shoulder nearly made her scream. She spun toward him, too full of a confused jumble of fear and fury and the sting of guilt she would not allow herself to feel to bother keeping her feelings off her face.

"What?" she shouted.

Ben flinched, snatching his hand away from her. Then he licked his lips, and his eyes darted away from hers, first to the firelight still flickering from within the stockpot and then to the children each in turn.

"I—um—I see what you mean now," he said, his voice flat and thin. He looked down and then to his left. "This isn't normal. I mean, right? This is—this is no good." His glance flicked toward her, but not to meet her eyes, settling instead on the pocket of her jeans, on the top of her key fob poking out just a little, reflecting the unsteady orange light. "How about you give me your keys," he said, the hesitation melting out of his voice, the words coming faster now but not smooth or calm. Jerky, forced. "I'll get them in the car while you go over your documents and lock them back up, okay?"

Ben lifted his gaze then, looked right at Amber, holding himself very still as he repeated, "Okay?"

He was lying to her.

"*Damn* it, Ben," Amber said, and it was only when his eyes widened in obvious fear that she realized, by the terrible sinking in her heart, that part of her had still been hoping she was mistaken, that he was only nervous and not about to betray her.

The sick hurt struck her all the harder because of its familiarity. Just like Hannah, always turning on Amber and ruining her life. Just like Nathan, refusing to speak to her in public. Just like her parents, only wanting her love on their terms.

"This isn't my fault," she hissed, because if she spoke any louder the tears—of betrayal, of rage—would come and the tears could not come, not right now. "I don't *like* it! I don't want to have to do this. It isn't fair! My *parents*, they did this to us—and now we don't have a choice! When the kids turn eighteen . . . do you think

Greg's parents will, what? Just let it all go? We'd lose everything." Fury swelled then, easing the tightness in her throat, so that she could repeat in a hard voice rather than a wobbly whisper, "I would lose everything."

Amber reached for Marigold.

Ben scrambled to put himself between Amber and the children, his eyes still wide and his face still pale, but something about his expression put her in mind of the way he behaved when he got home from the firehouse.

There was a hardness there that sparked fury in Amber even as it broke her heart. Ben didn't notice, or didn't care. He grabbed the kids and swiveled, dragging them behind him and keeping his body between them and Amber. She pivoted in place, breathing fast, thoughts frantic. How could she get this back under control, how could she fix this, if only she still had the gun—but she didn't, she didn't, and Ben was backing the children toward the exit from the kitchen, in the direction of the front door. Amber kept them in view, desperately searching her mind for something, *anything* to say to stop Ben from ruining everything, forever.

Not half a second after Ben had pushed Xander and Marigold both into the entryway, the sliding back door slammed closed. The kitchen window fell shut with a bang. A single long crack appeared running up the center of it.

In the same instant, violent orange light flared behind Amber. Scorching heat washed over her from behind and she ducked forward with a yelp.

CHAPTER 20

LOOK AT ME

NOVEMBER 2020

Amber spun. The flames roared above the rim of the stockpot now. Above the stove the plastic casing on the microwave sizzled. From behind her Ben shouted something Amber didn't catch and then her husband lunged past her, reaching for the fire extinguisher mounted on the wall. With a series of sliding sort of *clicks*, the window and door locked. Amber straightened, whirled. Nothing—no one—had turned those locks.

Ben got one hand on the extinguisher.

He hesitated, cocking his head.

The whispering had begun. Now Amber wished she had let Ben talk more about the haunting; had he heard this voice before? Would he know that this time, it sounded different? No longer diffuse. No longer directionless. The tone, too, had shifted; whatever words the voice whispered now were not for Amber.

All the better. Ben was distracted, no longer between herself and the children.

Turning, she rushed toward them, stooped to grab their hands without looking into their half-lidded, expressionless eyes.

And stopped.

The whispering had grown louder. No . . . that wasn't quite right. She'd drawn closer to it. Near enough to hear the tone, an urgency that made Amber's stomach sink. The susurrus echoed with half-understood emotion, something that should have been warm but that wormed into Amber's guts as a twisting fear. Swallowing hard, Amber tried to push the squirming unease away and call back her certitude. The time had come to act, not to stand frozen with her throat constricting at the sound of one soft, almost gentle voice.

But a tiny movement caught her eye. Amber crouched to peer more closely. Mari's curly hair swayed near one ear, as if being blown by soft breaths.

What was the voice saying to the children?

The question chilled Amber to her bones. She glanced at Xander; the boy's tilted lean diminished. His eyelids fluttered gently at first, then more quickly. Amber's breath caught in her throat. What were the whispers telling them? She forced herself to breathe, tried to still herself in spite of a trembling spreading to her limbs.

Over the soft murmurs a *click* sounded out, a clasp coming undone.

As Amber turned to spare one quick glance for the sound, Ben spoke, his voice surer than he'd seemed all night. "It's not safe, you better get out, Amb—" He spun, holding the fire extinguisher, and stopped short when his eyes landed on Amber and the kids. Practiced firefighter confidence gone in a heartbeat, he let the extinguisher clatter to the ground as he jumped for them, gasping, "I told you two to run!"

As soon as "run" left Ben's lips the whispers took it up, repeating the word over and over, faster and faster, louder and louder. Amber scrambled to stand without losing her grip on the children as Ben came to an abrupt halt just behind her, reaching around to pry her hands off Xander's and Mari's wrists. A brittle, hollow feeling cracked open in Amber's chest, and she twisted as Ben pulled her back from them and wrapped his arms around her.

At the same moment Marigold sucked in a deep breath and Xander blinked hard, his body stiffening.

"What's happening?" Xander asked. Beneath the tremble of confusion, his voice rang with hard suspicion.

His eyes moved from Marigold to Amber and Ben, and when he looked at Amber his lip curled into a scowl. When Amber met his eyes, her mind slid away from the fundamental fact of who he was. As if they had never before met, as if she hadn't been raising him for years. Like a familiar word spoken too many times, the child did not change yet became abruptly alien to her.

Wild with fearful protectiveness, the boy darted forward and grabbed his sister's arm, pulling her to him. He wrapped his arms around her shoulders, his breath coming fast. The incongruity of the gesture, such an adult action from such a small boy, hit Amber with the force of a blow. Tears burned in her eyes, obscured her view, and the gut punch of guilt took her breath away even as she struggled to make herself understand. Who were these children? Why should their faces fill her with this terrible shame?

"What's happening, Xander?" When Mari spoke her big brother's name—her voice thick with the confused misery of a lost little girl—it blew away the fog of strangeness that hung over them.

They were only Marigold and Xander, and Amber had to get away from her husband and catch them.

Ben, however, dragged her toward the back door, shouting past Amber at the kids, "Run!"

This time they listened, Xander grabbing Marigold's hand in a grip so tight Amber could see his knuckles whiten as he half dragged her into the front hall.

"Let go of me, Benjamin!" Amber snarled, writhing in his arms, but Ben was a firefighter, he knew how to haul a panicking adult out of a building. He was almost to the back door already and Amber's burning fury with him was tempered only by an ache in her chest so deep she thought she might fall into it forever, because even when he'd turned on her, even when he'd forced her to realize that if she didn't get rid of him he'd ruin everything forever, even now he was trying to save her life, too. "God *damn* it, Ben," she cried, "just let me go!"

"No!" For an instant Amber thought he was answering her, but the panic in his voice didn't fit, and she craned her neck to see his face. He pivoted abruptly without taking his eyes off the exit from the kitchen, shouting, "Not that way! Don't go that way!" Ben shoved Amber roughly toward the back door, heedless when she stumbled over the discarded fire extinguisher, as he dove for the front hall. Amber pushed herself up and turned in time to see Xander and Mari disappear, not through the front door, but up the stairs.

Before Ben could leave the kitchen in pursuit, the flaming stockpot on the stove shot into the air. It crashed into the underside of the microwave and spun, trailing smoke, to land on the floor.

The fire didn't merely spread from the stockpot, it raced out as if alive. Twin lines burned across the floor, one leaping to cut Ben off from the kitchen's exit, the other circling the room from the opposite direction. Amber clawed her way to her feet and back from the sliding door just as the flames raged across that space.

Amber and her wayward husband were hemmed in on all sides by a wall of deadly flames. Smoke billowed and Amber didn't know if it was too much, if it filled the room too fast to be natural; Ben would know but she couldn't ask him, she could hardly see him in the choking, ember-flecked darkness.

When the smoke detectors let out their first blast of noise, Amber almost screamed. The alarm went on, piercing and painfully loud, a shrilly shrieking reminder of the one other mundane fire safety device she'd completely forgotten about.

The fire extinguisher.

Ben had dropped it, she'd tripped over it, and now she needed it—to fight the fires or to swing at Ben and fight past *him*, Amber would decide when she had it in her hands. Pulling her shirt over her mouth and nose, she scurried in the direction it had rolled away in.

Hands of smoke and shadow appeared from the writhing darkness. They lashed out at her. Hot, sharp fury spiked through her—*don't touch me*—and she tried to seize the feeling and hold it between herself and the terror. The hands shoved again, striking her chest, driving the air from her lungs. When she staggered backward, they dissipated. She sucked in a breath but got a lungful of scorching hot smoke. Gagging, she stumbled over her own feet, bent double, and coughed so hard she vomited. Disgust and smoke together choked her.

Pathetic. Weak.

The fury driving her sputtered and faded, leaving Amber trembling. She couldn't even make herself stand upright again, her mind spinning in helpless circles. Still bent over, she fumbled again in the direction of the extinguisher. Adrenaline and terror rendered her body jittery and clumsy.

The whispers snarled her name as the hands from the shadows drove her back again, a blow to the gut this time. She slipped in her own sick mess and fell hard on her tailbone. Though the smell of her vomit made her bile rise again, down on the floor the air was less hot, less suffocating.

Remaining low, Amber tried to scoot forward.

Something tangled itself in her hair and yanked her head backward. The pain in her scalp was sharp and bright and nothing to the pain in the back of her skull as it struck the floor, hard. She lay dazed, her limbs loose, colors wobbling before her eyes.

When her focus returned it came with fury. She'd shown *everyone* who'd ever tried to push her around. This bullshit wasn't going to beat her now.

The fire extinguisher. That was the only thing that mattered. Rolling onto her hands and knees, she scrambled for it.

The phantom hands slammed into her spine this time, knocking her flat on the floor. Hatred surged in her, as strong as the fear, all sharp edges cutting at her insides. She clutched that hatred, rode it. Let it drive her. It filled her voice as she finally gave words to the crawling fear and burning fury.

"*Stop it, Nathan!*" she screamed into the floor.

In the ringing echo of her shout, a lull fell. The flames still burned but their crackle and pop quieted enough that Amber could hear her own ragged, rasping breaths again. The smoke lightened, just a touch.

This time when Amber tried to stand nothing tripped her up or knocked her down again. But when she stepped toward the extinguisher the smoke swirled unnaturally, drawing in, gathering with ember and shadow, forming shapes between Amber and Ben.

Figures.

Not one, but two.

The blazing fire couldn't touch the cold in Amber's bones, the dizziness of the world whirling out of control. Her head spun and her stomach dropped. No, no, this was no time for more mewling and fear. She had to get herself under control! She tried to dredge up more of that hatred.

"*Na-Nath-Nathan-athan-an?*" The whispers from the two figures repeated the name, bouncing it back and forth between them, dripping with scorn. They materialized further, grew more distinct.

"No," Amber rasped, struggling to breathe.

Limbs separated from the mass. Heads reared up. Each had a strange, small spot of glittering silver at the end of one arm. One of the figures lurched higher than the other. Both grew more defined.

Amber couldn't blink, though her eyes burned.

Shadow turned to something like skin but crackling black. Featureless heads became faces, skulls exposed until spectral flesh began to form, eyes fire-bright and rolling. Amber didn't look at those faces, didn't meet the smoldering eyes. Told herself it was because they were too gruesome.

No other reason. No. *No.*

On the left hand of each, those silver glitters reflected the surging orange light.

"Not . . . Nathan," one of them said. Didn't whisper. Didn't scream. The voice was harsh and cracked, but it touched something painful in Amber's chest.

She knew it.

Amber gasped and choked. Ben tried to speak but coughed too hard for Amber to make out the words, to tell whether he spoke to her or the fiery specters. Whether he, too, recognized them.

The fires leaped higher around her, dazzling her eyes. She covered her face, her whole body shaking.

"Look at us, Amber," that voice said, no louder but full of command. "Look at *me*."

Bitter terror swelled through her. If she looked, she might finally lose her mind. But she couldn't help herself. Amber dropped her hands and turned her burning, watering eyes up to the figures looming between her and Ben.

They had their old faces again, at last.

CHAPTER 21

THE RIGHT LIE

NOVEMBER 2020

The half-insubstantial shadow things exuded a thick reek of burnt meat and singed hair and rot. The stink of charred human flesh. Even as Amber watched, their spectral forms smoldered, flesh forever burning away without diminishing. Standing motionless, lips closed, the hateful whispers nevertheless drifted from them once more. They stared at Amber with eyes that reflected the spreading fire.

No, not reflected—magnified it, burned from within.

And they were unmistakable.

Amber wrapped her arms around herself and tried to speak, but all that came out of her mouth was a dry, cracked wheeze. She licked her lips and shuffled backward, then tried again.

"Hannah," she breathed.

An ache squeezed her heart and her eyes burned from more than the smoke. She fought to inhale, battling the potent and painful blend of love and hatred she had thought she would never have to feel again. Words failed her.

"*How?*" Ben gasped the question Amber couldn't force out of her throat, and in that moment of desperate relief to be facing this with somebody else, Amber could have forgiven him almost any betrayal.

Greg's eternally immolating ghost half turned, his whole form guttering like a candle about to blow out, and between one flicker and the next he stood not side by side with Hannah, but directly before Ben.

Ben recoiled with a shout, catching himself an instant before stumbling into the flames eating at the room's periphery, blackening the walls, but Greg did not pursue him. Amber's late brother-in-law merely held out his left arm, skin—or what looked like skin—burning and splitting and peeling and re-forming and burning again. Something glittered at the end of that arm. Amber's eyes flicked down to Hannah's left hand. She wore a silver-bright ring, the firelight giving it a molten appearance.

Amber's eyes locked on that small, shining point as one moment flashed across her mind—one single, inconsequential irritation in a long list of irritations on the day they'd moved into this damned house: Xander crashing into her legs in the front hall. Amber dropping a stack of boxes. The wrought iron and silk jewelry box falling open. The movers had been impatient, so Amber had scooped up scattered necklaces and earrings as fast as she could . . . and in such a hurry to get out of their way, she'd dismissed as unimportant the jewelry that had fallen down the vents. There'd been no time to check the ducts then, and it had slipped Amber's mind later; she'd never felt the lack of the missing jewelry.

Hannah and Greg's wedding ring set.

The only things salvaged from the fire the night they'd died.

"It's been *you* all along?" Amber said, voice rasping out of her dry throat, fighting a cough with every word as smoke filled and filled the kitchen. The fire crawled over the countertops, climbed the curtains, charred the cabinets and the walls, but did not spread any further.

Between one choking breath and the next Hannah moved, from the center of the kitchen to inches from Amber's face without a heartbeat between. Sweat already seeped down Amber's back, dampened her underarms and dripped down her forehead and nose, but the heat that poured off of her dead sister was so much worse, suffocating and furious.

"How dare you act surprised," Hannah hissed, the voice coming from her mouth but also from the smoke and the fire itself, overlapped by whispers Amber couldn't make out as, over Hannah's shoulder, Greg leaned nearer to a cringing Ben. Even so, Amber heard the pain beneath the rage. Especially when Hannah went on, her voice cracking and the fire dimming for one sad little moment, "How *could* you?"

In that moment the terror fell away, and though the burned and reeking thing before her didn't change, it was just . . . Hannah. Just Amber's little sister—an annoying, bossy tattletale; a tagalong when it suited her; one of the first people Amber ever hated and one of the few people Amber ever loved, and once upon a time the only friend Amber had. Hannah being argumentative, Hannah throwing accusations around, Hannah failing to hide the beseeching quaver that reminded Amber of what it had felt like to be protective of her sister. She'd never wanted to see Hannah again, and at the same time hearing her voice from the other side of death made her heart hurt, and that didn't feel like a contradiction—it had always been this way, and the grave between them could not change that.

It was that familiarity that drove Amber's quick, easy denial, years of habit pushing the words out of her mouth—words that Amber knew were wrong a second too late to stop herself: "What are you *talking* about, Hannah?"

The specter of smoke and shadow recoiled as if slapped. The kitchen seemed to close around Amber as the flames leaped again, scorching the ceiling, spreading along the blackened walls. To Amber's left something thumped hard but Amber couldn't tell what because Hannah was right there, right in her face, and the familiarity burned away with the rage pouring off the ghost. Hannah gave voice to a wail like Amber had never heard from her in life, hollow and echoing and vast. *"I'm talking about the night you killed us! You were my sister, and you killed me! You stole—"*

"I didn't!" Amber yelped, cowering, raising her hands as if to protect her head or to block out the madness around her.

"*Liar!*" Hannah screamed.

The heat grew beyond mere discomfort, her skin stinging like a sunburn, a small pain that nevertheless filled Amber with absolute dread. Amber's mind raced like a caged mouse, she couldn't breathe, she couldn't think, there would be a right thing to say, there had to be, this was *Hannah* for god's sake, her perpetually smoldering corpse-self leaning into the arm Greg's ghost put around her shoulders in a gesture so familiar and human that it made Amber want to squeeze her eyes closed against the incongruity. The right lie or deflection or story wouldn't come, though, and all that was left to Amber, in the end, was the truth.

"I wanted to!" she cried, her shrill voice nothing in comparison to the ghostly scream of her sister.

Silence fell over the kitchen again, and Amber lowered her hands to better see the thing that was her sister, who gaped at her as if dumbstruck.

Amber wrapped her arms around herself and said again, "I wanted to . . . but I couldn't. I told Ben he had to do it because he could fake it better, but the real reason was because I couldn't."

The thought of killing Hannah had sickened Amber in a way murdering her parents years later hadn't, and she'd made Ben take on that burden instead, then lied to him about why. Once it was done, she'd buried those feelings so deeply she could have spent the rest of her life tricking herself into believing they weren't there . . . if only Hannah hadn't shown up to ruin everything even now, forcing from Amber the honesty Ben had been after for four years, the thing she would never admit to him.

Did Ben understand what she meant, did he grasp how she'd misused him? Amber's gaze flicked past Hannah and Greg to—wait, Greg? When had he stopped menacing Ben?

Amber jerked in a tight turn, the ghosts not forgotten but for this one moment ignored. Ben was gone. There was a gap in the flames right at the entryway into the kitchen from the front hall.

She ran. She didn't wonder where Ben was or why Greg had let him go. Self-preservation took over and Amber did not have one single thought other than the image of the front door and desperation for a breath of that cold November air.

Hannah and Greg flickered into being in the front hall, in the exact center of the spot where Amber had left her mother, her father, and her accomplice dead on the floor nearly a year before. It was fire, not blood, that spread from the ghosts, and Amber almost couldn't stop her headlong flight in time, almost tumbled right into the inferno. Pain seared her face along with every inch of skin exposed to the heat, and sweat slicked her body and made her clothing cling to her.

"I said it wasn't *me*!" Amber cried, scrambling backward. To her left were the two sets of stairs, one leading all the way to the second floor and the half flight of stairs leading to the lower area of the split-level, both terminating in darkness untouched by the fires in the kitchen and now the front hall, too.

"*That's not good enough*," Greg snarled, and for one ridiculous moment Amber wanted to snap at him to mind his own fucking business, this was between her and her sister.

Hannah didn't give her a chance, cutting in with the most terrible, gut-wrenching cry Amber had ever heard in her life. "*You stole my babies!*"

Xander and Marigold. Amber's stomach plummeted. In the furor, she'd forgotten the kids, the way they'd been acting . . . Amber's deadly plans for that night. . . .

Did Hannah know? *Did Hannah know?* Despite the scorching heat a chill skittered through Amber, cold to her bones, because of course Hannah knew. Of course she did. After all, the children had not been burning Amber's papers of their own volition, had they?

Run. She had to run. She had to run, she had to run now, run now, run *right now*, but the back door was lost in a sea of flame and Hannah and Greg burned between her and the front door, so where could she run *to*—

The garage.

Amber pivoted and dashed to the abbreviated staircase, leaping down into the living room in a single bound, ignoring the flicker of hateful orange in her periphery as Hannah or Greg appeared by the living room window, flames bursting from them. She threw herself around the corner into the hallway so fast she collided with the opposite wall and rebounded, still running, desperate to reach the garage door before—

Burned hair stink and pain, a vicious yank, and Amber reeled backward almost before she registered the flaming hands in her hair, dragging her away as the garage door combusted with a roar. Another cruel jerk of her hair and Amber toppled onto her ass. The pressure let up but not the pain, not the burning, the burning. Amber's hair was on fire, her scalp blistering, she was screaming, scrambling to her feet as if she could escape her own body, beating desperately at the back of her head until the flames were out even as she staggered back up into the entry hall.

Tears streaming down her face, Amber did not pause. She scrambled up the next flight of stairs, tripping over her own feet and going up on all fours after that. There was only one other way she might escape, just the one, but Hannah knew this house as well as Amber did. They'd grown up here. She'd think of it, too. Which meant Amber needed the children.

Unless they'd gotten out of the house; if they got out then Amber would die—

No, no, no, she'd seen them run up the stairs, and as she climbed she found she could breathe easier. The smoke stayed downstairs. The fire stayed downstairs. Hannah and Greg would not let their children burn.

The quiet, the cooler air, and the blue night-light in the upstairs hall felt like something out of a dream after the raging heat and fury below. Amber's skin stung all over, the back of her head throbbed, heat pouring from it. She stank, and when she flexed her hands the pain in her scorched skin brought tears to her eyes. All she wanted, in the whole world, was to stand in this hushed dimness and let everything that had just happened be another awful nightmare.

But the smoke detectors continued shrieking, the orange glow from the bottom of the steps grew stronger, and from Xander's room came the low and desperate murmur of Ben's voice.

Ben.

That asshole had left her alone with Hannah and Greg to chase after Xander and Marigold, even now?

Fine. *Fine.* Amber would deal with Ben just as soon as those fucking kids got them safely out of this house.

She meant to storm over to Xander's door and wrench it open, but at the first step she took, something let out a long, groaning creak from Xander's room. Amber shivered, sucking in a harsh breath. It was the closet door, and when Ben's voice spoke again it was not in a pleading murmur but a tight, frightened stammer that Amber could hear clearly from the hall.

"No! Wait! I—I was trying but they're under the bed—I can't, I can't get them to come out to me . . . Well, no, but wait, no, I didn't want to scare them—yes, I swear. Okay. Okay!"

Who was in there with Ben and the children? Hannah? Greg? Or . . . Amber glanced down the stairs again, her mind full of the ground-floor windows with their eyeless reflections and the safe, dark night beyond . . . maybe both of them were in Xander's room and she could go for it right now.

How could she know? She couldn't, not at all, it would be a gamble, but maybe—

Xander's door slammed open and Amber spun back toward it with a little scream, quickly stifled because the shapes bursting from the room were not the terrible ghosts. Ben ran out, Marigold clinging to one of his hands and Xander to the other. Ben's eyes snapped to Amber and he let out an alarmed shout, dashing across the hall and into their bedroom, dragging the children along.

Their bedroom—with the window that led to part of the roof where a tree grew too near, its roots threatening the foundation but its branches offering escape.

He was going to get the children out and leave Amber here to burn.

With a despairing cry, knowing she would never catch them in time, Amber gave chase. She lunged to the doorway and there was Ben, across the room, sliding Marigold out the window. Xander waited just beyond, crouched low on the roof, one hand gripping the windowsill from outside and the other steadying his little sister. Ben lifted one leg and stuck it through the window, following the children, and Amber would never make it.

So she took a dive.

Amber faked a trip, took a tumble, landing with an exaggerated gasp near the foot of their bed. She pushed herself halfway up and reached for her husband, crying, "Ben, *please*, I'm sorry!"

And he hesitated.

Tears of pure, unfiltered relief flooded Amber's vision as Ben pulled his leg back inside and turned around, hurrying to Amber's side, where he belonged. It had worked. He skidded to a stop and reached down for her hand. The door behind them slammed with a resounding *crack*. Amber grabbed Ben's wrist. The closet door slid open with a *rattle* and a *bang*. Amber tightened her grip on Ben's sweat-slicked skin, but she didn't just let him pull her to her feet. As the window Ben had left open slid shut and latched itself, Amber yanked him down while she shot to her feet, shoving with her shoulder when he was off-balance. The force sent Ben, eyes wide with betrayal, staggering sideways into their bed.

As he lost his balance and fell onto the mattress, it burst into flames.

Amber recoiled with a scream that she could not hear over the sound of Ben's bellows. On either side of the bed, Hannah and Greg flickered into existence, and Amber could not help but stare at them as they watched, impassive, while the bed and Ben burned. When Ben lurched to sit, his blistering and bubbling arms pushing him toward the edge of the bed, Greg leaned forward and shoved him back.

Amber should have been edging away, going for the window while they were distracted, but the terrible spectacle pinned her in place. Ben, her Ben, the only person who had ever stood by her to the . . . well, almost to the end . . . was dying in agony, and Amber could not make herself look away. He writhed and tried to roll off the side of the bed, but Greg reached out again. Where the ghost's hand closed over Ben's arm, the flesh blackened faster. Greg yanked Ben toward the center of the bed.

"Why?" Ben screamed, the word drawing out and out, his hair burning and his clothing scorching and his flesh melting as the inferno ate him faster than any natural fire could have. "Why?"

But the ghosts did not answer. Not until after Ben fell silent and still.

"Because," Greg whispered, one still-burning corpse to another, "you were my best friend until that poisonous bitch"—Hannah turned to Amber at these words, but Greg had eyes only for Ben's body, almost indistinguishable now from the ghosts—"made you into somebody who would murder me in my bed, you shithead."

Now both ghosts faced Amber, and a terrible swooping dizziness struck her at the realization that she'd missed her chance—maybe her last chance—to run.

"Hannah, you don't want to do this," she said, her voice reasonable, imploring. "I'm your *sister*—"

"No," Hannah snapped, fury in her eyes and in her voice and in the fire that filled the air around her with the word. "You don't get to say that to me. Not after what you've done. You murdered me, Amber. You stole my babies! My god, you were going to—"

"It was supposed to be *me*!" Amber shouted, unleashing years of impotent indignation that was easier than facing the terror and grief and rage. "I was supposed to be the first one to have kids, but you knew if I did, Mom and Dad would stop paying more attention to *you* all the time. You *knew* Ben and I were trying, and you and Greg weren't even married yet but you got pregnant anyway and you never—never—never fooled me, Hannah. I knew it wasn't an accident, you just couldn't let me win, and I thought raising Xander and Mari would be good enough but it wasn't. They never loved me like they should've. Mom and Dad never came around. I deserve my chance to start the fuck over!"

Hannah's eyes flashed with fury and Greg's whole charred body billowed with choking smoke, and the temperature in the bedroom exploded, heat so thick it almost drove Amber to her knees.

"*Deserve?*" Greg bellowed, the ghostly echoes and ringing depth distorting his voice worse than ever. "Our children deserve their parents—they *deserve* their lives. What is wrong with you?"

"How can you look yourself in the eye?" Hannah hissed before Greg's roar had faded.

A tap at the window then drew Amber's attention, jerking her around with a burst of hope that the children might be trying to help her, but no. It was her reflection, pressed against the glass, tapping and tapping, forcing her to look her own terror in the face.

It had no eyes.

How can you look yourself in the eye?

"How can you sleep at night?" Hannah went on, advancing now, the fire crawling ahead of her, but Amber's attention went to the bed between the ghosts, her husband's corpse still burning there, and her mind spun through every sleepless night since she'd moved into this godforsaken house.

"You—you were *fucking with me*?" Amber gasped, turning to Hannah.

She finally found it then, her last resort, her ultimate shield, the fury that could keep the terror at bay and let Amber find her way out of this mess, waiting for just the right affront to bring it roaring to life. She leaned into it, stoked it, forcing a hard laugh as she shouted, "This whole haunting was—what—Hannah the tattletale, *still* nagging me? Grow up! This is so like you; death hasn't given you one ounce of perspective, has it?" The idea, her salvation, it struck her then, and Amber felt a vicious, victorious smile stretch her lips. She bared her teeth with that smile and said, "You can't hurt me. This house is going to burn down and good riddance, but your kids can't get off that roof by themselves."

Hannah closed the distance between them in a flicker. Amber had no time to react, hardly time to realize her sister had moved at all. Hannah grabbed her. The burning of her scalp when the ghosts had yanked her by the hair was nothing to the agony of her sister's scorching hands closing around her shoulders. White-hot and total. Amber knew herself to be screaming but could not feel it rasp in her throat, and the world spun but she could not feel herself turning, and then her face was pressed up against the window just as her reflection's had been.

"Look," Hannah commanded, and when Amber did look she cried into the glass, a wordless howl of hurt and terror.

Because that damnable busybody Mrs. Jones stood in the dark lawn outside, bony old arms outstretched. Marigold huddled at her feet, sooty and shell-shocked but out of danger. Xander sat on a low tree branch, his grip on the bough white-knuckled, his eyes locked on Mrs. Jones as she reached for him, her lips moving, her eyes frightened but sincere.

He shifted his weight as if to leap, but then he turned and glanced at the window first. His gaze met Amber's and she sucked in a breath. It was on her lips to scream for help, but Xander's focus didn't linger on her. He looked beyond her, and his eyes widened, lips parting as if in a gasp.

"No," Amber moaned.

The fear on Xander's face dropped away—like he forgot the fire, forgot Amber's peril. In place of the fear, marveling recognition softened his eyes.

"Hi, my baby," Hannah whispered, not the hateful hiss but a tear-choked murmur that Xander could never have heard. The ghost made a sound like a gasp and repeated, "Hi, my baby. Oh, I love you so much."

As if he had heard her after all, Xander made a half-hearted gesture, reaching up with a limp hand and hesitating before he let it fall. His eyes stayed fixed beyond Amber, his face wonderstruck, as his lips formed a single word. *Momma.*

Then Mrs. Jones shouted, "Come *on*, boy!" Amber heard it through the window it was so loud, and it snapped Xander out of the moment. In the next instant he was down out of the tree, clutching the old woman as she lowered him to the grass next to his sister, and behind Amber her own sister sobbed.

But the moment Xander was away, Hannah's burning grasp spun Amber to face her.

"How," Hannah asked, eyes bright with fire instead of the tears that filled her voice, "can you live with yourself?"

Hellish fire leapt from the dead sister to the living one.

Hannah didn't even stay to watch.

As Amber's skin bubbled and peeled, the ghosts turned their backs on her and simply vanished, bright metal falling from the nothing where their hands had only just been, leaving their wedding rings and the inferno behind.

Screaming, alone, Amber died.

EPILOGUE

IT HAD TO GO

DECEMBER 2020

Xander leaned against the siding of an unfamiliar house, in an unfamiliar backyard, listening beneath a window he'd purposely left open a crack before slipping outside. It was winter, but not the kind that counted, not even with the brightly colored lights decorating houses throughout the neighborhood. As far as Xander was concerned, it wouldn't be for-real winter until some snow fell. The last week had been full of slushy rain instead. He sat on mucky, squishy ground because there wasn't anywhere dry. Icy water seeped into his pants and he pulled the bottom of his coat out and tucked his knees up inside.

The window cast a square of light onto the grass in front of him, and he kept his eyes fixed on it. Shadows moved across the yellow illumination, and Xander breathed slowly and quietly through his mouth, making sure he could hear every word of what the social worker was saying to the people who lived in this house.

His grandparents.

Xander made himself think it again—his grandparents—but the words still didn't fit in his brain.

He put his hand on the lid of the cardboard box sitting next to him in the flower bed, its bottom already soggy. Xander picked at a rain-softened spot on its top. The social worker had set it down in the foyer, and nobody had bothered to keep an eye on it. They weren't used to kids in this house, Xander figured. They hadn't hidden the matches too well, either.

"The Hugheses' next-door neighbor, Samantha Jones, gave her statement. She says it looked like Amber Hughes was in the master bedroom helping the children out the window when she succumbed to the fire," the social worker said.

Amber Hughes.

Xander dropped his hand to the grass, pulled it up one blade at a time and dropped the bits in a muddy little pile. Amber Hughes. He'd spent as long as he could remember thinking she was his mom, thinking his name was Xander Hughes. But she'd never been his mom. She was his aunt. And his dad . . . *Ben* . . . had never been related to him at all. He wiped his palm on his coat, leaving a streak of wet grass pieces on the slick fabric, and settled back.

If he closed his eyes as tight as he could and concentrated hard, hard, *hard*, he *almost* remembered his real mom and dad.

What he remembered better was a feeling more than a face, of being confused around Amber and Ben Hughes way back when he was still basically a baby. Remembering how he hadn't always thought Amber and Ben were his mom and dad didn't count as remembering his real parents, though. Xander knew that.

"The reports state that the fire started in the kitchen, looks like a cooking accident," the social worker continued, voice stilted like he was reading the information off a page. A second after Xander thought that, papers ruffled. He would have smiled at the confirmation of his guess, except his eyes slid out of focus and his hands curled into fists, fingernails digging into his palms.

The kitchen. Orange light. Smoke. Marigold, next to him.

Someone shouting. Someone whispering? Xander blinked hard. Tried to think.

There was nothing else.

The social worker went on. "The experts can't figure out how it spread so fast—the burn patterns don't suggest accelerant, apparently—but it must have been intense. Mr. Hughes was a firefighter, this shouldn't have happened. Do you happen to know what his mental state was before the fire?"

"I'm sorry," said Linda—his grandmother, Xander thought, but the word didn't work; grandmothers were old ladies wearing aprons and gray buns under bonnets in cartoons, not sad-eyed women with dark hair and soft hands. "After the fire—the, the first fire"—her voice broke, she sniffed, then went on—"after Greg and Hannah passed away, Amber and Ben took custody of the kids and cut us off. They told us they'd take care of everything. Said they didn't want us to burden ourselves or worry. Ben and Greg had been friends, you know, in college. And they promised—they *promised* we'd all still be close, after the funeral, when everything was calmer, but we never saw them after that. . . ." She trailed away, crying softly.

Greg and Hannah. Those were his real parents. Greg and Hannah Edwards. And the man and woman who lived in this house were Greg's parents. He couldn't remember meeting them before the night of the fire, though they had spent a lot of time during the month Xander and Mari had been living there showing off pictures of themselves holding him and Marigold as babies. And pictures of baby him and baby Marigold being held by Hannah and Greg. Those he pored over in secret, sneaking out of bed at night the way Marigold had been doing at the old house, pulling out the albums and going over and over the photos.

Xander's grandfather, Tim, cleared his throat and grumbled something under his breath that Xander couldn't catch. Linda said his name like he was in trouble, and Xander heard the sound of a swat.

"Actually, ma'am," the social worker said, sounding apologetic, "we found some evidence in the house that the late Mr. and Mrs. Hughes were intentionally separating the children from anyone who might be . . . suspicious, if an accident were to befall them. The police discovered some troubling search history items on a laptop recovered from the scene."

Someone gasped—probably Linda. After that, no sounds came through the window for several long moments. Xander clenched his fists, gritted his teeth. His chest tightened, his eyes burned, and he took a long, shuddering breath. Hurt churned in his chest and his gut, the weight pushing his shoulders down. They'd never been his parents. They had never cared about him, loved him. They'd never—the hurt turned to fierce, protective outrage—they'd *never* cared about Marigold, either.

"No! They'd never!" Linda gasped.

"I believe it," Tim said, his voice dark.

"I'm sorry to have to ask you this, but have the children mentioned anything happening to them in the care of their aunt and uncle?"

"I just can't . . ." Linda murmured, then, more loudly, "No, they haven't said anything. It seems . . . outlandish, honestly."

"Not to me, it doesn't," Tim said. "That Amber . . . Ben was an all right kid before he started hanging around her. Always polite, real nice but kinda dull. Impressionable. You know the type. But his wife? I wouldn't be surprised if she had . . . I dunno. Bad ideas, buried way down."

Xander nodded.

The fire was a foggy blur in his mind, the whole last day at the house nothing more than a bunch of broken pieces. His memory jumbled together in fuzzy bits, except for two moments.

Just before the fire spread beyond the kitchen, Xander knew, more than he'd known anything in his life, that Amber wanted to do something *bad* when she'd grabbed him and Marigold, pretending she wanted to help.

And after . . .

Xander squeezed his eyes shut, inhaled sharply before he opened them again, and looked down at the box next to him.

This backyard didn't have a fire pit like the one his dad—*Ben*, he reminded himself, but his lip trembled—had built in the last yard. But there was a simple, almost spherical barbecue on the patio, and that would work.

The social worker and his grandparents were still talking, something about recommended counseling and optional parenting classes, but the rest of the conversation didn't matter. If they'd figured out anything else about what Xander had seen or learned on the day his fake parents died, they would have talked about it already.

Nobody knew anything else.

Nobody knew that after he got through the window, he'd turned and looked back. Nobody knew he had seen a woman in the fire, holding Amber inside. She should've been a stranger, but Xander knew her when he looked at her. His heart hurt and his tummy flipped, and he tried not to think about it, except . . . if *she* could come back, maybe anybody could.

Xander lifted the metal lid on the grill with quiet care, keeping it from scraping or clanging. He set it down in the grass, then hefted the box of papers. It was all that was left from the last house. Of Amber and Ben.

It had to go.

Xander set the box on the grate, then snapped four matchsticks in half trying to light one. When he finally got a tiny flicker of flame, he set it on top of the cardboard and watched for a few moments, to be sure it caught. Satisfied, he put the lid back into place, slow and cautious. He didn't want anything to get out of hand, after all.

Everything was done. Everything was safe.

While his grandparents ushered the social worker out the front door, promising to call if they needed anything and thanking him for coming over at the end of his long workday, Xander snuck in the back and crept up the stairs, shedding his shoes and his coat inside the doorway of his new room.

He didn't stay there, crossing the hall to Marigold's room to check on her, instead. He stood in the middle of the room—almost really set up for a little kid now, no longer just thrown together in a hurry—and watched his sister sleep. There was no hint that she'd ever had a hard time sleeping in her bed. After a moment he climbed onto her bed and lay next to her, atop the covers. Her steady breathing, slow and even, soothed him.

It took a long time for him to finally fall asleep. Once he did, he slept deeply, untroubled by nightmares or worry.

ACKNOWLEDGMENTS

I drafted *These Familiar Walls* over the summer of 2020, and it's not only the book that got me started writing horror, it's also the book that served as my introduction to pursuing traditional publishing—I entered the first draft manuscript of this book into Pitch Wars, a mentorship program that deeply impacted my writing, my publishing endeavors, and the incredible writing community I've found. So my thanks, first and foremost, go to my Pitch Wars mentor Roxanne Blackhall, the first person ever to read the earliest little draft of *These Familiar Walls*, who helped me through an intensive three-month revision process, who did so much to demystify the process of querying literary agents and pursuing publishing, and who has been a kind and supportive presence for the last five years. Thanks also, of course, to Brenda Drake, the founder of Pitch Wars. And always, my thanks to my Pitch Wars friends—one of the coolest experiences of my debut year with my last book, *The Cut*, has been to get to meet some of you in person for the first time.

My gratitude to my family for their support of my writing and belief in me can hardly be expressed. I love you all so much. And a special thanks to my son, for saying all the creepy, eerie stuff you used to come up with when you were little—I think you're starting to get tired of hearing the story about how the initial idea for this book was inspired by one very creepy phrase you uttered when you were almost five years old and we'd just moved into a new house, but I'll never get tired of telling that story.

Thank you to my agent, Chris Bucci, for helping me realize my authorial dreams, and for being patient when I come to you with a bombardment of a million questions at a time. And of course, thanks also to the team at Aevitas Creative Management.

Many thanks to my editor, Michael Homler, for helping me find excellent ways to make this book even more upsetting and scary than it was before, and for getting it out into the world. My thanks, as well, to everyone at St. Martin's Press who worked on *These Familiar Walls*: Madeline Alsup, Stephen Erickson, Sara LaCotti, Kiffin Steurer, James Sinclair, Lizz Blaise, Jennifer Rohrbach, Lani Meyer, Lynn Varon, Ervin Serrano, and the whole St. Martin's team; I can't say how much I appreciate the work you've put into my books.

To my beta readers and critique partners, whether you read the whole book years ago or took a look at the last three chapters after heavy revisions, your feedback and friendship have meant so much to me—Mo and Erin, by whose powers combined are MK Hardy; Roxanne Blackhall (I know I mentioned you earlier, but you deserve it again); and Rose Black.

I have had so many amazing friends who have helped keep me sane through the years of writing, querying, and subbing, and who have now helped make my debut year so incredible: Mo and Erin again, Hester Steele, Ash Waters, Dave Goodman, Briana Una McGuckin, Erin Adams, Courtney Floyd, Alex Fox, Meg Quisenberry, Tony Gagnon, Marty Amos, Branden Hershberger, Robert Rodriguez, Amanda Farrenholz, and the incredible community that is the Inklings.

ABOUT THE AUTHOR

C. J. Dotson possesses the statistically average number of body parts for a human being to have. She and her husband, stepson, and children (all of whom also appear human) share a cabin in the woods with more bugs than she would ever like to see. In her limited spare time she enjoys reading, video games, painting, baking and decorating cakes (with . . . questionable success), and petting her dog and six cats.